THE
House on
HALLOWED
GROUND

Mysteries by Nancy Cole Silverman

The Misty Dawn Mystery Series

THE HOUSE ON HALLOWED GROUND (#1)

The Carol Childs Mystery Series

SHADOW OF DOUBT (#1)
BEYOND A DOUBT (#2)
WITHOUT A DOUBT (#3)
ROOM FOR DOUBT (#4)
REASON TO DOUBT (#5)

THE House on HALLOWED GROUND

A MISTY DAWN MYSTERY

NANCY COLE SILVERMAN

HENERY PRESS

Copyright

THE HOUSE ON HALLOWED GROUND
A Misty Dawn Mystery
Part of the Henery Press Mystery Collection

First Edition | September 2019

Henery Press
www.henerypress.com

Trade Paperback ISBN-13: 978-1-63511-551-2
Digital epub ISBN-13: 978-1-63511-552-9
Kindle ISBN-13: 978-1-63511-553-6
Hardcover ISBN-13: 978-1-63511-554-3

Printed in the United States of America

To My Better Half

ACKNOWLEDGMENTS

It takes inspiration to write a book, and for that, I thank Misty Dawn, who jumped off from the pages of my Carol Childs books and insisted on her own story, as well as the very special group of fans and friends who helped me to bring her to life.

To better understand Misty, I interviewed a number of psychics — not for readings of myself, but to get an idea about the types of people they saw, the questions they were asked and their experiences with spirit guides. They were, as I expected, varied and intriguing. But this book would not have been as divinely inspired were it not for Patti Negri, a Hollywood psychic, who in the course of my interviewing her, insisted I stop and told me to just trust myself, that — in essence — I had this.

I also want to thank my good friend and Sister in Crime author, Rochelle Staab, who worked with me through numerous transitions and believed in Misty and Wilson as much as I did. I chatted nonstop with about spirits and their powers with my hiking partner Rhona Robbie, who read and offered terrific advice on an early draft. My keen-eyed proofreader, George Marlowe, caught errors that my less than keen eyes missed. And of course, my husband, Bruce, cheered me on throughout the process. Thank you all.

And to the entire staff at Henery Press, my editor Marie Edwards, Christina Rogers, who funneled numerous emails back and forth between myself and Henery's staff, and worked hard to develop the cover for this new series, and most especially, my publisher Kendel Lynn: you make dreams happen. I am forever thankful for your belief in me.

Chapter 1

The house on South Norton Drive looked like any other mid-century cottage on the same quiet tree-lined street. A two-bedroom, two-story Craftsman with a deep-set front porch surrounded by a white picket fence. There was nothing out of the ordinary about the home. Certainly nothing wraith-like. No cobwebs or darkened windows. Just a nice, quiet little house. But then, that was before I moved in.

In my defense, psychics can't read themselves.

My name is Misty Dawn, formerly Hollywood's leading Psychic to the Stars with a clientele that once read like the Who's Who of Hollywood. A respected consultant to the FBI on major crimes, and confidant to a former First Lady who had me on her speed dial. After such an illustrious career—thirty years at the top, doing late-night talk shows and private consults—I never imagined I'd find myself in the latter part of my life with a diminished clientele. I had outlived most of the big names I had read for, and with limited resources, I found myself in need of a place to live. But, like I said, psychics can't read themselves.

It was my client Denise Thorne, a Realtor, who came to my rescue. The Craftsman had been her brother's home. The recently deceased Wilson Thorne, a flamboyant, self-absorbed, and very fey Academy Award-winning Hollywood set designer who had died suddenly in his sleep. The home and all its contents had been left to his sister, who because of a temporary upset in the real estate market, was undecided what to do with the property. She made me an offer I couldn't refuse.

It was one of those rare, rainy Southern California days. I had just made Denise and myself a cup of tea, and we were seated at the kitchen table inside my aging '68 Volkswagen Van, my sole possession, where I had been temporarily living with my cat Bossypants.

Denise said, "Misty, I have an idea. Why don't you move into my brother's place? It's certainly better than these cramped quarters, and you could hang out your shingle and start afresh."

It was a tempting offer, considering my rusted trailer had begun to leak with the rain.

Denise assured me I'd be doing her a favor. Her brother Wilson had been a collector. Every inch of every room in the house had something from a television or movie set or stage production he either worked on or fawned over, and liquidating the house was going to take some time. If I moved in it'd give me a decent place to live and save her from making a rash decision as to what to do with the place.

I replied while Denise's offer was very generous, I was concerned what I would do with my van. I couldn't just walk away from it. Parking it in a lot would be an expense I didn't need. "It's part of who I am," I said. "I'd have to find somewhere safe to keep it."

"You can park it in my brother's drive for all I care. As for your cat, long as she doesn't knock things over I suppose it'll be fine. Wilson was extremely fastidious about the house. Lots of collectables and artwork. He never had pets of his own. Always worried they'd make a mess of things. Truth is he was highly allergic. Fussy sort. Sneezed at the thought of a feline. But now that he's gone I suppose it shouldn't matter. Come on, Misty, what have you got to lose? The house would be perfect. Great

location. Corner lot. Just off the boulevard in the valley. And..."
Denise raised her brows teasingly. "As we say in Realtor speak,
it's got great curb appeal. For someone like yourself, there
would be a lot of passersby. People out walking their dogs.
Couples. Potential clients." Mentally, I could see Denise had
already moved me into her brother's cottage and was calculating
what I feared might be rent. "Of course, I'd have to charge you."

There it was, my excuse. Money. I didn't have any and
could afford absolutely nothing. While I had earned a good
living in my glory days, I had always been a soft touch, and
financial planning had never been my forte. I'd probably given
away as much as I'd ever made. I somehow believed tomorrow
would always take care of itself.

Then there was Denise. The woman was a psychic junkie.
She had made a hobby of going from psychic to psychic to
compare readings and, had I allowed it, would have seen me on
a daily basis. At age forty-five, Denise had developed a kind of
teenage girl crush on the actor Hugh Jackman. She was
convinced if they met, Jackman would leave his wife of nearly
twenty-two years and ask her to be his life partner and join him
on stage. Thus rekindling what had been a flailing acting career.
Delusional was not a word Denise understood. She believed she
and Jackman were soul mates. Like Katharine Hepburn and
Spencer Tracy, the big screen was waiting for them.

"I don't know, Denise, I—"

"Stop. We can make this work. It'll be a win-win for us
both. Unlimited counseling sessions for me, none of this once a
month stuff. And you? Aah! Misty, you could make a comeback.
Give it a year. What harm can it do?"

I can't say Denise twisted my arm. The fact was both my van and
I were in varying degrees of disrepair. My van needed the

obvious: new tires, new transmission...new everything. And me? Between my arthritis, my cataracts, and overall age-related ailments, I wasn't much better. Hence, I accepted Denise's offer on her brother's cottage sight unseen and told her I would move in. On one condition. While I'd be happy to oversee the care and maintenance of the home, I could not, under any circumstances, make myself available for unlimited counseling sessions.

"It just doesn't work that way, Denise. Reading someone more than once a month isn't something I can do. And any honorable psychic would tell you the same." Most psychics, the real ones anyway, aren't fortune tellers, but enablers. I like to think of my job as helping people help themselves. Put them in touch with their dreams and their higher self by teaching them to focus on what it is they really want to bring about in their lives and help them to do it.

Denise dropped her head and stirred her tea, clanking her spoon annoyingly against the side of the china cup. Clearly, this wasn't the response she wanted. I reconsidered my position. While Denise's intentions violated my psychic code of right and wrong, I sensed my response had been too heavy-handed, and relented.

"I will, however, since it's your brother's home, put on a pot of tea now and then and—"

"And invite me in, often as I like?" Denise raised her head from her cup and dropped the spoon on the table.

I closed my eyes and nodded. Even as I did, I knew this was going to be a problem. But there was no point in arguing. Denise believed this was a win for the both of us. I needed a win right now as much as I needed decent shelter over my head.

The house was exactly as Denise had promised. Charming. The yard green and well-manicured. Every blade of grass appeared to have been lovingly combed and neatly coiffed into place. A large flowering magnolia tree shaded the front walk, and on the porch, two white wicker rockers with green striped cushions set on either side of a brightly painted cherry-red front door.

With my cat Bossypants in my arms, I stood on the front porch and inserted the key into the front lock. Despite the fact I could feel the latch turn and the deadbolt slide open, the door remained locked. I readjusted the cat in my arms—Bossypants gave me an anxious meow—and I twisted the handle again, shaking it to make certain the latch had engaged. Then I gave the door a strong second shove. No luck. I tried again. Perhaps the rain had caused it to swell and all it needed was a little more effort on my part. With my shoulder against the door, my cat squirming beneath my arm, I gave it another try. When that didn't work, convinced something was blocking my efforts, I stood up on the tips of my toes and glanced through one of the three small square-shaped windows at the top of the door.

Was it my imagination or did the lights from the hallway chandelier flicker? Nonsense. It must have been the sun's dappled light filtering through the old magnolia as it hit the glass. Determined not to be bested by the likes of a cherry-red door, I hugged my cat firmly to my chest, twisted the key in the lock another time and pushed against it with all my might. This time with more force than I'd used before. The door remained resistant. Not to be outdone, I gave it one more try. I took a large step back, a deep breath, and with all my might, plus fifteen pounds of cat, heaved myself against the frame.

Like a jack-in-the-box, the door sprang open. Suddenly, I was an unstoppable force. With my cat in my arms, I went flying onto the entry's wooden floor and landed like a sack of potatoes. Bossypants screamed and sprang from my arms. Before I could stop her, she disappeared beneath the staircase directly in front of me. As I lay on the floor and tried to catch my breath, I stared up at the Tiffany-styled chandelier. This time it wasn't my imagination. The light flickered three times. And as I started to get up, I heard a sneeze.

Achoo!

That was when I knew the house was haunted. Experience had taught me it was best to let whatever ghost-like spirit inhabited the house to play out its frustration. Ghosts can be unpredictable, particularly when their turf has been encroached upon unexpectedly. When mortals invade their space, temper tantrums are never unusual. Most spirits prefer to deal with humans only when they're good and ready and always on their own terms.

Best to wait him out.

For the next day and a half, I proceeded with my move and pretended as though nothing was amiss. As I did, I witnessed all kinds of amateur hauntings designed to send someone less experienced running from the house. The copper pots that hung above the stove would sway whenever I entered the kitchen. The water pipes would clank randomly, and the doors, particularly those to the upstairs bedrooms, would bang shut for no apparent reason.

I volleyed back with a few tricks of my own.

The first was relatively simple. I took all the magazines off the coffee table, volumes of *Architectural Digest*, *The Hollywood Reporter*, and books on famous Hollywood homes, and put them on the floor. I replaced them with items of my own: an aloe vera plant I'd been carrying around with me for years, a glass vase a client had made for me, and a large magnifying glass I used from time to time to help me read.

All of which immediately disappeared, which prompted my second move: the armoire.

Upstairs in the master bedroom was a mirrored, wooden wardrobe that looked as though it might have once graced an eighteenth-century castle. Inside were several identically matched men's suits, perfectly spaced an inch-and-a-half apart, and a burgundy, black and gold striped smoking jacket, which I appropriated for myself. Knowing this wasn't going to go down well, I retreated to the master bath where I took a long, hot shower. Refreshed, I took my bra and panties, flung them over the shower rod, and donned the smoking jacket. I then retreated downstairs to the study, where I had seen a cigar box on the desk. I picked what I felt certain might be a favorite—a Cuban—cut off the end, seated myself in a fine leather chair, and with my legs up on the desk, lit up. A sure sign to my overseer who I knew was watching, I didn't plan on retreating.

The next morning I found my bra and panties on the kitchen table, along with my burlap bag and the keys to my van.

Game on.

I responded by retreating to the living room. Grabbed a gold statue off the bookshelf, opened the front door, and jammed the statue up against the base like a doorstop.

As though the house had shuttered, I felt a gust of wind come from behind me. Smiling to myself, I determined it was time I took a seat, and was about to sit down in one of the green-striped wicker rockers and contemplate my next move, when I heard my name.

"Misty!" Denise had parked her late model Lexus across the street and came trotting up the walk with a package in her hands. She stopped mid-path, held the package to her chest, and put a hand to her mouth. "Oh, no. Misty, this isn't good. I should have warned you."

"What about?" I doubted Denise had any idea about the haunting of her brother's house.

Denise gritted her teeth and pointed to the statue like it was a snake about to strike. "The Academy Award, Misty. It...it was Wilson's. You're using it as a doorstop."

"Am I?" I picked up the statue, looked at the engraved nameplate–Wilson Thorne–then cradled it against my chest. "You're right. I guess I am. Careless mistake on my part. Won't happen again. The door's been banging open and shut all morning. I grabbed the first thing I could find. I thought I might air the place out."

"Probably a good idea. The house's been closed up for a month." Denise took the statue from my hand, replaced it with the package, and put the statue on the entry table next to the study. Immediately the upstairs bedroom door banged shut. "You alone?"

"Other than my cat, yes, but she's in hiding. Beneath the staircase, I think. As for the banging upstairs, I left the windows open. Must be a breeze." I pointed to the L-shaped staircase directly in front of us where I believed Bossypants had taken refuge.

Denise ignored the staircase and turned left to the living room. As though she was drawn to it like a child in a candy store, she approached the couch in the center of the room and ran her long fingers across the back of it. "You know I've only been inside this house once or twice. My brother never wanted me here. Look at this, would you? It's a museum. This couch, it was Norma Desmond's sofa from the set of *Sunset Boulevard*. Wilson worked on the Broadway production and shipped it home as a souvenir. And these," Denise took a step toward the dining room and picked up one of the elaborately hand-carved, silver candlesticks from the table. "They were from a TV show, I think. *The Addams Family*, maybe. A bit over the top, but then, if you knew my brother, so was he.

"Quite the collector," I said.

"To say the least. Every room has something from some set he either worked on or fawned over." Denise put the candlestick down and dropped her wrist. "And I do mean fawned over. The man had such a sense of style. Loved pretty things. Didn't matter who or what. Male or female. Long as it had–how'd he put it? Pizzazz. The man was wild about pizzazz. I think that's why he never wanted me around, he was afraid I'd walk off with one of his prized possessions." Denise laughed, and I felt a sudden chill in the room. "Crazy, huh? But that's not why I'm here. I thought I'd drop that off." Denise took the package from my hand and unwrapped the brown paper surrounding it. "It's a shingle. I thought you should have it. I had it made for you yesterday."

The sign read, *MISTY DAWN. Psychic Readings. Inquire Within.*

Chapter 2

After our initial tit-for-tat exchange, the moving of each other's items around the house, the banging of pots and pans, and the slamming of doors, Wilson Thorne made himself scarce. So scarce in fact, I began to wonder if perhaps he had moved on.

It wasn't until one of my consults, an attractive young woman who had come to me for romantic advice, had left, I realized that wasn't the case.

"You call that a psychic reading?" Wilson appeared, leaning over the banister at the top of the L-shaped stairs. With his dark hair slicked back, and tortoiseshell glasses, he was dressed as I had seen him in photos: in a pair of pleated trousers, a blue collared shirt, suspenders, and a bow tie.

I tempered my surprise—this was the first I had actually seen him, and with a measured response, I replied, "If you think you could do better, Wilson, you're free to sit in."

"You can see me?" Wilson stood upright, straightened his tie, and looked back over his shoulder. He pointed to himself. "You know who I am?"

"Tsk. Of course, I know who you are. You're Wilson Thorne, the recently deceased, former Hollywood set designer. And apparently, for lack of a better way to describe it, you're stuck."

"Stuck?" Wilson skipped down the stairs like a dancer, his lithe body taking the steps two at a time. When he reached the bottom, he stopped and did a perfect three-sixty pirouette in front of me, and with the palms of his hands upward, smiled. "And exactly what do you mean by stuck?"

"Between two worlds," I said. "In short, Wilson, you're in limbo."

"Limbo?" he scoffed and brushed the sleeves of his shirt. "Nonsense. I can't be in limbo. I've never believed in such a thing or any of the rest of it for that matter. Heaven or hell. I've never given it a lot of thought."

"Doesn't matter," I said. I moved from the entry into the living room and settled myself on the Norma Desmond couch, where I picked up a magazine and, ignoring him, started to thumb through it.

Wilson followed me into the living room. "What doesn't matter?"

"Whether you believe it or not," I said. I put the magazine down and stared directly at him. "You can choose to believe whatever you like, but the fact of the matter is, you're stuck. You're what people in my business call a shade."

"A shade?" He looked down at himself, patted his body, then put his hands on his hips and paced the room. "And exactly, Ms. Dawn, just what is a shade?"

"You can call me Misty if you like. Everyone does. And a shade is a person who hasn't fully passed on. It happens. Not often, but sometimes. Particularly when a person dies suddenly or unexpectedly. They get stuck."

"Well unstick me then. Or whatever it is you do. Use some of that witchcraft or psychic voodoo you use and bring me back." Wilson stopped pacing and raised his hand above his head dismissively as though all I had to do was wave my magic wand or some such ridiculous thing and voilà, suddenly he'd be back to his old self.

"I'm afraid I can't do that. I'm not a witch, and what I do, despite what you may think, is not voodoo. Not by any means. But I do believe I may be able to help."

"Help?" Wilson chuckled. "Just what is your idea of help? And let me add if it's anything like the advice I overheard you giving that young bobblehead this morning, I doubt you've much to say I'd find of any interest."

"Well then, it's up to you. We could exchange insults all morning, or you could choose to listen to what I have to say and make up your own mind."

"Fine," Wilson said. "We'll do it your way."

"You might like to sit." I nodded to the chair.

"I don't believe I need to."

"Entirely up to you. But to start with, you'll need to understand a few rules."

"Rules." Wilson fluttered his lips, like a horse expelling air, and gave me a Bronx cheer, displaying his displeasure. "I've never been particularly good with rules. I prefer to make my own."

"You won't now. The universe won't allow it. So, if you'd like to get unstuck, you might as well learn what they are and get on with it."

"And I suppose I've no choice in the matter, just as I had no choice in the matter of roommates or that wretched creature you brought into my home," Wilson took the chair and crossed his arms. "Because if I had, mind you, I would have preferred someone a little younger, perhaps with a little less padding around the middle." He pointed at my midsection like he would have liked to poke me in the ribs.

I gave no credence to Wilson's rude remark. In fact, I considered it less of an insult and more of an attempt on Wilson's part to test my mettle. I may not be the sweet young thing he would have preferred to take up residence in his house, but I like to think of myself as a wizened senior citizen, a woman of indeterminable age, with style all her own. One I haven't changed in years. My hair may be gray, and my wardrobe not fancier than the long skirts and tie-dyed shirts and moccasins I came to California with, but I'm quite comfortable in my own skin.

I squared my shoulders and fired back. "You can stop right there, young man. I'm well aware of your preferences. Some of which, I might add, may well account for your present situation. Not that I'm judging. I've always been a bit of a love-and-let-love type myself, but you should listen up. Your future may depend on it."

"Humph." He sat back and crossed his arms. "Alright, Misty. Have at it. Just what are these rules of yours?"

"Again, not my rules, the universe's. To start with, as far as your physical being goes, you're no longer part of the material world, and much as you may enjoy the pot banging and door slamming, it needs to stop. It's very amateurish and really unnecessary."

Wilson tilted his head up and gave me another of his Bronx cheers.

"And second, you have a job to do. You're a shade, you exist between two worlds, and at times I will need you to assist me in my readings. Which means, when it's necessary, you make contact with those spirits who have crossed over and channel their message back to me. Ultimately whatever you do to help me, helps yourself. One way or the other."

"That's it then, I'm to be an interpreter?"

"It's not as easy as it sounds. The work can get complicated, but we'll do the best we can with the time we have. However, you have to understand, this is a temporary assignment. And I should warn you, don't get too settled in, things can change in a flash. Hopefully, the powers that be, or however you choose to interpret them, will find favor with you, and your actions here will either earn you your wings or—"

"Or what?" Wilson scoffed.

"Or not," I said. I put the magazine back on the table. I was done for the moment. I needed a cup of tea and my noonday nap. "It's entirely up to you. Think about it. Your future may depend on it."

Chapter 3

After an initial flirtation as my sidekick, sitting in on my readings and reluctantly relaying messages from the other side, Wilson informed me he thought the work beneath him. He saw no reason to assist me in what he believed were whiny women seeking advice in dead-end relationships or hoping to reconnect with long-lost loves. Content with his limbo state, Wilson retreated to the study, which he now called his sanctuary, sans my cat, and barred my entrance.

We were in the midst of an argument with me on one side of the study's door, reminding Wilson he couldn't remain in his limbo state forever, and him on the other side, protesting, when the front bell rang. I excused myself and answered the door.

Standing on the porch was a petite, young woman dressed in a short, floral cotton dress—too flimsy for January's colder temperatures—a leather jacket, and Ugg boots.

"May I come in?" The girl wrapped her arms around herself and her small feet tap danced a jig, as she glanced over her shoulder back at the street. "I need to talk to you, and it's cold out here. You mind?"

I recognized the young actress instantly. The curly-haired, baby-faced blonde, known to the world simply as Zoey, was as close to Hollywood royalty as it gets. Like Beyoncé or Madonna, Zoey was one of the few Hollywood elites who didn't need a surname. Although, as a Chamberlain, a fourth-generation thespian with a lineage going all the way back to her great-grandfather and the days of silent movies, her ancestry didn't hurt.

"Are you alone?" Celebrities, particularly those of Zoey's ilk, seldom traveled without an entourage. I felt certain at any moment paparazzi would come speeding up to the house and my front lawn would be swamped with flashing cameras and rude reporters.

"I am now, but if I stand here any longer, I won't be." She glanced over her shoulder, bit her lip, and looked back at me anxiously. "Please?"

I opened the door and pointed toward the living room.

"Zoey, right?" I said the name just loud enough so that Wilson, who I knew was standing with his ear to the study door, might know that today's caller was no ordinary caller, but the one and only, hugely popular Zoey. Granddaughter of Clifton Chamberlain, one of the most revered Hollywood stars of the twentieth century. "Please, come in and make yourself at home."

"Thank you." Zoey stepped inside, her arms still about herself as her eyes scanned the living room, taking in the furnishings and bookshelves. Going to the couch, she ran her hand across the sofa's smooth satin finish and stopped. "This looks familiar."

"The former owner was a set designer," I said.

"*Sunset Boulevard?*" Zoey patted the couch. "I recognize the set."

"Each room in the house is different. Upstairs, the bed in the master bedroom was from a production of *Cat on a Hot Tin Roof.*"

Zoey laughed. "If only that bed could talk. Right?"

I wondered if Wilson could hear us. "Sometimes I think it does," I said.

Zoey twisted a long strand of her blonde hair around a finger and continued to inventory the room. "I've never been to a psychic before. I guess I was expecting something different."

"I can't say I'm surprised. The house is different for me, too. I've only been here a short while, but if it's crystal balls and cards you're looking for, I don't use them. Unless of course, you'd like me to." I cleared the magazines and a stack of Wilson's books off the coffee table and put them on the floor. "I do find a cup of tea will do much the same. Not to read leaves of course, but to warm you up. How about I make us some? You look like you could use a hot cup."

I left Zoey in the living room and went to the kitchen to make a pot of tea. Forsaking my own glass teapot, I used Wilson's silver tea service, complete with two cups from a Windsor China set I found in the cabinets. Fancier than I might have ordinarily used. When I returned, I found Bossypants purring contentedly on Zoey's lap.

"I see you've met my cat." I was about to scurry her off when Zoey stopped me.

"Don't. She's fine. I like cats." Zoey stroked the cat's long hair.

"She must like you, too," I said. "She's been playing hide-and-seek with me since I moved in. If her food bowl wasn't empty each night, I might think she had run off."

Zoey scratched beneath Bossy's chin, and as I leaned over to put the tray on the coffee table between us, the cat suddenly screeched.

Roww!

I heard a sneeze and took a quick step backward, just in time to avoid Bossy knocking the tray from my hand as she scampered back to her hiding place beneath the stairs. Out of the corner of my eye I caught Wilson—confirming my belief cats can see spirits most humans can't—and without losing a beat, steadied my tray and placed it on the table.

"You'll have to excuse Bossy," I said. "She's still a bit skittish from the move."

While Zoey adjusted her skirt, Wilson took a seat on the back of the couch. Like Rodin's Thinker, he balanced himself with his feet on the cushions, his chin rested on his fists, and stared at Zoey as though she was an alabaster statue he might worship.

"Ahem." I raised my brow in Wilson's direction—a subtle hint he needed to move—and poured tea into Zoey's cup. "Cream?" I asked.

"Sugar, please." Zoey reached with the silver tongs and took two sugar cubes and plopped them into her tea.

"Look at her, would you?" Wilson stepped in front of the couch. Like a director, he framed Zoey's face with his hands as though he were about to take a shot. "Those eyes. Her cheekbones. Her brows. She's the image of her grandmother. That woman could light up the stage with her presence. One smile and she had the audience in the palm of her hand. And this one, with her mother's genes as well, she's even better."

I scowled. I was not amused. Wilson knew better than to speak. I had been very clear about the rules. Spirits, like children at a fancy dinner party, were to be neither seen nor heard, particularly in the presence of clients. Not that Zoey could see or hear him, but I could and didn't appreciate the interruption. I had work to do. Wilson's job was simply to observe until called upon.

He gave me an overly dramatic head roll and turned his back.

Proceeding as though nothing were amiss, I sat back in my chair and stirred my tea. "So, Zoey—I assume I can call you Zoey?"

"Everybody does," she said.

"Tell me what it is you'd like my help with."

"It's not me." Zoey looked down and a lock of her blonde hair fell across her pale face. "It's my house. It's haunted."

"Haunted? Oh, now this is interesting." Wilson moved back to the couch and took a seat next to her.

With my head down, I continued to stir my tea and muttered under my breath so that only Wilson might hear. "Now you're interested?" Two weeks of consults and never a peep from the man and now he was interested. And only because it was Zoey. Wilson was as starstruck as he was stuck in his limbo state.

"Pardon me?" Zoey asked.

I cleared my throat. "I said, that's interesting. May I ask, why do you think the house is haunted?"

"I don't think," Zoey said. "I know. I'm sure of it, but nobody believes me." Zoey put her tea down. "The thing is, I haven't lived there very long. I just bought the place. The Pink Mansion? The old Mediterranean-style ranch house off Fryman Canyon? You must know it."

I nodded. Locals called the salmon-colored, red-tiled-roofed home "The Pink Mansion." It was a historic home, built in the early 1900s, and nestled atop the hills in Fryman Canyon. The area was popular with the Hollywood set, and backed up to hiking trails that offered views of the city and valley below.

"It needed a lot of work. Both inside and out. I did a big remodel before I moved in. At first, when I started to hear things, I thought maybe I had just imagined it or that maybe the house was settling. You know, like older houses do. Creaking floors. But then I started to hear other things..."

"What kind of other things?"

"Footsteps. Music. And always in the middle of the night. Sometimes I'd even think I heard someone playing the piano. I have a large baby grand, and I swear I'd hear someone playing

'Clair de Lune.' My mother used to play it late at night after I'd go to bed. But when I get up and check, the house is silent. Later, when I'd go back to bed, I'd hear footsteps. Like someone was tiptoeing up and down the hall. Chad, my fiancé, he thinks I'm imaging things."

"Your fiancé doesn't hear them?" I put my cup down and leaned a little closer.

"No, but Chad's not always home. He has a band and when he's in town he works late. Maybe you've heard them? Echo Chamber?"

I shook my head. Modern music wasn't my forte, particularly tunes that appealed to the younger set with a loud, ruckus beat and tone to it.

"Yeah, well, you're not alone. But it's what he does, and when he's not writing music, recording or rehearsing he's either chasing some gig in town or he's got one on the road." Zoey picked her cup up again and took another sip of her tea. "Actually, so am I. On the road that is, but right now, I'm home—at least for the next couple weeks anyway. I've been working on a movie, and most days I have to get up early to be on the set. But it's a ghost. I'm sure of it. It's not only the piano and footsteps, it's other things, too."

"Like what?"

"Like things from my jewelry drawer have disappeared. Not expensive stuff, but stuff my mother gave me before she died. Pop beads and mood rings. Trinkets from when we used to visit Venice Pier when I was a kid. It was her favorite place, and I like to keep some of the mementoes she bought around me. They remind me of her."

I remembered pictures of Zoey and her mother together before her mother had died. They were on every tabloid in every supermarket in the country. Cara Chamberlain, the beautiful, successful blonde actress with her adorable daughter. Cara had passed far too young, as had Zoey's famous father. Their untimely deaths left Zoey heir to the family fortune, and her fans wondering if rumors of a Chamberlain family curse might be true.

"Are you telling me you believe this ghost has taken things of yours?" I asked.

"Yes, but only temporarily. It's more like whoever's doing the taking is really borrowing my things. Moving them around."

"Because you find them later? In another location?" My eyes went quickly to Wilson then back to Zoey. Wilson and I had played this game ourselves.

"Yes! In fact, I found a whole stash of things under the stairwell in the kitchen. It's as though whoever took them had hidden them there." Zoey put her teacup down. "How did you know?"

"I've seen this before. It's not entirely unusual. Some ghosts consider it entertaining." I glanced back at Wilson, my eyes narrowed.

"Is that wrong?" He raised his palms up and shrugged.

My eyes clicked back to Zoey. "It may be nothing more than just a game of wits."

"I'm right then? There is a ghost in my house, and you can help me?"

"I can't promise anything—"

"For God's Sake, Misty, you're not going to turn her down." Wilson towered over me. The thought that I might not accept this assignment clearly agitated him. "The girl needs your help, Old Gal. What else are your talents for if not to help her?"

Old Gal? Where did that come from?

Zoey stood. "Please, Misty, I need your help. I don't know where else to turn. Whoever or whatever it is, it's got to stop. I can't sleep, and it's affecting me on the set. I can't remember my lines and Chad's growing irritated with me. You've got to help me."

Wilson stepped closer to me and whispered in my ear. "Look at her, Misty. The poor, bereft, little thing. No mother. No father. She needs your help. You can't turn her down."

"I don't know, Zoey," I said. "I'll have to think about it."

"Please." She grabbed my hands and squeezed them between her own. "I really need you. Chad and I are planning to get married. We want to be married in the house when I return from Italy next month. I'm shooting the final scenes there, and when I return I want everything to be perfect. Please tell me you'll do it."

"Misty!" Wilson put his arm around me. "What's there to think about? Tell her you'll do it. If you will, I'll..." Wilson raised his eyes to the ceiling and shook his head. "Well, I'll help you."

I paused long enough for Wilson to realize he had pledged himself to the effort, then bowed my head, and bit back my smile. I had Wilson exactly where I wanted him.

"I'd be happy to help, Zoey. Jot down your address on a piece of paper, I'll be over tomorrow. What time's good for you?"

"Any time after one. I have a quick shoot mid-morning, but the afternoon should be fine."

"One it is, then." I showed Zoey to the door, bid her goodbye, and turned back to Wilson. "I hope you're up for this. Things are never as easy as they may seem."

Wilson didn't answer. Instead, he sneezed and disappeared back into the study.

"Gesundheit," I said.

Chapter 4

Zoey hadn't been gone thirty minutes before the front bell rang again. It was Denise, and the minute I opened the door, I knew this would be no quick visit. She barged through with a large bag over her shoulder and waved a deck of tarot cards above her head.

"I know you don't read cards, Misty, but I can't help myself. This is just too big." Denise went straight to the living room and dropped her bag on the floor in front of the fireplace. "I've just come from another reader. Don't be angry with me, but it's important. I need you to verify something she's told me."

I picked Denise's bag up off the floor and dropped it on the end of the couch. A bag on the floor invited bad luck. I'd told her that numerous times, but Denise, despite her obsessive-compulsive disorder, never seemed to remember.

"You know I won't do that," I said.

"You have to. She told me she saw me meeting a man. That he's an important person. Someone I might not ordinarily cross paths with, but that the stars have aligned. And because of that, we'll meet under unusual circumstances." Denise slapped the cards on the coffee table. "It's all here in the cards. She said he's working on something to do with Hollywood, and that we would have a lot in common. In fact, she said he could be my soul mate. Misty, you know what that means?"

"No, Denise, I've no idea what it means. And even if I did, I wouldn't comment on another psychic's reading. It's just not done."

"But this is it, Misty. Don't you see?" Denise took my hands and shook them, forcing me to look her in the eye. "It's Hugh Jackman, I'm sure of it. He's in town for the Golden Globes, and this is my chance. I just need to know if you see it, too. Please, look at the cards and tell me." Still holding onto my hands as though she were afraid I might run away, Denise leaned down over the table, and, with one free hand, fanned the cards. "Please, look at the cards and tell me."

Before I could pick them up and stuff them back in her bag, Wilson slipped back into the room and swept the cards from the table, dashing them helter-skelter to the floor.

"Tell her to go," Wilson said. "I can't have that woman in my house."

"I can't do that," I said.

Denise and Wilson hollered back at me in unison. "Why not?"

"Because, Denise," I turned my back to Wilson, and leaned over to pick up the cards off the floor. "I don't read cards, and I won't be party to your stalking this man."

"I'm not stalking him. I'm not some crazy fan following him around and harassing him. That would be beneath me."

"Oh, right." Wilson put his foot on top of the cards and slyly pushed several beneath the couch. "Here it comes, my sister's belief she's God's gift to the stage. Wait for it."

"You know I'm not just some groupie, I'm an actor." With an accent on the last syllable, Denise put her hand to her throat and raised her head to the ceiling, as though she expected some shining light to come bursting forth to confirm her affirmation.

Wilson rolled his eyes.

"Just last year I played Maggie in *Cat On A Hot Tin Roof* at the Pasadena Play House. The critics are still talking about it."

Wrrrao! Wilson screeched, like a cat.

Denise continued. "You of all people, Misty, know how difficult it can be for a mature woman to find a leading man who can be a match for someone like myself." Denise did have a point. At six feet tall, she was bigger than most leading men on stage today. And in an industry that considered any actress over the age of thirty or bigger than a size two as both a has-been and obese, she was fighting an uphill battle. "If Hugh and I were to meet, things would be different."

"That's it, I'm out of here." Wilson threw his hands above his head, retreated back to the study, and slammed the door behind him.

Denise startled. "Really, Misty, you have to do something about the draft in this house. That door banging would drive me crazy."

"Believe me, I'm working on it."

Chapter 5

Zoey's house, the "Pink Mansion" as it was popularly known, was less than a mile and a half from Wilson's cottage, but getting there was more of a to-do than I had anticipated.

"Do you mind telling me how it is you expect for us to get there? Were you planning to fly us over on your broomstick? Or did you think we'd take that rattled old hippie van of yours, which, by the way, I wouldn't be caught dead in." Wilson stopped me at the front door.

"You are dead." I pushed past him. I didn't appreciate the implication I might travel by broomstick nor the knock on my hippie van. "And no," I snapped back, "I don't plan on driving myself. I plan to Uber. Broomsticks are so yesterday."

Wilson put his hand on the door, blocking my exit. "Cancel it. I'll drive."

"You?" I took a step back. Not that ghosts can't drive or operate machinery, but I hadn't considered Wilson as a chauffeur.

"I have two cars in the garage. A '54 silver Jaguar XK-120 in mint condition, and a vintage Rolls Royce. Both right-hand drive. Which, under the circumstances, Old Gal, works in your favor."

"Old Gal?" I winced. This was the second time Wilson had referred to me as Old Gal. Was this some new pet name, a subtle indicator our relationship had advanced from adversarial to more of a partnership, or was he mocking me?

Wilson gave me no chance to ask. With his hands on my shoulders, he hustled me out the back door to the garage where he pointed to the two cars.

"Which do you prefer? The windows on the Rolls are blacked out. The roadster has a canvas top. If you sit on the left-hand side, like most American drivers, people would assume you were driving, and nobody would notice. Dead or alive, Misty, I'd wager I'm a better driver than you are."

Wilson had a point. My driving skills, like my eyesight, were less than stellar, and my patience with LA's busy streets and inattentive drivers had grown weary over the years. I had to admit, his offer had a certain appeal. Which was how Wilson came to be not only my roommate and limboed-spirit guide, but my driver.

For our first trip, Wilson insisted we take the Jag. He said he hadn't had it out for a spin in quite some time and the old roadster needed a little road work. Once behind the wheel, he revved the engine until the car hummed like a caged cat, then, with his foot on the accelerator, released the brake. Showing little regard for the speed limit or red lights—or me!—he whizzed in and out of traffic like a madman.

I held onto the grab bar until I couldn't feel the circulation in the tips of my fingers. "What are you doing? Are you trying to get us killed?"

"Relax, Ol' Gal. This is exactly what you need." Wilson pressed his foot to the floorboard and with little or no warning, took a hard right onto Zoey's street. My body slammed against the Jag's door. "Gets the ol' heart pumping. Not to mention clears the fuel lines. Gets the kinks out."

"Stop!" I yelled.

Ahead of us, the street was blocked. Two black-and-white

police cruisers were parked with their lights flashing in front of the Pink Mansion, along with an ambulance and several large television news vans. On every level it spelled trouble.

Wilson pulled the Jag onto the side of the road and parked beneath a large pine tree. Far enough away that no one would notice the car's British configuration and me getting out on the passenger side.

"Wait here. I'll check the house." With my bag over my shoulder, I took a deep breath and began to hike up the street.

I was no more than five feet from the car when I heard Wilson holler to me. "Hold on there. We're a team, remember? Where you go, I go."

I turned around and exhaled. The care and training of a ghost in limbo is no easy task. Wilson had slipped out the window on the driver's side of the car so as to not open the door and stood waiting for me like a soldier at arms.

I marched back to the car.

"Okay, Wilson. As long as you remember the rules." I resisted the urge to point a finger at him, lest anyone see me and think I was talking to myself. "You're to be neither seen nor heard. And more importantly you can look, but you cannot touch. We're here in search of a ghost. You got that?" I realized Wilson had agreed to come along because of his interest in the Chamberlain clan and whatever historical memorabilia he might find inside the house. I reminded him, sternly, he was here to assist me, to stay close by my side, and resist whatever urges he might have to wander off.

"At your service, Old Gal." With a salute, Wilson smiled and fell in behind me. I felt as though I was about to accompany a minor through a candy store.

The Pink Mansion stood elevated from the street by a slight slope, surrounded at its base, by six-foot fencing with an elaborate wrought iron security gate. In front of the gate, yellow crime scene tape had been strung. Looky-loos and paparazzi had already started to arrive. Behind the yellow tape, the gate was open, and up the hill I spotted Zoey dressed in a long robe, standing huddled beneath a huge white California Oak with branches the size of tree trunks. The arms of the tree spread like a giant octopus from one side of the property to the other and crowned the front of the Pink Mansion like an umbrella. Standing next to Zoey were three people I didn't recognize. Combined with the natural shade the tree provided, and the reflection from the flashing red and blue lights of the patrol cars, the light beneath the tree cast an unusual aura. A kind of dusty, mustard glow I had encountered in the past when dealing with the FBI on criminal investigations. I glanced back at Wilson. I had an uneasy sense of foreboding in the pit of my stomach. Something terrible had happened here.

"Misty?" Zoey came running down the drive toward me, her eye makeup smeared, her face red and blotchy. "I forgot you were coming today. Thank God you're here. Lacey's dead."

"Lacey?" Zoey lifted the crime scene tape that separated us and hugged me to her as though I was a security blanket. Instinctively, I wrapped my arms around her and allowed her to bury her head on my shoulder. "Who's Lacey?" I asked.

"My best friend. Lacey Adams. The actress? We look alike. Some people think we're sisters."

I hadn't followed *Who's Who in Hollywood* since I'd stopped reading for Liz Taylor. The younger generation had come along so fast, and with such fury, it was more of a bother than a necessity to keep up. But I did remember one of Zoey's movies where she appeared with a similar looking curly-headed toddler who had been cast as her sister.

"What happened?"

"She drowned." Zoey grabbed my hand and walked me up the hill toward the house. "I don't know how it happened. Lacey came by last night to go over lines with me for a scene I'm working on. We were sitting in the kitchen, the windows were open, and Lacey thought she heard a sound outside. There have been feral cats around. I had seen kittens hiding beneath the spa decking earlier and she wanted to go check. It was getting late, and I needed to go to bed. She told me not to worry. She'd let herself out like she usually does, so I took a sleeping pill and went to sleep. That's the last I remember. I just assumed she had gone home."

Zoey and I reached the front patio, an atrium entrance with a walled water fountain that fed into a small koi pond. Zoey paused, and with her back to the house, looked back down the drive to the street.

"When did you find the body?" I asked.

"This morning, about seven thirty. Jose, my gardener, found her. Chad and I were still in bed. I didn't have to be at the studio until nine and Chad got home late last night from a recording session. We were sleeping in." Zoey glanced back over her shoulder at the house and shuddered. "Jose said it looked like Lacey's long hair got caught on the drain and she was pulled under." Zoey closed her eyes and shook her head. I could see she was trying to shake the dark vision that surrounded her.

"And the paramedics," I asked, "you called them?"

"Right away, but I knew she was dead. There was no way she was still alive."

"What about the police?"

"They showed up right after the EMTs, and so did the news." Zoey nodded at the news trucks parked in the street and a growing number of looky-loos and paparazzi. The only thing holding back the crowd was a thin line of yellow crime scene tape.

I put my arm around Zoey and turned her away from the gawkers and the flash of cameras.

"Don't you think it'd be best if you went inside?"

"Maybe." Zoey wiped a tear from the side of her face. "There's a detective inside now. He's been asking all kinds of questions. He wanted to know what time Lacey came by and why she was here. Did I know she'd gone out back by herself? That kind of thing. He said it was just a formality, but he didn't want me in the backyard while they were working. Chad and I came out here to get away from it all."

"Did the detective give you his card?"

"Ah-huh." Zoey pulled a business card from within her robe, her hand shaking. "His name's Detective Romero."

We were almost to the front door when I caught sight of the detective. His gold shield caught the morning light as he came through a small, wooden gate that separated the front and back yards. Tall, gray-haired, middle-aged, and handsome enough to play a leading role, the man looked like he could have come from central casting.

"Excuse me, Zoey? This yours?" The detective held out a small, clear plastic ring. "Found this in the bottom of the Jacuzzi. Looks like Lacey may have tried to get it out of the spa and accidentally turned on the bubblers. Caught her long hair in the whirlpool return and it sucked her right under. I'm sorry for your loss."

Zoey wrapped her hand around the ring and made a fist. With her eyes closed, she held the ring tight against her chest and pursed her lips.

"Are you okay?" I asked.

Zoey opened her eyes, looked up at the sky, then pinched them shut again. A tear slipped down her cheek.

"By the way," Romero asked. "The gate in the backyard, the one leading to the park, was open. Your gardener says it's usually locked and he doesn't have a key. You leave it that way?"

"Maybe. I...I don't know. Chad and his friends use it to get to the trails." Zoey shrugged. "You should ask him."

"What about smoking?" Romero asked. "Did Lacey smoke?"

"No." Zoey shook her head.

"How about you?"

"Sometimes, why?" Zoey frowned.

"Probably nothing, but I found a cigarette butt out behind the spa. Had lipstick prints on it. I wouldn't worry about it. Probably been out there for a while."

Zoey stood numb, her face pale. I doubted she comprehended anything the detective had just told her.

"You can go back inside now if you like." Romero tilted his head toward the backyard. "The coroner's got the body bagged. He'll bring it around in a few minutes. I'll call if we need anything else. Again, Miss, I'm sorry for your loss."

With the ring still clutched to her chest and her other arm wrapped around herself, Zoey stood motionless, closed her eyes, and turned her head up to the sky. I pulled her close and felt her collapse like a rag doll against me.

"What is it?" I asked.

Zoey opened her hand. "The ring," Zoey whispered, "it was my mother's."

Chapter 6

The minute I entered the house I knew why Zoey had chosen to wait outside while the police had completed their investigation. Despite the presence of paparazzi and news reporters, the front atrium with its secluded entry was the only area that didn't face out onto the backyard. Inside, the house had been built with floor-to-ceiling picture windows and French doors from every room that wrapped around a back patio and offered an unobstructed view of the pool and spa. If Zoey had remained in the house, there was no way she could have avoided seeing Lacey's body as the coroner pulled it from the Jacuzzi.

"Make yourself comfortable." Zoey pointed to an oversized brown leather couch beneath a wrought iron chandelier. The couch faced out onto the patio and a spacious, well-groomed, park-like backyard. "I'll be out in a minute. I need to check on something."

Wilson, who had been by my side the entire time, followed Zoey like a shadow down the long, entry hall into what I assumed must be the home's west wing or private quarters. So much for following my orders.

The living room—or the great room as it might be called in such a grand house—was an immense step-down affair: viewable from the entry and complete with a bar, fireplace, and black baby grand piano, creating three distinctly different conversation areas. Next to the great room was the dining room, an equally formal-looking room. The entire area was separated from the entry by a long gallery-like hallway complete with Spanish arches that ran the width of the room.

While I waited on the couch, the three people I had seen Zoey huddled with outside beneath the big oak tree, entered the house. The tallest of the three, a young man whom I sensed was Zoey's fiancé, spotted me sitting by myself, and stepped forward.

"You must be Misty. I'm Chad." He offered me his hand. "Zoey told me about you."

Twenty-something, tall, about six feet, slim and crushingly handsome with light blue eyes and blond hair, Chad looked like he could have stepped out from an Abercrombie & Fitch catalog, forever tanned and healthy.

With a nod to his friends, Chad introduced me to his drummer Zac, and Zac's girlfriend, Kelsey. The two looked remarkably similar. Exact opposites of Chad. Both had mid-length dark brown hair tied back in a ponytail and were dressed in jeans, a black T-shirt, and dark, heavy military-type shoes.

"I called Zac and Kels right after we found the body. Zoey was hysterical. We were lucky they were close by."

"Down the street actually," Zac said.

"Jerry's Deli," Kelsey added. "We had stopped for breakfast and just ordered pancakes when we got the call."

"And we came right over." The two not only looked alike but finished each other's sentences with ease. Zac grabbed Kelsey's hand, and they took a seat at the end of the sofa.

"I gave Zoey something to calm her down," Chad said. "If she seems off, that's why."

"What did you give her?" I asked.

"Xanax. Her doctor prescribed it for her right after we moved in. Between finishing the remodel, the movie, and now this, I don't know how much more she can take."

"How long have you been here?" I glanced around the room, taking inventory. Several large black and white Hurrells—pictures of Hollywood stars from an era gone by, including one of Zoey's great-grandfather, William Chamberlain, hung on the wall. Other large prints had been stacked against the bookshelves waiting to be hung. Behind the piano, a moving box had yet to be unpacked, but for the most part, the room looked comfortable and as though the furnishings had been permanently arranged.

"'Bout a month," Chad said. "Zoey bought the place better than a year ago, but she wanted to do a lot of remodeling. She knocked out some walls. Re-did the bathrooms. Updated the kitchen. And then the pool. Took a lot more time than we expected."

"And money." Zoey walked back into the room. She had changed clothes and was wearing a pair of black palazzo pants and a tight T-shirt. "The pool was Chad's idea. I never wanted it."

Chad got up from the couch, went over to Zoey, put his arm around her and nestled his nose against her neck. "It's not your fault, Zoe."

"I know it's not my fault. But it still happened, didn't it." Zoey pulled away from Chad and turned to me. The tension between the two was palpable, and I wasn't the only one aware of it. A quick look between Zac and Kelsey told me they also felt a chill in the air. "Misty, come with me. There's something I want to show you."

I followed Zoey down the long gallery-like hall toward the east wing of the house. Kitchen, den, and staircase that led to an upstairs area. Zoey stopped just short of the kitchen and pointed to a small door beneath the stairs.

"One day I noticed the door wasn't quite closed, and then, well...you need to see this." Zoey opened the door and climbed inside.

I knew before Zoey came out what she was going to show me. Over the years, I've worked with enough ghosts to know that some kept lairs, hiding places for those things ghosts felt empowered by.

Zoey reappeared with a small, white wicker basket in her hands. "This is where I found some of my mother's things. Whoever or whatever took them from my dressing table moved them here. Chad thinks I'm making this all up. That I'm stressed and imagining things. But I swear to you, just like I didn't drop the ring Detective Romero found in the spa this morning, I didn't put these things here either." Zoey reached into the pocket of her pants, pulled out the ring, and held it up for me to see. "The ghost did."

I took the basket from Zoey's hands. On top was a delicate hand towel, monogrammed with the initials A.M.M. Beneath it was a small gardening shovel with a pink handle, a doll-sized porcelain teacup with matching saucer, and more jewelry. Pop beads, bangle bracelets, and barrettes like a child might wear in her hair.

"The jewelry and hair clips are all from my dressing table. They're things my mother gave me before she died. Why they're here, I don't know."

I picked up the strand of pop beads from the basket and held them in my hand. Sometimes, if items have been worn by the bearer for a period of time, it's possible to get a reading from them. Usually, it's more with items made from precious metals, but it was worth a try. With these I got nothing. They remained cool in my hand, as though I'd just picked them up off the shelf at a toy store.

But what I did get was Zoey's concern.

"You don't believe Lacey's death was an accident. You think it was something else."

"It wasn't an accident. I'm sure of it. I think Lacey was drowned. Deliberately. And whoever did it, I think they thought it was me. I need your help more than ever now. I need to find out who killed Lacey and why. The cops think it was an accident, and Chad thinks I'm stressed from work and the house. But I don't think so. I think there's a ghost in this house, and it wants to kill me."

The front doorbell rang. From the hallway, I heard the sounds of voices. I looked at Zoey.

"That's Crystal, my personal assistant. She's here to take me to the studio. Chad didn't think I should go alone."

"You really think you should be working today? Wouldn't the studio give you the day off?"

Zoey put the basket back in the closet under the stairs and stood up. "Any other time maybe, but I need to finish this morning's shoot. We're behind schedule, and the shoot can't be postponed. If it had been me, I suppose they would have to, but since it wasn't, I need to go. I'm an actress. I'm paid to turn it on and off anytime the studio wants. In a way, I suppose I'm lucky. It's a way of escaping. And tonight, because of what happened today, I can get the studio to put me up at a fancy hotel. I can tell them I can't go home, and they'll be more than happy to put me up at the Ritz if I ask." Zoey smiled at me, her face lit up like the young ingénue her fans all knew her to be on the screen. "But tomorrow...tomorrow I'll need you to come back here and help me. 'Cause I'm scared."

Chapter 7

Wilson and I didn't talk on the way home. I needed to digest everything that had happened, and by the time we arrived back at the house, Denise was on the doorstep. Sans the tarot cards, she was carrying the same large, oversized bag, and dressed in heels and a colorful sheath dress. Her Realtor Outfit. Soon as she saw the Jag, she waved her hands above her head and ran to greet me, exactly as she'd done before.

Only this time, it wasn't because she wanted a reading. She had obviously seen the news.

"Oh my God, Misty! You were at Zoey's house. Poor girl. How is she?"

Wilson parked in the drive, and I pushed myself from the passenger seat and banged the car's door shut. For all the Jaguar's sporty features, comfort wasn't one of them. "Good as can be expected," I said.

"But Lacey." Denise put her hand to her throat. "She was so young, and vibrant...and she was Zoey's best friend. It's hard to imagine she's dead. Zoey must be terribly upset."

Without answering, I ambled toward the house, doing the best I could to stay ahead of Denise with my arthritic knees. Denise paused halfway up the walk.

I stopped, knowing what was about to come, and turned to see Wilson as he slipped from the driver's seat and out the window like an Olympic gymnast.

"Were you driving Wilson's car?" Denise furrowed her brow and looked back at the Jag.

"I thought it would be okay. The key was on the key rack in the kitchen, and you did ask me to keep the place up. I assumed that included the cars. Was I wrong?"

"It's just—"

I switched the subject, the less said about Wilson and his car the better. "I'm sorry, Denise. I know you want to talk about Zoey, but, I can't. She's been a client for a while now, and you know I can't talk about her. It's not professional."

I went up the steps to the porch and put my key in the lock.

"Even a little?" Denise asked.

"Even at all," I said.

"Then at least tell me about the house. I haven't been inside in years. What's it look like?"

"You're asking me as a realtor then, not as a fan?" I turned the lock on the door.

"If it'll loosen your tongue…a realtor." Denise smiled coyly. What did I have to fear?

I pushed the door open and Denise followed me inside while she continued with her comments about the house.

"For your information, realty wise, I think Zoey overpaid for the place. It stood empty for nearly ten years. The last owners were jet setters. Never home. Owned houses all over the world and then priced the property so high realtors refused to show it. I heard Zoey paid six million for the place. Six million. Can you imagine? That house wasn't worth a dime over five. And then she spent a fortune remodeling. And insisted the place be painted pink. Like it was originally. Who does that today? Pink, of all colors."

Denise's interest in the property matched my own. As a realtor, I understood her curiosity about what improvements

Zoey might have made on a six thousand square foot mini-mansion that had everything from a wine cellar to an upstairs gym. But it was Denise's understanding of the history of the property that made me think she might know something that would help me better understand what was going on inside the house.

"Well if all you want to know," I said, "is what she's done with the place, I suppose I could share with you a little of what I saw."

Wilson glared at me from the front porch and swept past me to the study. A not so subtle reminder he didn't want his sister in the house. Anticipating his intent to slam the door, I grabbed the handle and closed it quietly behind me, then nudged Denise in the direction of the living room.

"There's a book on the coffee table you should look at. It was your brother's. *Historic Hollywood Homes.* I was looking through it yesterday after Zoey left. You might find it interesting."

Denise settled herself into one of the wingback chairs with the book on her lap.

"You know," she said, "the entire Fryman area was once owned by Tom Mix, the silent film star. The man made a fortune in real estate. The property Zoey's house is on, Mix lost in a bet to another actor named Clayton Mann. He was the original owner and built the Pink Mansion for his wife and daughter back in the early forties."

"Were you ever inside?" I asked.

"Once, years ago for an open house. The listing agent back then had worked up a one-sheet with the house's history. The Manns didn't live there long. They sold the house back in 1943, three years after they moved in. Rumor had it the couple had a four-year-old daughter who drowned in the backyard pool during a birthday party. If that happened today, a realtor would have to list it on the property records, but that was so long ago. I doubt there's ever been any reference to it."

"A little girl?" My mind flashed on the cache of items hidden beneath the stairs Zoey had shown me. The pink trowel, the pop bead jewelry. Things a child might treasure and maybe hide.

"Yes, and sometime either before or after the Manns moved out, the pool must have been filled in. It wasn't there when I attended the open house. Then again, the property's always been a bit of a mystery and changed hands half a dozen times before the last owners finally agreed to sell. Poor Zoey. She must blame herself for putting in a new pool and spa."

"She's very upset," I said. "To lose your best friend like that. It can't be easy."

"I tell you, it's the family curse. She's just lucky it wasn't her."

Everyone in Hollywood knew about the Chamberlain family curse. Going all the way back to Zoey's great-grandfather, the Chamberlains had experienced as much fame and fortune as they had tragedy. None had survived past fifty, and all had died as the result of some freak accident.

Denise's wrist phone buzzed. "Ugh. I've got to go. I have a showing down the street, and since I was in the neighborhood, I wanted to stop by and see how you were doing. Plus, I have a bit of good news." Denise raised her hand and crossed her fingers.

Denise's good news could only mean one thing. "You got a meeting with Hugh Jackman?"

"Almost," she said. "I met his publicist. Hugh's doing *The Ellen Show* tomorrow, and she promised to get me in." Denise shook her hands beside her head. "It's happening Misty. It's really happening."

"It appears so," I said.

Denise crunched her shoulders to her ears, kissed me

goodbye on the cheek, and promised to call back with a report. I showed her to the door, then turned to find Wilson standing outside the study with his arms crossed.

"I assume you heard all that?" I said.

"The part about my sister stalking Hugh Jackman or the history of Zoey's house?"

"Let's stick with Zoey's house for the moment, shall we?" I reminded Wilson while I was talking with Zoey, he had slipped away—something he had promised not to do—and I was anxious to know what he had seen. "Did you find anything unusual?"

"Like what?" Wilson asked.

"Like a ghost," I said. "It's what we went there for. I thought that's why you wandered off. That you considered that to be an excusable offense and had connected with something."

"Well, you thought wrong. I've rethought things."

"Again?" I wasn't surprised. Lacey's unexpected death had changed the purpose of today's visit, and shades, by their very nature, can be easily upset by the sudden death of others.

"Look, Misty..."

Misty? Was Wilson really calling me Misty again? Was it a slip of the tongue or a change of heart? I wasn't sure. Only that I'd gotten rather used to him calling me Old Gal. His return to the proper use of my name concerned me.

"I know you asked me not to go snooping around, but if you thought I was going to go ghost hunting and give up the chance to comb through the Pink Mansion, well...I'm sorry. It just wasn't going to happen. I was much more curious as to what Zoey had done with the place and what collectibles I might find from the Chamberlain estate than to chase after some ghost."

"You didn't see anything? No ghosts at all? Lacey or anyone else?"

"I told you, I wasn't looking." Wilson walked back into the study and began perusing the bookshelves.

I followed as far as the doorway. "And what happened to your promise to help me? To help Zoey?"

"You mean so I might earn my wings?" I sensed a note of sarcasm in his voice.

"That was the plan," I said. "Or has that changed now that you've been inside the Pink Mansion?" I couldn't believe we were going back and forth on this again.

"Yes, well, after giving it some thought, I've decided differently." Wilson ran his index finger along the bookshelves, then stopped, and finding a bit of dust, rubbed the first two fingers on his left hand with his thumb and blew the dust in my direction. "You see, Misty, aside from my sister's occasional visits to my home, I'm not at all certain I object to my current state. I'm in no pain. I've no bills to worry about, and other than your intrusion into my life, I'm not all that unhappy."

I stepped into the study. Shades were known to live in a state of denial and waffle on their commitments. I needed to confront this head on.

"Perhaps, Wilson, if you were not so self-involved you might feel differently. But since you are, let me explain it this way. Nature, my friend, abhors a vacuum. If you don't do something to attract positive energy in your direction, just like that dust you've chosen to blow at me so dismissively, you'll be swept up with negative energy. When that happens, you'll be gone. Poof!" I snapped my fingers. "In my experience, shades in your position don't always end up in such a happy place." I turned my back and got as far as the door when I heard a loud bang on the desk.

Wilson had taken a book from the shelf and slammed it onto the desktop. "What is it you want from me?"

I counted to three and then smiled obligingly. "I believe our ghost is a little girl, about four years old. Your sister says the original owner of Zoey's house was an actor named Clayton

Mann."

"Ugh." Wilson made a sour face. "My sister again. I wish you wouldn't quote her to me."

"Regardless, I'm going to need your help. Your sister believes the Manns had a daughter, and that she drowned in a pool accident. I thought somewhere in this grand library of books you have about Hollywood, there might be something about Clayton Mann and his family that may help to identify the girl."

"It's a possibility." Wilson turned back to the bookshelves and ran his finger along the spine of several books, then finding what he wanted, stopped. "In fact, this might be exactly what you're looking for. It's an almanac of Hollywood stars from the thirties and forties and their homes."

Wilson placed the book on the desk and began to thumb through it. He stopped at a large black and white photo of Clayton Mann and his wife Margaret with their daughter Alicia Mae Mann.

Chapter 8

I was still thinking about Alicia Mae the next afternoon as I worked in the garden behind Wilson's cottage, transplanting my herbs from their clay pots in my van into the ground. If Alicia Mae was the ghost that haunted Zoey's home, she had been dead or ghost-like for nearly seventy-five years. While that may have been a long time, she was still a child. One thing about child ghosts—they rarely age.

And they don't kill people.

Child-ghosts, unlike Hollywood movies like to portray, are seldom violent or vengeful. Experience has taught me child-ghosts can be whimsical and playful. Above all things, they enjoy a good tease. Which might explain the disappearance of Zoey's jewelry.

Thinking about all the possible scenarios as I tucked a small sprig of rosemary into the ground, my cell phone buzzed. I brushed the dirt from my hands, reached into my apron, and retrieved my phone.

"Misty?" Zoey's sounded stressed. "Thank God you're home. I need you to come back to the house."

"Are you okay?"

"I'm fine, but the house...it's a mess. Someone trashed the place last night. Can you come and take a look?"

I assured her I'd be right over. Difficult as it is for me to move quickly, I hobbled into the house to find Wilson. He was in the study reclining in his cane back chair with his feet up on his desk, dozing. Ghosts don't sleep. They may hibernate or cocoon, adopting an almost trance-like state, but sleep is something only humans do.

"Wilson?" He sat upright as though I'd surprised him. "Zoey called. She needs me back at the house."

"Is she alright?" Wilson's concern for the young starlet didn't surprise me. He may well have been on the fence concerning our ghost chase, but access again to the Chamberlain estate was an entirely different matter.

"She says someone trashed her house last night. I need you to drive me."

I would have thought news of a possible break-in at the Pink Mansion might have motivated Wilson to put the move on, but instead of the Jag, which I knew could move through traffic in record time, Wilson suggested we take the Rolls. Evidently, he had always made it a practice of rotating his rides, and since we had taken the Jag out yesterday, the Rolls it was.

All of which was fine until I realized the Rolls moved at a snail's pace. I could have walked the mile and a half from Wilson's home to the Pink Mansion in less time than it took to drive. The only good thing about the Rolls—other than being an exact copy of the car Princess Grace had once owned, which pleased Wilson to no end—were the blacked-out windows. So dark it was impossible for anyone to see inside and notice the argument I was having with Wilson, trying to get him to put on a little speed as we turned onto Zoey's street.

Zoey met me at the front door. She looked tired, her eyes strained, her skin even paler than the day before. I doubted even heavy stage makeup could camouflage the weary look on her face. Without saying a word, she opened the door wide, swung around and held out her arm. Like a game show host, she waved a hand to the mess behind her that only yesterday had looked like a room ready to be photographed for *House Beautiful* or *Architectural Digest.*

Today it looked like a tornado had hit. Lamps had been tossed to the floor. Tables and chairs were tipped over. Every seat cushion and back support from the couch had been pulled from its frame, and decorator pillows had been stripped of their covers and lay scattered about the great room, leaving a dusty trail of duck feathers.

"And this isn't all," Zoey said. "Every room's the same. The kitchen's even worse. The drawers have been emptied, the cabinets are a mess, and there's food everywhere."

I stepped into the great room with Wilson behind me. On our drive over, I had instructed him, in no uncertain terms, that he was to case the place. We needed to find our ghost. No skirting the issue. Not like last time. With a slight nod, Wilson left my side and slipped down the hallway in the direction of the west wing.

"This happened last night." The tone of my voice could have been as much a question as it was a statement. Either would have been appropriate. For psychics, time and space tend to blend together. It's not always easy to pinpoint an exact time, but the damage was obvious. Whoever or whatever had torn the house apart wasn't just angry, but wanted to send a message. And while an ordinary intruder would have left after such a scene, I sensed an anxious energy in the air, as though the presence still remained.

Zoey nodded. "I don't know what time it was. I wasn't here. The studio put me up at the Hotel Amarano in Burbank last night. I told them I couldn't go home. Not after what happened. Chad met me at the hotel, and we spent the night together. We didn't come back here until this morning, and then…this is what we found."

Zoey's fiancé appeared from the west wing. "I called the police as soon as we realized what had happened. Once the cops left, Zoey insisted we call you." Chad put his arm around Zoey's shoulder and kissed her lightly on the cheek. "Don't worry, Zoey, the police will find who did this."

Zoey bit her lip and Chad excused himself and said he was going outside for a smoke.

I waited until the front door closed. "But you don't think so."

Zoey shook her head. "Before I left for the studio yesterday, I asked my assistant Crystal to hire a cleaning service to come in. I wanted them to scrub the place top to bottom. I didn't want anything in the house to remind me of what happened yesterday. When the detectives arrived with their forensics team this morning, they dusted for prints. If they found any prints at all, they'd be Chad's or mine."

I took Zoey by the hand and led her away from the front door lest Chad return and interrupt our conversation. "Let's you and I talk. How about the kitchen?"

The kitchen was as much of a wreck as was the great room. Cabinets were open. Plates, pots, and pans were everywhere. I cleared an open space for us on the window seat to sit down, and, with our backs against the window so Zoey couldn't see the backyard, asked her if the reason she had called me was that she thought the ghost had done this.

"Who else?" Zoey buried her head in her hands. "Chad doesn't believe me. He thinks this is all a reaction to the sleeping pills I'm taking. But I know there's a ghost in this house. I can feel it. And I think he wants to kill me. Even worse, I think when the ghost learned it wasn't me in the spa who died but Lacey, he came back last night to find me. And when he didn't, he trashed the place."

I took Zoey's hand away from her face and held it in mine.

While I could understand Zoey's fear, I didn't feel she was in any danger or that the ghost intended her any harm.

"I don't think so, Zoey. I believe you have a ghost, I really do. And I agree with you, I think a ghost may have done this," I gestured to the mess in front of us. "But, not for the reason you suspect."

"No?" Zoey grabbed a tissue off the kitchen counter and dabbed her eyes.

"I think it's something else." I had seen things like this before. My own experience with Wilson had taught me how upset ghosts can be about the movement of their things. I shut my eyes. In my mind I saw Detective Romero and the ring he had found in the spa. The vision of him handing it to Zoey. The look of surprise on her face. "Did you take your mother's mood ring with you when you left last night?"

"I put it in my bag when I left for the studio, why?"

"Because I don't think the ghost meant to hurt you, but may have been looking for the ring instead. You said yourself the ghost had taken it before."

"You really think so?" Zoey squeezed my hand, a look of hopefulness in her eyes. "Then you don't think I'm in any danger? That the ghost was here last night, looking for my ring?"

"I know one way to find out." I said.

"How?"

"Leave the ring on your dressing table tonight."

"And stay here?" Zoey pulled back, her brow wrinkled, eyes narrowed. "You think that's wise?"

"I don't believe you're in any danger and, if you want to, yes. By all means stay here. If I thought for a second you would come to any harm, I wouldn't suggest it. But if you leave the ring on your dressing table and it's not there in the morning, we'll both know who took it."

"The ghost?" Zoey whispered.

I nodded. "I think she's been looking for it."

"She? You think the ghost is a woman?" Zoey's eyes widened.

"I think the ghost is a small child. About four years old."

"A child killed Lacey?"

"No. Not at all. I think what happened to Lacey was probably an accident. Exactly like Detective Romero said. After you and Lacey finished running lines, Lacey went into the backyard to check on the presence of a kitten and for some reason, was attracted to the spa and saw the ring. Maybe your little ghost had dropped it there, and when Lacey went to reach for it, the unfortunate happened. She leaned over, her hair got caught on the drain, and she drowned."

"You said probably." Zoey tilted her head skeptically and raised a brow. "You don't know for sure? I thought a psychic could tell something like that."

"There's a lot of things psychics know, Zoey. I could tell you when I walked in the house yesterday I sensed something terrible had happened here, but as to how Lacey died, I wouldn't know. For something like that, I'd have to spend more time in the house. But before I do, let's see what happens with your ring tonight. Shall we?"

"If you're certain I'm okay, I'll stay. Chad's convinced whoever came in and trashed the place was a fan who was following the news about Lacey's death and used it as an opportunity to break in. I've had stalkers before."

It wouldn't be the first time a fan had broken into a celebrity's home while they were away. Celebrity break-ins had become all too common. It was easy for fans to track their favorite stars' comings and goings. A group the press had dubbed the "Bling Ring" had burgled the homes of several high-profile celebrities and had made off with more than three million dollars in cash and jewelry before they were finally arrested and convicted of their crimes. Anyone watching Zoey's house, particularly after hearing the news of Lacey's death in the spa, might have guessed Zoey might not be home. That she would take a day or two to process Lacey's death before returning. With easy access to the Pink Mansion's backyard from the canyon trails, it was conceivable a hiker might have broken in and trashed the place looking for valuables. But Zoey hadn't reported any jewelry or cash missing.

"I don't think it was stalkers any more than I think there's an evil spirit in this house. However, I will agree with you. You do have a ghost, but like I said, she's a child ghost, and I don't believe she means you any harm. Spirits, regardless of their size or age, are subject to our control. They don't dominate our sphere of existence—our here and now. We do. If your little ghost comes back tonight and bothers you, all you need to do is to tell her to leave. Use that actress voice of yours and command her to go away. She'll leave."

"For good?" Zoey sounded skeptical.

"Probably not until I've spoken to her and learned what it is she wants. But temporarily, yes. It's a bit like sending her to her room. Meanwhile, my sense is, she'll come back tonight, take the ring and leave. You'll never know she's been here until tomorrow morning. You've nothing to worry about."

"Excuse me, Zoey. I'm sorry to interrupt." Chad stood in the doorway to the kitchen, his cell phone in his hand. "Crystal's on the phone. She needs to go over your schedule with you. She tried your phone, but you didn't answer."

"I suppose that's my cue to leave." I hugged Zoey goodbye and added, "Call me in the morning. You'll be fine."

Chapter 9

There's a curious thing that happens to me when I begin to work a new case. I don't know about other psychics, but for me, it's as though the universe begins to throw breadcrumbs at me. Over the years, I've learned there are no accidents. People, ideas, or breadcrumbs, as I like to refer to them, often appear to me when I'm in a state of luminary-acceptance, and while on the surface some of the people and events may not seem to be connected, invariably I find they always are. And as Wilson and I drove home, I began to feel as though I was being pelted by breadcrumbs. They were coming at me from every direction.

The first crumb was innocent enough. We were two blocks from Zoey's house when I spotted a string of nursery school kids dressed in their brightly colored coats with their little backpacks strapped to their backs. Like ducklings, they lined up at the school crossing and waited for the light to change. Holding on to their parents' hands, the crossing guard escorted them all safely across the street. My mind flashed to Alicia Mae. Had her mother dressed her and sent her to school in the same fashion? Walked her to the local schoolhouse? Was there even a school here in the forties? Probably not. Most of this area back then, with the exception of the land around the Pink Mansion, had been citrus orchards. Hollywood's outback for ranches and rural living. But the image of a small child, holding tightly to her mother's hand, persisted. I let it find a home in the back of my mind, knowing at some point as I worked to connect with Zoey's ghost, it would all make sense.

The second crumb was Denise. She called my cell phone as Wilson drove the Rolls past the school and stopped for a light at the corner of Laurel Canyon and Ventura Boulevard, just blocks from Wilson's home.

I answered the phone and accidentally put it on speaker. My arthritic fingers, not very adept at pushing small buttons, did this more than I care to admit.

"I need a favor, Misty. I'd do it myself, but I'm at an open house and I can't leave."

Wilson scowled at the sound of his sister's voice.

"What do you need?" I asked.

"That book on the coffee table you showed me yesterday. The one about historic Hollywood homes? I need you to bring it to me. I've got a client coming by who says she grew up in the Pink Mansion. I thought it'd be fun to show her the book. My open house is just two doors down from Wilson's. Could you bring it?"

I glanced over at Wilson, his jaw tight, his hands even tighter on the steering wheel.

I put my hand over the remote speaker, and whispered, "Better me than her coming to us. Unless, of course, you want your sister coming in and combing through your things." I knew the answer to that and told Wilson not to worry. I took my hand off the speaker. "Not a problem, I'll bring it by. See you in a bit."

Heather and Allen Jefferies were meeting with Denise when Wilson and I arrived at the open house. The three of them were in the kitchen, and Heather recognized me immediately when I walked in. Wilson, true to his nature, remained sight unseen and made himself at home behind the counter.

"I know you. You're...you're—somebody famous." Heather snapped her fingers in an effort to recall my name.

"Misty Dawn." Denise took the book from me and laid it on the kitchen counter.

"Right." Heather tapped her husband on the shoulder. "The psychic. I used to see you on one of those afternoon talk shows my mother used to watch."

"And this," Denise opened the book and pointed to a photo of Zoey's house, "is the house Heather grew up in."

There it was, like it had been dropped from the sky right in front of me: breadcrumb number three.

Heather leaned over the book. "Oh my goodness. That's it. Is it still pink? That's how we described it to everyone. The Pink Mansion with the big tree in front."

"It's still pink," Denise said. "It's been repainted several times. Different owners, different colors, but Zoey," Denise made air quotes around the name, "liked its original coloring and that people called it the Pink Mansion. From what I understand she's restored it, much as she could. So, yes, it's pink again. And the tree's still there as well."

Heather studied the photo. "I never knew it was so special. To me, it was just a house my father bought back in the late seventies with a great backyard and plenty of room for us kids. Hum..." She paused and tapped her finger on the window on the far left-hand side of the house. "And that...that was my bedroom. It's funny looking at it now. I used to think that house was haunted."

I glanced up at Wilson then looked closer at the photo. The front of the house had only three windows. Two on the right side of the house, arched windows that opened onto the long gallied entry inside, and a third window on the left side of the house, opposite the center atrium. All of them in the photo looked black, but there was something different about the window Heather pointed to.

"Haunted?" I asked. "Do you remember why you thought so?"

"Oh, it's silly," Heather tapped the page with the tips of her fingers, "back then, I had an imaginary playmate. At least that's how my mother described her, but to me, she was as real as you and me. She'd visit me, and we'd play for hours."

Without moving my eyes from the page, I stared at the window as though I might will myself to see behind the glass and into what was once Heather's bedroom. "And what did you play?"

"Dolls," Heather said. "Like most little girls. I loved my dolls, and we used to have tea parties. I remember I had this elaborate tea set, white with little pink roses on it." I flashed onto the small teacup Zoey had pulled from the basket beneath the stairs inside the Pink Mansion. Another breadcrumb. "I'd set it up on a table with my favorite doll in the backyard beneath this big weeping willow tree. She'd come for tea with her doll, and we'd play for hours. We had such fun. I really believed she was real. Even today I think of her as though she was."

"Do you remember what she looked like?" I glanced over at Wilson. If he had seen the ghost, I needed him to listen carefully so that we might compare notes later.

Heather tapped the tips of her fingers lightly against her lips. Clearly, she was trying to recall a memory, dimmed but not forgotten. "It's been a long time, but like I said, I still think of her as real. From what I remember she was small or smaller than me anyway. I was six, and I think maybe she was about four. Mostly I remember she had these long, pretty blonde braids. French braids I think, and freckles."

"Did she have a name?" I asked.

"Lisa something, maybe? I'm not sure. But I do remember

she had a lisp. She had lost her front teeth and couldn't say anything with an 's' sound, and when she said her name, it came out like Litha or something like that."

There it was, another breadcrumb. My eyes met Wilson's. "Alicia Mae?" I asked.

"Ahh! You are psychic." Heather put her hand to her heart. "How did you know that?"

"Misty knows lots of things." Denise picked the book up off the counter. A subtle clue she was anxious to show the house and not divert her client's attention with talk of ghosts any longer. "And I'm sure, Heather, if you'd like, she'd be happy to do a reading for you. She lives a couple doors down the block, in my brother's old house. The Craftsman on the corner."

"Could you?" Heather fisted her hands and tapped her knuckles together excitedly. "I'd love that. My mother tried to convince me I had imagined her. She said all young kids have make-believe friends, and Lisa was mine. If we hadn't moved away when I was six, I think she'd still be with me."

I left the book with Denise and started back down the walk to the cottage with Wilson close behind me. When we got home, two things happened almost simultaneously, both of them revealing.

First, Wilson sneezed soon as we walked in the door. A clear indication he was still new to his limboed state. Newer shades often maintain a lot of their former physical ailments like allergies, indigestion, or headaches until they're closer to their final transformation. And second, my cat reacted most unusually. Rather than scamper off, as I had expected her to when Wilson entered the room, she approached him. With her tail up and a soft meow, she bunted against his leg. A sure sign things had begun to change between the two.

"She sees me?" Wilson pointed to the cat and sneezed again.

"She does." I put my bag on the entry table and walked into the living room.

"But Heather Jefferies didn't. I stood right next to her, and she couldn't see me. Yet she saw Alicia. How is it she could see Alicia then, and not me now? And that damn cat of yours she sees me too."

"Animals and small children, Wilson. They see things differently." I took a seat in the chair where the cat had been napping. "Children because they haven't been taught not to. That is until they make the mistake of telling their parents about their invisible friends, and adults convince them their visions are nothing more than make believe. We all have intuitive talents. We're born with them, but by the time we reach adulthood, most of us have been taught not to trust them. In a sense, it's bred out of us. As for animals, they see because they can. Once they realize you're part of the household, they cease to be surprised by your existence. You're just another being in their presence."

Wilson took a seat on the back of the couch, back to his thinking position. Feet on the cushions, elbow on his knee, chin in his hand. "Heather described Alicia as though she had just seen her. Exactly as I saw her at Zoey's house today. Small. Blonde. And missing her two front teeth."

"Ahh." I raised a finger. Wilson hadn't mentioned what happened when he left me at Zoey's and gone in search of our ghost, he had been pensive and elusive on our drive home. "So you did see Alicia Mae today?"

"Of course I did. You asked me to go looking for her, and I found her."

"And?" Wilson paused. Back to his thinking position. "Did you speak to her?" I asked.

"No. She saw me, but she avoided me. I was in the hallway, outside Zoey's bedroom, and she ran right past me. Like she might be afraid of me."

"She's a child, Wilson. What did you expect?"

"I've no idea. Children have never been my thing. I've always thought of them as someone else's problem, and childhood a necessary sloppiness we all pass through until we arrive at who we are. But I will admit there's something special about this one."

"I believe you're right about that. And if I might make a prediction, things that bothered you as a mortal, like your allergies and attitude about children, the longer you remain in your limboed-state, the less they'll bother you. In fact, you may even grow to enjoy them."

Chapter 10

I wasn't at all surprised when the phone rang early the next morning. I knew before I answered it would be Zoey. She sounded elated.

"The ring's missing, Misty. I did exactly as you told me. I left it on my dressing table last night, and when I woke this morning, it was gone. Gone! Just like you said it would be. The ghost took it, I know she did."

I envisioned Zoey in her nightgown, dancing around her dressing table, elf-like, that she had made contact with the little ghost. I closed my eyes and tried to envision Alicia Mae, and wondered if she was doing the same thing—delighted to have had the ring returned—but the vision wouldn't come.

"Is Chad with you?" I asked.

"He's in bed," Zoey whispered. "I told him you didn't think the ghost would harm me. He still doesn't believe the house is haunted, but he was happy not to spend the night at a hotel."

"And you didn't see or hear anything last night?" I asked.

"No. I was exhausted after everyone left yesterday. The shock of Lacey's death and the house being turned upside down was more than I could take. But, after talking with you, I decided you were right, the ghost wasn't here to hurt me, and I took a sleeping pill. This morning, with the ring missing, I'm beginning to think it's like Detective Romero said, Lacey's death was just an accident. A terrible, terrible accident, but nothing more than that."

I didn't want to alarm Zoey, but there was something about the word *accident* that didn't sit well with me. I wanted to get back into that house to see if I might pick up something more on Lacey's death and why Alicia Mae, after all these years, was still in the house. I asked Zoey if it would be okay if I came by again.

"I was going to ask you. I'm not due back at the studio today until three p.m. Could you come by about eleven? There's so much I want to ask you. We really need to talk."

By the time Wilson and I arrived, Zoey wasn't alone. Three cars were parked in the drive, and I could hear the sound of people talking and laughing as I walked up the stone steps to the house. Before we reached the front door, I suggested Wilson continue his search to find Alicia Mae, this time outside beneath the big willow tree where Heather had said she and Alicia used to have their tea parties. I wanted to talk with Zoey inside the house, alone.

Chad met me at the front door. He was dressed casually in sweatpants and a black T-shirt with skulls on it. I wondered if he had any idea as to the significance of skulls. Most young people find them little more than provocative jewelry accessories. I found it oddly ironic. In ancient civilizations, the skull was considered to be a symbol of the recurring cycle of life and death, particularly the rebirth of the spirit. I doubted Chad was wearing the shirt out of any kind of respect for Lacey's passing, but I thought it a nice touch and said as much as I entered the house.

Chad looked down at his shirt as though he had forgotten what he was wearing and grunted. "Yeah, whatever."

Behind him on the couch, exactly where I had seen them

yesterday, were Zac and Kelsey and next to them, another couple I didn't know. Chad introduced them as Joel, Lacey's cousin and Nora, Joel's girlfriend. "I thought we ought to have friends in. Didn't think it was a good idea for the house to be empty at a time like this."

Before I could offer my condolences, Zoey entered and went immediately to Joel and Nora and greeted them tearfully, then took my hand and introduced me. "I assume Chad introduced you to my friend, Misty Dawn, she's—"

"Zoey's psychic," Chad picked up a pack of cigarettes off the coffee table, lit one, then sat down on the couch and put his feet up on the table. "Zoe's convinced the house is haunted."

"Misty's here to help me, Chad." Zoey flashed Chad a look that, had it been on the cover of one of the tabloids, would have been labeled, "Trouble in Paradise."

"You're a psychic?" Nora's eyes flashed wide. "Can I have your card? I'd love to talk to you sometime."

I fished through my bag for a card and handed it to her. "Whenever you like," I said.

"But not now. She's here to talk to me." Zoey grabbed me by the arm and hustled me off to the kitchen where we could be alone. On the counters were bags full of food Zoey said Chad had ordered from the local deli to sustain them through the mourning process. "I don't know that I need all this food as much as I need for you to look under the stairs and tell me if you see my mother's ring. I didn't have the nerve to look for it myself this morning, and I can't wait any longer. Just tell me if it's there."

While Zoey busied herself unpacking food and arranging it on platters to take to the living room, I opened the small doorway to the closet beneath the stairs. Inside it was dark and stuffy, and I tripped over a small, three-legged stool as I felt around. The basket Zoey had shown me yesterday wasn't there.

Aside from the stool, an old area rug, and a bucket full of rags, the closet was empty.

"I'm sorry, Zoey. It's not here, and the basket's gone as well."

Zoey stopped arranging the platter of cold cuts and looked at me quizzically.

"Gone? Everything?"

I nodded.

"But where? Did she move them? Has she left?" Zoey shook her head as though she was having trouble comprehending. "Please tell me she's not gone. I was beginning to like the idea of her being here."

I was about to explain how ghosts can move their cache with little or no effort. That it didn't necessarily mean Alicia Mae was no longer here, when Chad entered the kitchen.

"Excuse me, Zoey." Chad's face was colorless. "Detective Romero's here. He says it's important."

I followed Chad and Zoey back to the front door.

"Zoey?" Detective Romero stood in the entry with a clipboard in his hand. His demeanor more harried than his previous visit. His skin more sallow. "I'm sorry to bother you, but we need to talk."

"What's wrong?" Zoey shrugged a shoulder. Clearly, she had no idea why the detective had returned.

"I'm afraid I've bad news. It looks like whoever broke in yesterday knew what they were doing. Probably gloved-up. Must have known the security code and bypassed the alarm. The security company doesn't have any record of it going off, and none of your neighbors claimed to have heard anything. And unfortunately, our forensics team wasn't able to lift any prints, just yours and your fiancé's."

Zoey half-laughed and leaned over to me and whispered, "Yeah, maybe that's because ghosts don't leave prints."

"I'm sorry?" Detective Romero looked at me. "I didn't get your name the other day. You're?"

"Misty Dawn," Zoey said. "She's a friend of mine. And a psychic. Perhaps you've heard of her?"

I handed Romero my business card. He looked at it, back at me, and ran his eyes up and down my body as though he were scanning me for contraband. Another time he might have asked to search my bag for drugs and would have found a zip lock bag of herbs I carry. All quite legal in California. Fortunately, he passed. Which didn't disappoint me.

"So, you're Misty Dawn. The famous clairvoyant. The same Misty Dawn who worked with the FBI a couple years back. The one who found that college girl who'd gone missing."

"That and several other cases," I said. "Most weren't so well publicized."

"Huh." Romero tapped my card against his clipboard. "Never much believed in stuff like that myself. But 'round the station, a lot of guys think you're the real thing. Don't see how you'd be much help with a case like this though."

"Case?" Zoey wrinkled her brow. "What case, Detective? I thought you were here to tell us about the break-in."

"I'm afraid that's not the only reason I'm here, Zoey. I didn't come back to talk with you about the break-in. I'm here because the coroner told us Lacey was hit on the back of the head. Her death wasn't accidental. We're investigating a homicide."

Zoey gasped and stepped back. "I don't believe you. That's impossible. It was an accident. You said so yourself. Why would someone kill Lacey?"

"Miss, I think you should sit down." Detective Romero pointed his clipboard toward the couch.

"No. No, I don't want to sit. I want you to tell me why you thought my best friend accidentally drowned in the spa two days ago, and now you don't think so. Explain that to me."

"Like I said, the coroner did an autopsy and found evidence Lacey was hit on the back of the head. And—" The detective took a beat. A bit too rehearsed I thought. I had seen it before when investigators wanted to unsettle a potential suspect.

"And what, Detective?" Zoey's eyes swept from Romero to Chad and back again.

"And she was pregnant." The detective pinned his eyes to Zoey's and studied her response.

"Pregnant?" Zoey went pale.

"You didn't know?"

"No." Zoey shook her head. "She didn't say anything."

Romero made a note on his clipboard.

Chad put his arm protectively around Zoey. "You don't have to answer any questions, Zoey." Then to the detective he added, "You got a search warrant or something?"

"I'm not here to search the property, son. We did that the day Lacey died, and again after somebody tossed the place. What I want to do now is ask a couple questions that might help us to understand what happened here."

"You really think this is necessary?" Chad looked at Zoey then back to the group of their friends on the couch. "We're in the middle of mourning Lacey's death, Detective. This is hardly the time."

"I'm sorry," Romero said, "but I've got a job to do. Shouldn't take long."

"Chad, the detective's right." Zoey put her hand on Chad's chest and gently pushed him away. "What do you want to know?"

"When I was here the morning you reported finding Lacey's body in the spa, I told you we found a cigarette butt, with lipstick on it, out by the pool. You said Lacey didn't smoke, and the coroner didn't find any signs of her smoking either. So, I'd like to collect DNA samples from each of you. See if we can get a match to that cigarette butt."

Chad interrupted. "You're barking up the wrong tree, Detective. If you think Zoey killed Lacey because you found some cigarette butt in the backyard and you're trying to match it to Zoey, you're crazy. Zoey loved Lacey. We all loved her. Why would Zoey or anyone here want to kill her?"

"Hold on," Romero held his hand up. "Nobody's accusing anybody of murder."

"Murder? So now it's murder? And you're talking to us?" Chad wiped his hands on his pants. "Well, none of us were here that night, 'cept Zoey, and she was asleep. Isn't that right, Zoe? I was at the studio with Zac and Kelsey. We had a late recording session that night. You can check if you like."

Romero made another note on his clipboard.

"Besides," Chad nodded to the window to the backyard, "for all we know, someone might have snuck in through the back gate from the park. You said yourself it was unlocked. Park's closed at night, who knows if a hiker snuck in? Maybe saw Lacey by the spa, mistook her for Zoey, and killed her. Stars like Zoey always have stalkers."

"Stop it, Chad." Zoey covered her ears. "The detective's not here to accuse me or any of us. He needs our help. And if it helps to understand whatever happened to Lacey, I'm down with it. If you need DNA samples, we'll do it, and anything else, too."

The detective checked off something on his clipboard, then said, "I need a complete list of people who have been in the house the last couple of days, plus the names of anyone who may have known the security code."

Zoey answered, "As far as a list of everybody, I don't know. People come and go around here. Chad takes a lot of meetings at the house. As for as the security code, just me, Chad, and I suppose Zac and Kelsey. They stay over sometimes, and also my housekeeper, and my personal assistant."

"Ms. Martini?" Romero glanced back at the clipboard.

"Crystal," Zoey said.

"That's a name? Crystal Martini?"

"It is in Hollywood," Zoey answered. "But if you've issues with her name, you can ask her. I'm expecting her here soon. In fact," Zoey glanced through the window beside the front door. From behind her, I could see a woman outside in the courtyard. She took a final drag on her cigarette, then snuffed it out with the toe of her shoe and approached the front door. "That's her coming up the walk now."

Crystal Martini was tall, trim, and without an ounce of fat on a size two frame. I guesstimate her to be in her mid to late twenties, and hard. The type of woman who looked like she had been born to wear a business suit and comfortable in five-inch steel heels. Her hair was short. Sheared above the ear on one side of her head and cut geometrically on the other in a bleached blonde bob that shingled up the back of her neck.

Zoey let Crystal in and introduced the detective. "Crystal, this is Detective Romero. He's here because the coroner believes somebody may have murdered Lacey."

I would have expected a response, a look of surprise or a gasp at the very least, but Crystal was cool as her name. With a briefcase in one hand, Chrystal gave Zoey a quick hug, and with the other shook Detective Romero's hand.

"I'm sure there must be some mistake, Detective, but if there's anything you'd like to know, you can ask me. I was here for dinner the night Lacey drowned. The three of us dined together in the kitchen. I brought in a risotto from Angelinos. It's one of Zoey's favorites, and I left right after we finished eating so Lacey could run lines with Zoey. Zoey was tired, and she told me she didn't expect to work much past ten. I suggested she take a sleeping pill so she could get a good night's sleep. The next morning she called and told me Lacey had drowned."

The detective turned to Zoey. "And that was the last time you saw Lacey alive?"

"Detective," Crystal interrupted. "I think Zoey made it very clear the last time she talked to you that she and Lacey thought they had heard a sound. A cat or something outside. Wasn't that right, Zoey?"

Zoey nodded. "It was getting late. I was exhausted, and Lacey told me she wanted to check on it and would let herself out. We both thought it was just some feral cat. Nothing to worry about. And like Crystal said, I took a sleeping pill and went to bed."

"I'm sorry, Detective, I'm afraid that's all she can remember." Crystal stepped between Romero and Zoey and gestured with her hand toward the door.

Romero wasn't about to be put off by Crystal and putting his hand on her shoulder pushed her out of the way until he was face to face with Zoey. "And then the next morning, right after finding your best friend dead in the spa, you left that afternoon for the studio. Is that right?"

"Your point, Detective?" Crystal wasn't about to let Zoey answer any more questions and put her hand on the door and held it open.

"I'm just filling in a timeline."

"Then you understand deadlines. And know Zoey's working on a movie, and that she couldn't come back here after the accident. It was too awful. So the studio put her up at a hotel that night, and while she was out, I arranged for a cleaning crew to come in and clean up the place."

"You arranged for the cleaning crew?" Romero looked back at his clipboard, ready to check something off.

"I did, and I'm sure you understand, Zoey's very upset by what happened with Lacey. She's an artist and very sensitive.

Since moving in, she's had a fear that the house was haunted. She hadn't been sleeping well, and after Lacey drowned, she was afraid the ghost had something to do with it. Chad and I both agreed it might be a good idea to have someone come in and scour the place. That it might make her more comfortable. I'm afraid coming home the next day and finding the place tossed didn't help."

"I'm sure it didn't, Ms. Martini, but uncomfortable as it may be for Zoey, I'll need to talk to everyone here, including Zoey."

"Are you suggesting she's a suspect?"

"No, but right now we're conducting an investigation and difficult as it may be for you, working with a big movie star and all, I'm sure you understand the importance of cooperating."

Crystal stretched her hand out for Zoey. "Detective, you've made it very clear you have a job to do, but before you go any further, I need you to understand something. This movie Zoey's making, it's the biggest in her life. It's a multi-million-dollar production. Talk to whomever you like, but if you need to talk with Zoey again, you'll have to arrange it with her attorney."

Chapter 11

When Wilson and I got back to his house, I fixed myself a cup of lavender tea. I needed something to settle my nerves. I sensed Detective Romero's call on Zoey foreshadowed trouble, and asked Wilson to join me at the dining room table. If he had connected with Alicia Mae, perhaps she might know something about the night Lacey drowned, and if she did, I wanted to know.

"Tell me you've got some good news. That you did more than just observe our little ghost this time."

Wilson looked pleased with himself, and with the chair's back to the table, straddled the seat opposite me, cowboy style. "I should get Brownie points or whatever it is you give out for good behavior."

"Good behavior?" I put my cup down. "Need I remind you, Wilson, your work here is a kind of quid pro quo."

"Oh, that's right. That is how this is supposed to work, isn't it?" Wilson smiled and jiggled the back of his chair. "Well, then, you'll be happy to know, not only did I talk with Alicia, but she invited me to a tea party." Wilson paused and waited for my reply.

"A tea party? And how may I ask, is it you went from Alicia running away from you to inviting you for tea?"

"Simple. Girls love bling. I found a sparkly barrette on

Zoey's dresser, something that looked like Zoey might have worn as a child, and offered it to her."

"And for that, she invited you to tea?"

"She did, and not just tea. Turns out there's a playhouse in the backyard beneath the big weeping willow tree. In front of it is a child-sized picnic table. The playhouse is just behind the pool. Alicia said her father built it for her. It looks like a little gingerbread house with all the trimmings. But I suppose you haven't seen it since you mere mortals wouldn't be able to."

Wilson smiled, beaming with pleasure at his new found discovery.

"Indeed," I said. Noting the pleased tone in Wilson's voice, I added a little of my own. "However, now that you've mentioned it to this mere mortal woman of psychic powers, I'll be sure to look for it."

"You're welcome. And, if it helps to know, it appears Alicia's gone to live there, at least temporarily."

"Did she say why?"

The idea that Alicia was living in the playhouse didn't surprise me. If something had happened to frighten her—if she had seen Lacey drown—it made sense she would seek refuge in a safe place, and Zoey or anyone living in Zoey's house would never know the playhouse was still there. In reality, the playhouse had been torn down years ago, but in the spirit world, where Alicia lived and Wilson hovered between, it still existed. In its own sphere, invisible to those currently inhabiting the Pink Mansion.

"I didn't ask why she was living there. But I can tell you this, Heather was right, Alicia Mae has a lisp and the most becoming giggle. Not at all shrill or annoying like many little girls."

"Dare I say, it sounds to me like our little ghost has wrapped you around her little finger, Wilson."

"I wouldn't go that far, but I am curious." He got up from the table, walked to the window, and looked outside, "Is Alicia Mae stuck here like me? Is she a shade?"

I took another long sip of my tea before I answered. I didn't know, but the thought had occurred to me.

"Possibly," I said. "If she's been here since she drowned, all those years ago, maybe. If she was a ghost, it's more likely she would have come and gone, and if she had, she wouldn't be alone. Ghosts like company, they seldom travel alone unless they've attached themselves to someone for a specific purpose. And then it's usually temporary. The fact Heather remembers her as well makes me wonder if perhaps there's a reason why Alicia hasn't left."

"If she's a shade, why has it taken her so long to transition? You told me not to get too settled, that once the universe had made its mind up about me, I could go at any time. Certainly, the powers-that-be can't have any doubts about a child. Why would she still be here? All alone like she is?"

I looked down at my teacup. The spirit world was as full of mystery as the mortal world. In many ways, they're mirror images of each other. My only answer to Wilson's question was that we each have a mission to fulfill. When we've accomplished what we've been sent here to do, we leave. "My sense is, she's waiting for something or someone. Did she mention anything about the pool? Or Lacey? Or the accident?"

"We didn't talk about the accident or Lacey for that matter. But she did say she is afraid of the water. She won't go near the pool. She said her doll had fallen in once and she had gone after it. That her mother was very mad at her because of it. I got the feeling she felt as though she had been sent to her room and was waiting for her mother to come and tell her it was okay to come out again."

"That's a long time out," I said.

"Yes, but from this side, time is different. Tomorrow can be yesterday and yesterday hasn't even happened yet."

"An interesting observation, and one I will have to take into consideration." I thanked him for his work and told him I needed my meditation time. Time to think about what I had learned about Zoey and Alicia Mae. Why the two had found their way to me, and what it was I was meant to do.

I had never encountered a shade that had stuck around as long as Alicia Mae, but the fact she was still here, in the same house she had died in seventy-five years earlier, told me she had a very good reason not to leave. Perhaps Wilson was right. Maybe she was waiting for her mother to return. Or perhaps she had attached herself to Zoey like she had to Heather, because she identified with her. If so, why?

Chapter 12

The next morning, I woke with a sense of urgency and a need to get my hands dirty. I do some of my best thinking when I'm gardening. There is something about the soft feel of earth between my fingers that grounds my thoughts and allows that part of me that gravitates to the other side to come forward.

And as I tended to my nursery of young greens and herbs in the back yard, I let my mind wander freely. A myriad of thoughts, from the scene at Zoey's house, to Detective Romero's news LAPD had opened an investigation into Lacey's death, and back to Alicia Mae and Wilson's report to me about the playhouse in the backyard. None of my thoughts were fully flushed out, but I had an overwhelming sense of anxiety something was about to happen, when Wilson called to me.

"You best get yourself cleaned up, Old Gal, you have a caller."

Wilson stood at the back door, the screen partially opened. It wasn't yet nine o'clock, and I generally don't begin readings until at least ten a.m. But as I got to my feet, I realized I had been expecting something or someone since sun up. Hence my early morning rush to the garden.

"Who is it?" I asked.

"Crystal," Wilson said. "She's on the front porch. She looks upset."

Ah, so this was the cause of my early morning angst. I opened the door. Crystal pushed by me and stopped in the entryway.

"I need to see you," she said.

In her arms, Crystal hugged a large leather Hermes bag against her chest like a Roman shield. The cost of it more than my entire earnings last year. I sensed she feared I might cast some magic spell on her—thus the shield—and stepped back behind the door and gestured politely in the direction of the living room.

"Please come in." I might have added I had been expecting her, but I knew that might only add to her agitated state and instead smiled sweetly.

"I'm on my way to Lacey's memorial. I don't have a lot of time." Crystal got as far as the couch and spun around. "But first, you have to promise not to tell Zoey I was here."

I stopped short of entering the living room. Wilson behind me, his back against the study door. "Here it comes. The star's personal manager has come to intercede. Buckle your seatbelt."

With my teeth clenched and my lips barely moving, I told Wilson to *zip it*, then broke my smile and assured Crystal all my conversations were confidential. "But, I must add, if your visit is in regard to Lacey's death or anything related, you really should talk to Detective Romero."

"No." Crystal raised her hands to the ceiling. "It has nothing to do with Lacey or her death for that matter. It has to do with you, Misty."

Crystal pointed a finger directly at me. Like a dagger.

"Me?"

"I need you to back off."

Wilson let out another Bronx cheer. "Yeah, like that's going to happen."

"Are you threatening me?" Crystal wasn't the first person to object because I had gotten too close to a friend or revealed information their significant other didn't like and wanted me to back off. "You can interpret that any way you like. I tried to tell you the other day. Zoey's fragile. She's under tremendous pressure from the studio, and this nonsense you're feeding her about a ghost has got people questioning her sanity. I need you to stop."

"This nonsense *I'm* feeding her?"

"Yes, you. Until you came along this idea about a ghost was all just some fanciful thinking on her part. Something she manifested based on a few creaks and croaks she heard in the house at night. And now you've got her believing there really is a ghost living in the house. So how much is it going to take, Misty?" Crystal reached into her expensive Hermes bag and pulled out a checkbook. "A thousand dollars? Two thousand? Tell me. I'll write you a check right now, and next time Zoey comes by you can tell her you were wrong. That it wasn't a ghost at all. Make up any excuse you like, but tell her you can't see her again. I'll make it worth your while."

I rounded the coffee table and sat on the chair opposite the couch. "You can put your checkbook away. I won't take your money."

Crystal looked down at the floor. "Right. You want something else. A connection back to Hollywood maybe? Perhaps a late-night gig on a talk show?" Crystal put her checkbook back in her bag. "Something that might restore your former glory as a fortune teller?"

"Fortune teller? Is that what you think I am? Well, let me set the record straight. First off, I'm not a fortune teller, and I resent being called that. I don't read people's fortunes. I advise them based on the energy that surrounds them. What they do with it, and what they draw into their lives, is totally up to them. And second, I didn't seek Zoey out because she's some

Hollywood starlet. Zoey came to me because she thought I could help her. And just so you don't have doubts about it, Zoey's not as fragile as you may think, and I'm not feeding her any nonsense about some ghost. Zoey's not just imagining her house is haunted. It is haunted."

Wilson moved into the living room and rubbed his hands together. "Oh, this is getting good."

"You don't believe in ghosts, do you, Crystal?"

Crystal put her hand to her head. Poor girl. Anyone else I would have offered a cup of my lavender tea, fresh from the garden, guaranteed to soothe that annoying headache I could see was mounting between her temples.

"You're not serious?" Crystal said. "Why would you think I'd believe in ghosts? I'm a college-educated woman. I don't put my faith in old ladies who make their living trying to dupe people about things that go bump in the night."

Wilson pulled a book from the shelf behind the couch and let it fall to the floor. *Plop!*

Crystal's head jerked in the direction of the bookshelf.

"That doesn't mean they don't exist," I said.

Crystal picked the book up off the floor and dropped it on the coffee table. "You can try to scare me with your tricks, but it won't work. I don't have time for make-believe and tricksters like yourself. It's my job to take care of Zoey's schedule and to see there are no conflicts and that riffraff like you don't bother her."

"Riffraff!" Wilson fluttered the blinds at the window.

Crystal scoffed. "More tricks?"

"Drafts," I said. "It's an old house. It's drafty, no tricks. I don't need them." I shrugged my shoulders and held my hand up. A signal to Wilson to cool it.

"I'm warning you. I've got a few tricks of my own. I'll ruin you."

"I'm sure you'd like to try."

Crystal sat down. "Look, Zoey's stressed. She's working on a movie that's over budget, behind schedule and living in a house she should never have bought in the first place. Not to mention she's engaged to a man who, in my opinion, is more interested in what she can do for him than he is in her."

"You think he's using her?" I had sensed tension between Chad and Zoey. As to the cause, I didn't know. Chemistry not only clouds the vision of young lovers, but frequently those close to them as well. I made a mental note to spend more time with Chad to gauge his sincerity.

"I think Zoey could do better," Crystal said. "A lot better. The truth is, without her, Chad's nothing. He calls her his muse. You ask me, it's more like she's his financier. She pays for everything. His band. His travel. His studio time. And don't even get me started on his new drummer and his girlfriend."

"Zac and Kelsey?"

"Zac's an okay drummer. Kelsey sings...a little. Does backup stuff mostly and claims she's a writer, but so far nothing's happening. Chad needs a hit, and quick. His career's on the skids and Zoey, well...she's Zoey. She'll always have something. She's a Chamberlain, an heiress to a successful Hollywood franchise. But you know how it is in Hollywood when winners and losers hook up, it isn't always a match made in heaven."

Crystal glanced at her watch. "Look, I came here to tell you to back off. Between this Detective Romero snooping around and the paparazzi following Zoey's every move, she doesn't need to be fantasizing about ghosts. The more word gets out about it, the crazier she looks. So, if you really want to help her, stop encouraging her."

I stood up. "I'm afraid I can't do that, Crystal. It's not within my nature."

Crystal patted her bag and raised a brow. "Think it over.

You wouldn't be the first in Hollywood to be paid for your silence."

"I don't need your money. However, I do have a piece of advice for you."

"A premonition, from a psychic? Oh, I'm so excited," Crystal clapped her hands in mock delight. "You will forgive me if I don't ask you what it is."

I feel I should warn you, you might want to watch your step." I opened the door for her.

"Yeah, right. Like you'd know." Crystal brushed me, pushing me against the door, and started down the steps to the drive.

I bowed my head down and counted silently. *One thousand one. One thousand two. One thousand—*

Crack!

I didn't need to look up. I could have predicted it, psychic or otherwise. Crystal's heel had caught on the edge of the step. Fortunately, she had stumbled harmlessly onto the grass with nothing more than a broken heel and a bruised ego.

"Are you okay?" I offered her my hand. She rebuffed my offer and reached for her shoe.

"I'm fine, thank you." Crystal stood up, waved the shoe above her head, and hobbled towards her car.

I hollered from the porch. "Just so you know, that's not the step I wanted to warn you about."

"Yeah, right." Crystal flipped me a middle finger salute and hobbled back to her car.

"Seriously, you've put yourself on a mighty high perch, your next fall might not be so graceful."

Three hours later, Zoey was at my front door. She had come from Lacey's memorial and was dressed in black mourning attire. Her hair pulled up beneath a large black hat and her eyes hidden behind dark saucer-shaped glasses. In her hands, she had a rolled-up tabloid.

"Did you see this? I can't believe it." Zoey held the paper up for me to see. "Someone put it beneath the wiper blade on my car at the service. They think I'm a suspect!"

Zoey rushed in, threw her hat on the floor, and collapsed on the sofa with her head between her legs. The tabloid slipped to the floor. A banner headline screamed, "Zoey Questioned in Best Friend's Drowning. Lacey Adams dies in spa accident."

Beneath the headline was a photo of Zoey, her hands to her head with black mascara running down her face, her mouth wide open about to scream. She looked awful. The photo had to have been taken by one of the paparazzi the morning Lacey had died. I remembered trying to hustle Zoey back inside as members of the media hollered at her for a statement.

I skimmed the article. Nothing I didn't already know, but the picture it painted of Zoey was even more unflattering than the photo of her on the front page. I sat down on the sofa next to her and folded the newspaper on my lap.

"What's happening?" I asked.

"I don't know." Zoey shook her head, her eyes welled with tears. "I was hoping you could tell me. I can't talk to Chad about the ghost, he gets angry with me if I bring it up. I know you don't believe Alicia Mae's involved, but I was thinking, maybe she knows who killed Lacey, because I sure don't. But if you read the tabloids, they make it sound like it was me."

Zoey grabbed the paper from my lap and began to read. "'According to an anonymous source close to the investigation, Zoey and Lacey had had a recent falling out.'" Zoey put the paper back in her lap, "Which is a total lie. Lacey and I loved each other." Zoey picked up the paper again. And then it says, 'Zoey had been stressed-out with the filming of her latest movie,

A Little Romance, and the recent move with fiancé Chad Henderson into a new house, which, she believes to be haunted.' Shall I go on?"

"Has Chad seen this?" I asked.

"He's furious, and my agent's freaking out. She's afraid if this isn't settled quickly I won't be able to leave for Italy in time to finish up filming." Zoey bit her thumbnail.

"That's a lot on anyone's plate, Zoey."

"I've been thinking, what if you did a séance? Do you think Alicia Mae might show up? Maybe she knows who killed Lacey."

Chapter 13

Séances, aside from a round table, candles, and a quiet spot, require a precise order. The number of willing participants, or sitters as I like to call them, must be divisible by three. They should all possess positive energy, the ability to clear away any negative thought, and most importantly, a desire to make contact with a spirit that has crossed over. They're slightly more complicated than asking a medium or someone like Wilson to interact with a spirit from the other side. Had I been working with a more experienced spirit guide, I might have chosen to do that. But the problem was, Wilson was still new to the game. Easily disturbed and I couldn't depend on him not to waffle. Hence, I agreed to the idea of a séance, not only for Zoey's sake but as a teaching moment for Wilson as well.

I scheduled the séance for the following evening and asked Zoey to pick two close friends who she believed might best help her in our attempt to contact Alicia Mae. I chose Denise and her client, Heather Jefferies. As a psychic-junkie, Denise attended a number of my séances in the past and I knew I could depend on her for positive energy. Heather, because she knew Alicia Mae. The two had played together and shared a bedroom, and I felt Heather's presence around the table would help Alicia know our table was a safe place.

Zoey asked Chad, and Chad asked Zac. I was concerned

about Chad, but Zoey said she told him she needed a chance to prove once and for all there really was a ghost in the house. Chad acquiesced, but only if his friend Zac could come. I had worked with mixed groups of believers before, and told Zoey as long as they promised to remain open-minded I was fine with their presence. In fact, the additional male energy around the table would be a good idea. The men's presence would add a nice blend of male and female energies. In total, we had six people: Zoey, Chad, Zac, Denise, Heather, and me. The requisite number. I didn't count Wilson as he would serve as our spirit guide and would not need a seat at the table.

However, Wilson's presence brought with it one small problem: Denise. Wilson's sister had no idea of her brother's limboed state, and Wilson wanted to keep it that way. So, for the purpose of the séance, I asked Wilson to adopt a pseudonym. Another name his sister would not know. Wilson insisted upon Thornton, a name he chose based on his appreciation of Thornton Wilder, author of *Our Town*, the first stage play Wilson had ever worked on. Which, in a bizarre sort of way, worked. The play was about a ghost returning to a small town, and a stage manager who directed the audience's attention to the action on the stage. Not too dissimilar to the role Wilson would play as our spirit guide for our séance.

It helped that Wilson was a former set designer. In no time at all he transformed the dining room with its gently filtered light that streamed through the home's stained glass windows, into a dark, mysterious candlelit sanctuary. To do this, he hung green velvet drapes from the walls. Items he claimed to have rescued from the prop department when they auctioned off the set for *Gone with the Wind*. On the table, he placed a lace tablecloth from the set of *Arsenic and Old Lace*, and in the center of the table a tiered candelabra with six slim tapers from the set of *The Addams Family*. Next to the candelabra, I placed a dish of shortbread cookies I made along with a glass of milk. Bait for Alicia.

The pièce de résistance arrived when Denise and Heather rang the front bell. Much to my surprise, Heather presented me with a vintage Madame Alexander doll with rosy cheeks, dressed in a frilly pink and white frock with a matching hat. Exactly like she had been when Heather and Alicia Mae had their tea parties all those years ago beneath the tree in the backyard. The doll was the perfect addition to our little group, and I placed her on the table next to the plate of cookies.

Zoey, Chad, and Zac arrived moments later, and I made brief introductions. It wasn't necessary for them to exchange anything more than the minimum of formalities. In fact, in most cases, less is more. What was important was that each of the sitters knew they were here to help Zoey make contact with the ghost.

There's a pattern to a séance. A definite beginning where I light the candles and ask my sitters to hold hands and repeat a welcome chant or prayer, calling for our spirit guide to join us. A middle where our spirit guide introduces the visiting spirit or spirits and they make themselves known. And a very definitive end where I thank the spirits for their visit. It's important the pattern be followed lest a spirit feel slighted or as though a door has been slammed in their face. In all my years of doing séances, I had never had a problem, but I had heard of unhappy spirits following people home who hadn't followed instructions. And when they did, things got messy. Lives got complicated, personal effects went missing, and accidents happened.

I began by asking for everyone to take a seat around the table and hold hands. I then asked them to bow their heads and observe a moment of silence. When the room had settled and the only sound was that of our own breathing, I introduced Wilson, or Thornton as I would refer to him throughout the séance, as our spirit guide.

"Thornton's job is to bring together the spirits who want to speak to us tonight. You won't see or hear him. He'll speak to me, and whatever he says, I'll relay to you." Zoey sat next to me and looked up from her bowed head and squeezed my hand. Her palms felt damp. I could tell she was nervous. I squeezed back. "We've had a bit of luck because I happen to know Thornton has already made contact with your ghost. For those here tonight who don't know, her name's Alicia Mae, and she's four years old."

My sitters, even Chad and Zac, responded with a communal, "Awe." It's hard not to when told of the presence of a child ghost. Even the most hardened critic can find something dear about a small child so willing to help.

I paused long enough to recognize each sitter's willing connection with a child-ghost, then began with an opening prayer asking for the light of guidance and safety, and for everyone around the table to join with me in summoning Alicia Mae's spirit.

"Repeat after me," I said, and the sitters all followed in unison. "Alicia Mae, we're here tonight to welcome you. We bring gifts. Cookies and milk to refresh yourself. Come, join us in this celebration."

There was silence followed by a stillness in the room, so quiet I could hear the pulsing of my heart in my ears. I held tight to both Zoey and Chad's hands, reassuring them. The candle flickered. I squeezed their hands again, and in moments I heard the light sound of small feet—little hard-soled shoes—running across the dining room's wooden floor. The lilting sound of a child's laughter. I opened my eyes. Everyone at the table exchanged nervous glances. The six of us weren't alone.

Heather was the first to speak. "Does anyone else smell lemons? I smell lemons."

"I do." Zoey's eyes locked with mine, searching for some sign of confirmation. "I've smelled lemons before around my dressing table. I thought it was just my hand cream, but it's her, isn't it? It's Alicia Mae."

"It must be," Heather said. "She told me her mother used to rinse her hair with fresh lemons from their trees. Can you see her, Misty? Is she here with us?"

I nodded. For the first time, I saw Alicia Mae, peeking out from behind Heather's chair. She looked exactly like the photo I had seen of her in the book Wilson had shown me. Small, with blonde ringlets down to her waist. She was dressed in a pale pink chiffon pinafore with matching eyelet laced socks and saddle shoes. "She's standing right behind you, Heather."

Heather looked around, a look of happy expectancy on her face. "Why can't I see her?"

"She's shy," I said. "And she's playing hide-and-seek with Thornton. She won't reveal herself to you. Not now. Maybe when she's more comfortable."

Wilson, who had been standing in the doorway, walked around to Heather's chair, leaned down, and picked Alicia up. She wrapped her arms and legs around him, like a favorite uncle, and pressed her face against his. Then, spotting Heather's doll on the table, she stretched out her small hands. "Mira, Mira." she cried.

"Heather," I said. "She's seen your doll, and she's saying something. Mira, I think but I can't understand it. Does it mean something?"

"Mirabella!" Heather cried out breathlessly. "That's my doll's name. She remembers."

Wilson whispered the doll's name into Alicia's ear, and she giggled.

"She had a doll named Mariposa," Heather added. "I remember she'd bring her to tea."

Wilson nodded at the doll. "May I?"

"Please," I said.

Carefully, so as not to shock those around the table, Wilson picked up the doll and handed it to Alicia.

"Whoa!" Chad and Zac sat back in their seat. Gobsmacked.

"Shush!" Zoey hissed under her breath.

With their mouths open, Heather and Denise followed the doll's movement with their eyes as Mirabella appeared to float through the air and come to rest in Alicia's arms above their heads.

"It's all right," I said. "Thornton is showing the doll to Alicia. You needn't worry. This is all very normal." I paused while Wilson asked Alicia about the doll, then relayed, "Heather, Thornton says Alicia remembers the tea parties you used to have. But then you moved away, and she was very sad when you left."

Zoey interrupted. "Ask her about the dolls in my guestroom. Does she like them, too?"

"You can ask her yourself, Zoey. She can hear you. But remember, you're talking to a four-year-old, and she may not answer you directly."

Zoey asked about the dolls in the guest room. Did Alicia Mae like them? Wilson answered she did, but that she was too shy to answer for herself.

"They're my favorite," Zoey said. "I used to play with them for hours when I was little. I loved all my dolls."

Wilson cupped the back of Alicia's head, bringing her closer to his ear. "She says she loves the baby doll the best. Except..." he moved his ear closer to Alicia and listened carefully. "Except, she says, sometimes people come into the room and move them, and that makes her sad because she thinks they don't take care of them. She's afraid they might throw them out."

"No. No. That would never happen," Zoey said. "Tell her I'd

never allow that. Sometimes, when I have guests, they stay in the front guestroom with the dolls and they move them around. I don't think they mean to upset things."

Heather spoke next. "That used to be my room, Alicia. Do you remember? How we used to stay up late and play after everyone had gone to sleep?"

Alicia giggled and hugged Mirabella as she cradled her head on Wilson's shoulder. "She remembers," Wilson said.

I checked my tablemates. Not an eye had moved from the doll. Even Chad and Zac remained transfixed, frozen in their chairs.

"Alicia," Zoey leaned forward. "I need to ask, were you in your room the night Lacey fell into the pool?"

At the mention of the pool, Alicia buried her head in Wilson's shoulder and hid her face.

"What's wrong?" I asked.

Wilson hugged Alicia to his chest protectively, his hand cradling the back of her head. "She doesn't like to talk about the pool. Her mommy told her never to go near it." I translated as quickly as I could.

"Does she know what happened that night?" Zoey asked.

Suddenly, Alicia let go of the doll, and it fell face first in the center table.

Zoey screamed. "What is it? What's the matter?"

I repeated Alicia's mumbled words as best I could. "She says you were yelling at Lacey. You were mad at her."

Zoey gripped my hand tighter. "No, Alicia. No, I wasn't mad. I was acting. Lacey and I, we were friends. We were going over my lines for a movie. It was just pretend. It wasn't real. I wasn't angry."

Angry? Zoey's last word hung in the air and echoed, as though it had taken on a life all its own.

Another voice filled the room. A voice I didn't have to speak for. "No, you weren't angry, Zoey. But I was."

Zoey fell back in her chair. Her mouth open, her eyes wide. "Who is this?" I asked.

"It's Lacey. That's Lacey's voice." Zoey looked at me, the grip on my hand even tighter than before. "Lacey, why are you here?"

"I should have told you," the voice responded. "I didn't mean for it to happen, Zoey, but it did."

"For what to happen? Lacey, what are you talking about?"

"You don't get it, Zoey. You always thought you were so deserving, but it doesn't matter anymore. It doesn't make a difference now. It can't, and I'm here to apologize. I can't go on until I've told you everything."

"What do you mean, told me everything? What haven't you told me? Lacey, what's wrong?" Zoey voice trembled.

"You, Zoey. You're what's wrong. I was jealous of you. You had it all, everything I didn't, and everything I wanted. Money. Fame. Fortune. I had to have something. Something for myself. So when you weren't there, I had Chad."

"What?" Zoey looked at Chad. "What's she talking about, Chad?"

"He loved me, Zoey. Me! And you couldn't even see it because you're a Chamberlain, and you couldn't imagine Chad leaving you for someone like me. People think you're so great. But you're not. Chad, he—"

"No! No! You're not doing this." Chad stood up and dropped my hand, breaking the bond of the circle. The candle on the table flickered and went out. The room suddenly cold. Chad turned to the green curtains on the wall and began to tear them down. "This nonsense stops now."

Zoey screamed at Chad. Zac, Denise, Heather and I sat pinned in our chairs, unsure if we should move as Zoey flung accusations at Chad like darts against a dart board. When Zoey had said all she could, with tears streaming down her face she ran out the front door. Chad followed leaving the door open.

Before I could close it, I feared Lacey's ghost had followed them.

Chapter 14

The séance left me exhausted and had robbed me of a good night's sleep. I tossed in my bed. Anxious. My mind restless. I kept thinking about Zoey and Alicia Mae. How our group hadn't closed out the séance properly, thanking the spirits for visiting, and bidding them farewell. I feared Lacey's ghost had gotten the best of me. Her presence had been a complete surprise. Not that ghosts don't arrive unannounced at séances, but normally, I would have had more control over the situation. The only possible excuse I could give myself was that I was so taken by Alicia Mae—seeing her for the first time, and her interaction with Wilson—that I was thrown off my game. Wilson appeared affectionate, selfless, and almost paternal. So much so, that I was ill-prepared for Lacey's visit.

The next day I decided to make an unannounced visit to Zoey. I wanted to talk to her face to face about Chad. While I was there, I planned to make an inspection. If Lacey had followed either Chad or Zoey home, I needed to know. I wanted to do whatever I could to correct my mistake as soon as possible. Under the circumstances, one ghost in a house, despite the size of the Pink Mansion, was quite enough.

The security gate was wide open when Wilson and I arrived at Zoey's. An old, yellow Subaru sedan was parked in the Pink

Mansion's drive, the trunk open with boxes inside. I hobbled up the walk with Wilson at my side and stopped to catch my breath. I was about to continue my ascent up the hill when Zac and Kelsey came out of the house carrying boxes. The two were arguing and didn't see me. I stepped back beneath the big magnolia tree.

Kelsey waited for Zac to put his box in the trunk then slammed it shut. "I'm just saying we wouldn't be in this position if Chad had kept his head in the music and his fly zipped."

"You're just angry things haven't progressed as you wanted," Zac said.

"How could they? The man's a womanizer."

"Something you want to tell me?"

"Shut it, Zac. You know better."

I stepped on a twig. The two turned and looked in my direction.

"Misty," Zac called my name. "I didn't realize you were here. Need some help?"

"No. I'm fine. I wanted to stop by to check on some things. Everything okay?"

Kelsey slapped her hand on the trunk. "You have to ask after last night? I'd think you'd know."

Kelsey trounced back into the house. Zac behind her.

"More trouble in paradise?" Wilson asked.

"Looks like it," I said. I ambled up the last of the steps to the house and tapped lightly on the front door. "Zoey? It's Misty. You here?"

Moments later it wasn't Zoey who came to the door, but Chad. He looked like he hadn't slept. His hair a mess, his eyes weary. He said he spent the night on the couch at Zac and Kelsey's. The two of them had come back with him and were upstairs. As for Zoey, she had left for an early morning shoot and wasn't home.

"She kicked me out. You happy?" Chad turned his back to me and headed barefoot down the hall. In his distraught state, he didn't care if I came in the house or not.

Wilson left my side and went immediately in search of Alicia Mae, while I followed Chad as far as the master bedroom. Then stopped short of entering

I sensed another energy in the room.

"You alone?" I asked.

"Does it look like I have company?" The bedroom was a mess. Clothes on the floor, an open suitcase and a pile of what looked a lot like dirty laundry on the bed. Chad began sorting through them.

Across the room, sitting on the edge of the dresser in a racy, red negligee, was Lacey. She finger waved to me and smiled. I quietly finger waved back.

"You don't see her?" I asked.

"See who?"

"No one," I said. If Chad wasn't aware of Lacey's presence, perhaps I still had time.

I clapped my hands. Three times. Loud and vigorously. On the third clap, I whipped my index finger in the air, upwards toward the ceiling like a master wizard. That should have done the trick. Unfortunately, it didn't. Lacey remained.

"You okay?" Chad screwed his face up in a contorted smile.

"Better than you, I think. Look, I'm sorry, Chad."

"Yeah, right. You're sorry. A lot of good that does." Chad threw a couple of socks into the suitcase. "The cops think Lacey was murdered, and you got Zoey believing in ghosts. And now she thinks I was having an affair with Lacey."

"Were you?" I stepped over to the bed, picked up a lone sock, found its match, and tossed it into the suitcase.

"It's not like it sounds." Chad took a pair of briefs from the dresser, wadded them into a ball and threw them toward the suitcase. And missed. "You got to understand, Lacey came on to me. Zoey had been working crazy hours and I...I made a mistake, okay? I never meant for Lacey to think it was anything more than that."

Lacey picked up the briefs and, doing a little jig, threw them back into the drawer. Chad did a double take, shook his head like they might be another pair of like-colored boxers he had missed, and stuffed them back into the bag.

This was worse than I thought.

"You didn't kill her?" I asked.

"Me?" Chad drew his mouth awkwardly to one side of his face. "Do I look like a killer to you? I'll admit I was upset with Lacey, but I never would have killed her. I feel awful about it."

Lacey made a sad face, pouted her lower lip and rubbed her baby doll eyes with her fists.

"Any idea who did?" I looked at Lacey. She shrugged. The girl didn't have a clue, which isn't unusual. With some deaths, particularly violent deaths, the deceased blanks out all memory of the actual act and transition.

"How would I know?" Chad asked.

"What about Zoey? Did she stay here last night? Alone?"

Chad shrugged. "Probably. Crystal was here when I came in this morning. She said Zoey called her and she stayed in the guest bedroom."

"Did Crystal mention anything to you about the house or anything unusual happening last night?"

"You mean about the ghost?" Chad hissed. "No, she didn't mention anything about a ghost. You happy? And I wish you'd stop with this whole ghost-bit. There is no such thing as a ghost."

With her finger to her lips, Lacey pushed the suitcase off the bed.

"Dammit. Silk sheets. I hate 'em. Zoey loves 'em, but

nothing ever stays put on the bed. Slip slides in every direction." Chad smoothed the sheets then picked up the bag and put it back on the bed.

What could I say? If Chad chose not to believe in ghosts, or was simply ignoring the obvious, thinking it would go away, I wasn't about to change his mind. At least not yet. He'd find out soon enough. Lacey may not have had Chad in life, but as a ghost, she had every ability to haunt him. Poor man, he had no idea what he was in for.

The doorbell rang, followed by a heavy knocking on the front door. Chad threw a couple T-shirts into the suitcase and slammed it shut. "Now what?"

I followed Chad to the entry. Zac and Kelsey had just come downstairs with boxes and upon seeing me, did an about face, and went out the back way. Chad had barely turned the handle on the door when someone on the other side pushed it open.

"What the—"

"Morning, son." Chad stumbled backward as Detective Romero entered. "I think you and I need to have a little talk." Spotting me behind Chad, he added, "Well now, this is interesting. Misty Dawn. Have to say, I didn't expect to find you here. Certainly not at this hour."

"And good morning to you too, Detective." I stepped out from behind Chad.

"Doing a little investigating on your own are you?"

"More of a visit, if you really must know," I said.

"Well, this isn't." The detective slapped an envelope against Chad's chest. "Search warrant, buddy."

"For what?" Chad crushed the warrant in his hand. "You already searched the place twice. Now what do you want?"

"I'm looking for whatever might have been used to knock Lacey Adams out. You got any ideas?" Romero asked.

"Not a clue, and whatever you think you're going to find,

you're not going to find it here." Chad backed away from the detective and stuffed the warrant in his pocket. "'Cause even if I had killed Lacey—which I didn't—I wouldn't be stupid enough to hide something here. Not in the same house where she was murdered. I'm not a moron, Detective."

"But you are her baby's father," Romero said.

"Ugh, shit." Chad hung his head. "How?"

"DNA, son. The coroner got a match off the fetus growing inside your girlfriend's womb."

"She wasn't my girlfriend." Chad ran his fingers through his hair. "Look, this is all a big mistake. I can explain. Lacey wanted me to leave Zoey, but I never would have left Zoey for her. We were just fooling around. If you think I killed Lacey because she got pregnant, you're wrong."

"How about Zoey? We matched her DNA to the cigarette butt we found out by the pool. From the looks of it, that butt wasn't laying around too long. Couldn't have been there more than a day. Maybe the two of you killed her together."

Chad threw his arms up in the air. "You people."

Romero waved two plainclothes detectives through the door and told them to search everything. "Including the boxes Chad's buddies carried out through the garage. Go through this place like you were looking for gold." Turning to Chad, he said, I may not have enough to make an arrest yet, but I've got enough to tell you and Zoey not to plan on leaving town any time soon."

"How about the house? It okay if I leave here?" Chad nodded to more boxes in the hallway. "News flash, Detective, Zoey threw me out. I'm staying at my drummer's place. That okay with you?"

"Long as we know where to find you."

"Fine. Have at it. Search the place, I don't care. Tear it apart if you like. You're not going to find anything with my prints on it connected to Lacey's murder. 'Cause like I said, I didn't do it."

Chad walked back down the hall toward the master bedroom.

"One more question, Chad."

Chad stopped. "What's that?"

"The night Lacey died Zoey told us you came home late and she was in bed. That Lacey planned to let herself out."

"So?"

"So if Lacey was going to let herself out, where was her car?"

"Her car?" Chad scratched his head.

"Yeah, her car. How'd she get here?"

"I don't know. Lacey liked to drink. She knew she and Zoey would be working late. They sometimes drank when they worked. Maybe she took an Uber. There wasn't a car parked in front when I came home."

"And you didn't sneak out back and maybe have a little rendezvous with Lacey while Zoey slept?"

"I told you, I didn't see Lacey."

I thought now might be a good time to retreat back into the bedroom and corner Lacey. See if I couldn't convince her to vacate the premises. I told the detective if he didn't mind, I'd take my leave.

"Actually, Misty, long as you're here, I'd like to have a word with you too. I have a couple of questions."

"Concerning the case?" I couldn't imagine what more he wanted to ask me. He had made it clear when we last spoke, despite my reputation with the LAPD, that he didn't put much stake in my work or my profession.

"Maybe," he said. "Why don't you take a seat in the living room? We can chat when I finish here."

I did exactly that. Took a seat on the couch and stared out the big picture window at the backyard. The morning light on the pool's clear blue water created a serene, shimmering effect beneath the big weeping willow, its branches hung low to the grass as though it were hiding something. The yard was pristine, green and fresh with a colorful border of sweet peas and pansies. I concentrated on the scene in front of me and closed my eyes. Wilson had said beneath the tree was the playhouse. With my mind's eye, I recreated the scene in front of me: the pool, the shimmering water, and the big tree. When it was crystal clear in my mind, I opened my eyes. There in front of me, like a mirage, was the playhouse and the child's picnic table Alicia's father had built for her. Exactly as Wilson had described.

And sitting at the table were Wilson and Alicia.

This was the same table Alicia and Heather had used for their tea parties. The same table and playhouse later residents had destroyed. But, in Alicia's world, the table and the playhouse had remained, and for all the years since her accident, the safe-house where Alicia had stayed. Safe and sound, in her make-believe world. Right here in Pink Mansion's backyard. Waiting. But for what? Was Wilson right? Was she waiting for her mother's return? I watched as Wilson sat at the table with Alicia and played patty-cake. A game I doubted Wilson had ever played before meeting the little ghost. Now, to watch him, he looked like her adoring uncle, smiling and laughing. Did he understand this wasn't really her home? Did he know, like I did, that the day would come when it would be his job to send her away? To explain to her that the world she thought she knew was but temporary? That the friends she thought were real were not of her world, but another, generations later? I preferred not to think about it.

Chapter 15

I was still sitting on the couch in the great room when Detective Romero returned with the two plainclothes detectives. The two left with a large brown paper bag marked *EVIDENCE.*

Romero closed the front door then turned his attention to me. "I appreciate you staying to talk, Misty."

"That's alright. You did say when you were here last you wanted to talk to everyone. I just hadn't assumed that *everyone* included me."

"Let's talk outside, shall we?" Romero nodded to the courtyard. "I'd prefer whatever you have to say stay between us, and no one else."

"Wherever you like." I followed him outside.

"I wanted to ask you about Zoey. You mind telling me how long she's been a client?"

"Why? You think that has anything to do with Lacey's murder?"

"Maybe not, but asking questions is what I do. Considering your history with the department, I'd think you'd understand that."

"I suppose that's par for the course." I settled myself on the edge of the small koi pond and put my hand into the water. "But if you plan to ask me what it was we talked about, you have to understand, I consider all my consultations private and confidential."

The detective suppressed a laugh and looked down at his shoes. "I was warned you might say that, but the fact of the matter is, your *consultations* with Zoey don't fall under the confidentialities guaranteed by a doctor-patient relationship. If it makes it any easier, I'm not about to ask what you talked about, I'm only curious as to how long you've been meeting with her."

I cupped my hand and let the water trickle back into the pond on top of the heads of several curious koi. "Not long. In fact, I didn't know Zoey, at least not personally, before she showed up on my doorstep."

"And she was there because she believed her house was haunted. Is that right?"

"I thought you weren't going to ask me why Zoey came to visit me. It appears you've been reading the tabloids." I shook the water from my hand and stood up.

"I'm an investigator. I'll admit tabloids aren't my usual trusted source, but your name did come up in several of the columns. Along with Zoey claiming she believed her house was haunted. As a result, I thought we should talk."

I smiled. A detective reading the tabloids, particularly this detective, felt ripe for the picking. Another potential believer about to fall into my camp. "Do you believe in ghosts, Detective?"

"I believe in the things I can touch and feel and drag into court," Romero said.

"Then, unfortunately, I don't believe we have a lot to talk about. I don't know who killed Lacey if that's what you're thinking. Although, you'll be relieved to know, I don't believe it was the ghost, and I have a hard time believing it was Chad."

"He had a pretty good motive. Lacey was pregnant with his child, and he was engaged to Zoey. As for means and opportunity, look around. Lacey was here. Chad lives here. In my world, you put that together and he's a likely suspect. Lacey may have threatened him, told him she was going to tell Zoey. Or maybe Lacey told Zoey about her affair with Chad, and Zoey killed her. Or Zoey and Chad did it together."

"I don't believe that."

"You mind telling me what you're doing here today? Seems like every time I come by you're here."

"Am I a suspect?" I laughed half-heartedly. I couldn't imagine Romero thought I might be involved.

"Case like this, everyone's a suspect. 'Til they're not."

Romero's response caused me to pause. I picked up my bag from the ledge next to the koi pond and held it to my chest. "If you must know, Detective, I came by to check on Zoey and Chad. They broke up last night. I thought I should see how she was doing."

"And you know this how? Zoey call you or something?" The detective's eyes met mine and held steady.

"I suppose the fact I'm a psychic isn't a good enough reason?" I adjusted the shoulder strap on my bag and started toward the walkway. I had had enough of the detective's cold looks and penetrating questions.

"Like I said, I deal in facts, not the supernatural."

"Then you wouldn't believe me if I told you."

"Try me."

I stopped at the top of the stairs. "If you must know, I came by to check on Zoey because I was concerned Lacey might have followed her home after the séance last night, and—"

"A séance?" Romero raised his brow.

"Yes, Zoey insisted I do one."

"And just where did this séance take place?"

"My home, or the home I'm leasing anyway, off Norton Drive. It belonged to a former..." I stopped. There was no point in explaining.

Romero took a notepad from within his jacket pocket and began taking notes. "And exactly what happened at this séance?"

"Zoey wanted to see if we could get in touch with her ghost."

"The one she's been talking about in the tabloids?" Romero stopped writing.

"Yes. She's a four-year-old girl."

"A child ghost?" Romero rolled his eyes.

"Her name's Alicia Mae. She drowned in a pool accident in 1943. It was a big news story back in the day. You can check the papers. She fell in the pool just like Lacey fell in the spa. Both girls drowned. Which is why I probably should have figured she might show up."

"She?" Romero winced. "Who are we talking about? Lacey or this Alicia Mae?"

"Both really, but Lacey in particular." I hated when I had to explain myself to someone who so clearly doubted my talents. But if it helped to find whoever had killed Lacey, I was more than willing to put up with Romero's skepticism. I continued, slowly so as to not confuse him. "She, Lacey that is, showed up at the séance right after Alicia Mae, and starts confessing to Zoey how sorry she was for the affair. As you can imagine, Zoey lost it. She knew nothing about an affair, and when she realized Lacey and Chad had been carrying on, Zoey screamed. Chad stood up, and the séance ended on a bad note. A very bad note. Spirits hate to be slighted. And ending a séance before they've had their say can be messy, if not dangerous. Hence, I was afraid Lacey had followed Zoey home, and I came by this morning to check in on Zoey and Chad."

"I see." I was certain Romero didn't see at all, but he scribbled something on his notepad, then looked up at me. "And you would swear in a court-of-law this is what happened?"

"Spirits exist, Detective. Whether you choose to believe in them or not. They're here. Most people spend a lifetime unaware of their presence. But that doesn't mean they're not here or that we're alone. You for instance." I pointed to the detective's left hand. "I notice you still wear your wedding ring." The detective blanched, and I paused. "Your wife's passed on. It was unexpected. Cancer I think. But she's with you. And you can't tell me you don't still feel she's around you. You talk to her all the time. Oh, not in front of anyone, but when you're alone."

Romero put the notepad back in his pocket. His eyes broke from mine. I sensed he was uncomfortable with what he considered an intrusion into his personal life.

He exhaled. "She died three years ago. She was young, a teacher. You could have heard about it or maybe read her obit in the paper. She was popular, Teacher of the Year the year before she died. It got a little bit of press."

"But I didn't hear about it or read it in the paper, and I certainly didn't know about the trip the two of you always wanted to take. That Mediterranean Cruise you talked about? She wants you to take it." I reached for the Detective's left hand. "May I? If you like, I could read your ring."

Romero pulled his hand away. "Like I said, I'm not into psychics."

"It's not as frightening as you might think. It's entirely up to you, but you might want to consider it's time to take that ring off your finger. Your wife won't mind." I started down the front steps toward the street where Wilson was waiting for me inside the Jag and stopped. "Detective, you mind if I ask a question?"

"Go right ahead."

"Did you find what you're looking for today?"

"You mean did we find a weapon or something that might have been used to knock Lacey out?"

"Yes," I said.

"My detectives found something. You saw them walk out with bags."

"Mind if I tell you I don't think so?"

"Not at all, as long you understand it's the coroner who'll determine if what we bring back matches what the killer used."

"And what exactly do you think it is?"

"Don't know for sure. The coroner says it's something with a flat bottom. Could be a frying pan. Maybe even a shovel."

"Hmmm." I shook my head. None of that felt right. "Well, good luck to you."

I had almost gotten down the steps when the detective hollered back to me. "That your car, Misty?"

I looked back at him. "It's a friend's. I'm taking care of it for him. Pretty isn't it?"

"'54 Jaguar, right? Right-hand drive?"

I could tell from the way Romero cocked his head he didn't think I'd drive such a ride.

"Right you are," I said. "And you know what they say about little old ladies and sports cars."

"What? Go, granny, go?"

I waved dismissively and started back to the car.

Romero called after me. "Just don't go too far, Ms. Dawn. I've a feeling we may want to talk again."

Chapter 16

The following afternoon I was in the living room, snoozing with the newspaper on my lap, when I heard a knock at the door. By the time I got to my feet, someone had inserted a key into the lock, and the deadbolt slid open. Seconds later, Denise burst in and spotted me in the living room.

"You won't believe it." With the keys still in her hands, Denise did a little happy dance in the entry. "Guess who's got a meeting with Hugh Jackman tomorrow afternoon?"

"I thought you were meeting with him yesterday." I shuffled toward the study and pulled the door shut, lest Denise's voice alert Wilson to his sister's presence. *One less battle I needed on my hands.*

"Oh, yes, that meeting. Well, it didn't work out. His publicity manager Nina was supposed to get me into a fan meeting. A real exclusive she said. What a waste. I was one of three hundred people. Nothing more than a big cattle call. No way was I going to get any face-to-face time with Hugh. So I walked out, and when I did, guess who I saw?"

"Surprise me," I said.

"Nina! I mean, how lucky is that? I recognized her from photos I had seen of her in the trades, and there she was, right in the middle of a bunch of Hollywood industry types. All staring at their cell phones and about to get on an elevator. And guess what?"

"I'm afraid to ask."

"I followed her. Sidled up to her, all nice and cozy like. I mean she didn't know who I was or what I looked like since we hadn't met in person, and I pretended like I knew what I was doing, took out my phone and yada, yada, yada..."

"Yada, yada, yada what?" I asked.

"Well, if you must know the details. Nina was on the phone with an assignment editor from *The Hollywood Reporter*. Turns out the reporter who was supposed to meet with Hugh tomorrow afternoon has the flu. They were calling to tell her they needed to reschedule and would get back in touch. So..." Denise reached into her bag and produced a business card with *The Hollywood Reporter* logo on it and shoved it in my face. "I took the liberty of making a few business cards and calling Nina back. I told her finding a substitute was no problem, provided Mr. Jackman might be available slightly earlier than the original agreed upon time, and presto-gusto, I got the appointment."

I took the card from Denise and stared at it. *Denise Thorne, Reporter.*

Denise had done a lot of silly things in an attempt to meet Jackman, but this bordered on insanity, not to mention fraud. That is, if impersonating a reporter is a prosecutorial offense these days.

"What if *The Hollywood Reporter* calls back?" I asked.

"Oh, please. This is Golden Globes week. By the time they get around to finding another reporter, I will have met Hugh, and my mission will be...how do the French say it? A *fait accompli*." Denise grabbed the business card from my hand and asked if she could use the powder room beneath the stairs. "You mind?" Denise did a little tap dance. "I have to go."

"Go."

No sooner had Denise disappeared inside the powder room,

then Wilson poked his head out of the study. "Tell me that's not my sister."

I gritted my teeth. "I'm afraid so."

"Get rid of her."

"Easier said than done," I said.

Wilson gave me another of his Bronx cheers and was about to retreat back into the study, when the front bell rang. "You expecting someone?"

"No," I said. "And whoever it is, you're going to have to make yourself scarce. I can't be putting up with your sibling rivalry while I'm dealing with your sister and a guest. Now go."

I opened the front door and found Detective Romero on the porch. He was dressed in jeans, a jacket and T-shirt, and tennis shoes. And around his neck, like a neon sign, hung his gold LAPD detective's shield.

"You here to arrest me?" After yesterday's interrogation concerning my whereabouts the night of Lacey's murder, I had less than warm feelings for the detective.

"I'm here to talk, Misty. You got a minute?"

I glanced back at the doors to the powder room and the study to make certain they were closed then pointed Romero in the direction of the living room. My excuse for getting Denise out of the house had just materialized. I tapped lightly on the door to the study and whispered, "Five minutes, Wilson. Give me five minutes."

"Excuse me?" The detective stood in the middle of the living room and looked at me, puzzled. Was I in the habit of talking to myself?

"Please," I said, "take a seat." I picked the newspaper up off the end of the couch and waited for Romero to sit down, then sat in one of the winged back chairs opposite him. "Is there something I can help you with, Detective?"

"Maybe. Like I told you yesterday, I'm not a believer. No

offense."

"None taken," I said.

"But I thought I'd stop by and ask your opinion."

"About?" Out of the corner of my eye, I spotted Wilson. Curiosity had gotten the best of him. He had walked through the study door—as ghosts and shades can—and was now standing directly behind the detective. I shook my head slowly, side to side. *No funny business, Wilson, not now. I'm warning you.*

"This morning," Romero said, "I hiked up the trail behind Zoey's house. Thought I might have a look around. I wanted to see if I could find anything that might help with the investigation."

"Did you?"

Wilson moved from behind the couch and took a seat next to Romero. Crossing his arms and legs, he leaned into the detective in what I could only imagine a man like Romero would consider uncomfortably close.

Ahem. I cleared my throat.

Romero ran the fingers of his left hand beneath the collar of his t-shirt. "Is it hot in here?"

"Hot and cold," I said. "The house is drafty. I could turn the thermostat down if you like."

"No. It's not necessary." The detective shook his head. "I'm here because I found something on the trail, and I thought you should see it. It looks like someone dropped it in the bushes. May be nothing, but since I wanted to stop by anyway to ask a few more questions, I thought I'd have you take a look at it." The detective reached into his pocket and took out a small, round, plastic, cylinder-shaped item that emitted a crude tinny sound, like that of a feral cat or baby's cry. "I had forensics dust it for prints, but they came up empty. Nobody knows what to make of it, so I thought I'd bring it by for you to look at."

Romero put the small box on the coffee table between us. I

leaned forward and looked at it.

"You want me to read it? Is that why you're here? Because if you do, Detective, it's plastic. For me to really get anything off it, it'd have to be metal, like a ring or a necklace."

"No, I'm not going to ask you to read it. I just wanted you to have a look at it. See if you thought it might be relevant."

"To the case?"

Romero nodded.

"Most of what I do deals with the paranormal, and I know you're not here because you believe in such things. That is unless you had a sudden change of heart?"

"Of course not," Romero scoffed. "I told you, I don't believe in ghosts. But it seems to me this squawk box could be something the killer used to attract attention. Zoey did say she and Lacey heard what sounded like a cat outside the house the night Lacey died. From the sounds of this thing, it could be what the murderer used to get Lacey's attention. I wondered if maybe it might suggest something to you."

Before I could answer, the door to the powder room opened and the mood in the room changed. Ahh, the magic of chemistry. Like the birth of a new star, colorful fragments of light, unseeable to anyone else but myself and Wilson, filled the room.

Romero glanced up and, seeing Denise in the entry, stood and knocked Wilson to the floor.

The instant Denise's eyes met Romero's, I knew the detective was a marked man.

With the early morning light streaming in behind her, Denise looked almost angelic. She rubbed her hands together. The scent of vanilla hand cream permeated the air. She scanned the detective like a prized bull at the state fair.

"Misty, I'm so sorry. I didn't realize you had a consult." Denise took a step into the living room.

I made hurried introductions. Anxious to move Denise along. "Detective, this is my landlady, Denise Thorne. Denise, this is Detective Romero. Denise was just on her way—" I was about to say "out" when Denise brushed past me and extended her hand.

"Romero? Like in Romeo, but with an 'r'?" Denise winked. The detective took her hand and held it longer than I thought necessary. "And such a handsome detective, too. Are you here to talk with Misty about Lacey's murder? Do you know who did it?"

Romero cleared his throat, glanced at me then back at Denise, "Not yet, ma'am. But we will."

"Well, I can tell you this, it's not Zoey's ghost, that's for certain. But then, I'm sure Misty's already shared that with you." Denise fluffed the back of her hair and smiled.

Wilson slipped back into the study. From inside the room I could hear him slamming books to the floor.

Denise jumped, and the detective looked in the direction of the study door, his hand automatically to the gun at his hip.

"Not to worry," I said. "I left a window open upstairs. Must be the wind. You know how it is with old houses. Besides, Denise, the detective doesn't believe in ghosts."

Romero sat back down, and Denise took a seat next to him on the edge of the couch where Wilson had been sitting. She paused momentarily and looked on either side of her as though she might have thought or felt something odd, then shrugged. "So, Detective, if you don't believe in ghosts, what do you believe in?"

I answered. I wasn't about to give in to Denise's flirtation. "The detective's found what looks like a doll's squawk box on the trail behind the house. His forensics people don't know what to make of it." I pointed to the cylinder-shaped speaker on the coffee table. "He's here to ask me what I think."

Denise poked at the box. "Well, then, I should think that

settles it."

"Settles it how?" Romero asked.

"The newspaper said Zoey and Lacey heard cat-like sounds coming from the backyard before Zoey went to bed. If you found this in the park, then it can only mean one thing."

"What's that?" Romero looked amused, his lined face had a sudden glow about it. A glow I could only attribute to Denise's close proximity, and the smell of vanilla hand cream she had just applied. An aphrodisiac for some.

"Zoey had a stalker. Some crazed fan who knew where she lived and that her house backed up to the park. It wouldn't take much to break in through the gate and…Wham! Bam!" Denise punched the air like she was hitting something. "Suddenly Lacey's dead and our stalker's out of the gate and disappeared into the park. Never to be heard from again."

Romero bit back a smile. "It is a possibility. Although, in a case like this, we often find the victim usually knows their killer."

"Ah-huh," Denise took a quick breath. I could see she was mentally calculating the list of possible suspects in her mind. She looked at me, then back to Romero. "I assume Misty told you what happened the night of the séance?"

The detective's eyes slid from me and back to Denise.

"You haven't told him?" Denise asked.

"I have," I said, "but—"

"Because if you were there, you would have seen it—or heard it anyway." Denise was adamant. "Lacey showed up and confessed to Zoey she'd been having an affair with Chad and Chad went off the deep end. Tore the curtains off the wall, and then there was this big argument. Do you think it could be Chad? That maybe he wanted to silence Lacey?"

"I'm afraid I can't address your concerns," Romero said. "At least not about the séance, but we're still checking on Chad's whereabouts the night of the murder."

Denise pointed at the newspaper on the coffee table. "Yes, well, it's probably not Chad. The paper reported he was at some recording studio that night, so I suppose it couldn't have been him."

"We don't get our facts from the newspaper, Ms. Thorne."

"Denise, Detective. Please, call me Denise."

"Denise, then. And I appreciate your interest, but—"

Denise put her hand on the detective's. "Then where do you suppose Chad was? I mean, he's Zoey's fiancé. And a rock star. It's not quite like he could hide."

Romero looked down at his hand and gently removed it from Denise's.

"That's what we're trying to verify now. The man who runs the studio's been out of town. Chad assures us he can back his story up, but for the time being, we haven't been able to pin down the exact time when Chad was at the studio or when he left."

"Was he alone?" Denise pressed forward, shoulder to shoulder with the detective.

I pulled Denise away from the detective. "You'll have to excuse Denise, Detective. She's caught up with news of the murder. Perhaps, Denise, we should give Detective Romero a chance to ask if there's anything more he needs from me and allow him to go on his way."

"Actually, Misty, that's quite alright. Denise asks a good question, and I don't mind answering. According to Chad, he was at the studio with Zac and Kelsey."

"And you're looking at them as suspects as well?" I asked.

"Right now, everyone's a suspect."

"Everyone?" There it was again. The subtle hint the detective wasn't just talking to me because he thought I might be helpful in identifying the squawk box, but because he had his doubts as to whether or not I might be involved.

"I'm following up with everyone who was at the house the morning Lacey's body was found. Nothing for you to be concerned about."

"Perhaps not, but all the same, I had assumed—incorrectly evidently—after showing me this squawk box, you were here to ask for my help. That you had reconciled yourself to my talents. However, since that appears not to be the case, I'm afraid I'm going to have to ask you to leave."

"Misty!" Denise snapped her head and looked at me like she couldn't believe what I had just said. "You're being rude."

"Perhaps," I said. "But while I don't mind answering a few questions, being the subject of an investigation is an entirely different matter." I lumbered to my feet, "And for that, Detective, I'm afraid you'll have to go. You too, Denise. I've work to do. My own investigation if you don't mind. And I don't need either of you around to do it. Now go. Both of you."

I walked both Romero and Denise to the door, and once they were both out, gave it a good shove.

Chapter 17

Crystal called the following morning. She was hysterical. Somebody had put a doll in her closet at the mansion, and she was convinced that somebody was me. I couldn't see why Crystal would be so upset about a doll. Zoey had lots of dolls around the house, and she kept most of them in the guest room where Crystal was staying. It wasn't until she described the doll that I understood her angst. The doll's head had been smashed and her dress bloodied.

"What are you trying to do, frame me?" Crystal was convinced the doll had been used to murder Lacey and that I had somehow found it and mysteriously moved it into the guest room where she was staying.

I hung up the phone and looked at Wilson. "Please tell me you didn't tamper with any evidence you may have found when we were at Zoey's."

"Would that be wrong?" Wilson grinned.

"Ugh!" I raised my head to the heavens. *Why me?* "Let me remind you, Wilson, your time here is temporary. What you do. Who you help. Who you don't help. It all weighs in on where you go from here. You do understand that?"

"I don't see anything wrong with returning things to their proper place. All I did was take the doll Alicia found by the pool the night Lacey was murdered and return it to the guest room with the other dolls. The police never would have found it, and you know how fastidious I am about things being out of place."

"Are you telling me Alicia Mae had the doll? And that it might have been used to murder Lacey?"

"Well, I don't know if it was used to murder Lacey or not. But I do know Alicia said she found it by the pool the night Lacey drowned and took it back with her to the playhouse."

"I thought you said she didn't see anything."

"She didn't. But when she heard Zoey and Lacey arguing—"

"Rehearsing," I said.

"Alicia went from the guest bedroom where she had been staying to the playhouse. When the arguing stopped, she peeked out of the playhouse window, saw the doll by the pool and went and got it. The police never would have found it there, because the playhouse doesn't exist. At least not in their world. Alicia was very upset the doll had been hurt and wanted me to fix it. I told her I couldn't fix it, not right away, but that we needed to return the doll to the nursery. Which, in Alicia's mind, is the closet in the guest room where Crystal had moved all of Zoey's dolls."

"You placed the doll there, in the closet, right after the police searched the house the *second* time?"

"I did. I suppose that should count as a good deed, right? I mean if I'm racking up points to earn my wings so to speak, that's got to count for something."

I exhaled. "Get the car keys. I need to see Crystal."

Detective Romero's car was parked in the drive when Wilson and I pulled up in front of Zoey's house. I ambled up the steps, not relishing the idea I was about to run into the detective again, and stopped halfway up to catch my breath. While Wilson disappeared into the house ahead of me, I spotted Romero beneath the atrium's arched entry. He appeared to be waiting for me.

"Crystal call you too?" He asked.

"She did," I said. With my hand against my chest, I felt my heart race. Whether it was the surprise of seeing the detective on the steps, or the steps were more strenuous than either my heart or I was prepared for, I wasn't sure. I took a deep breath and exhaled. If the detective was going to treat me as a possible suspect, best I get on with it.

Romero stepped down from beneath the portico and held out his hand. "Need some help?"

"I suppose we could all use some." I took his hand reluctantly.

If offering me help up the steps was in some way an apology, I wasn't ready to forgive the detective for yesterday's accusation that I might possibly have been involved with Lacey's murder. But the help up the steps I could use. Together, we climbed the remaining steps and met Crystal on the front patio. The door to the house was wide open behind her.

"Detective." Crystal greeted Romero formally, and with a chill I felt she had reserved for me, said, "Misty."

"Crystal." I mimicked the short, terse tone in which she had used my name and smiled curtly.

"Humph." Crystal walked back into the house. "I'm glad you're here, Detective. I've something to show you, and I suspect Misty knows damn well what it is and why it's in my closet."

"Well, then, suppose you show me what it is." Romero stepped ahead of me.

Crystal shut the door behind us and led us down the hallway to the guest bedroom where she was staying. The room was furnished with a king-size bed, a marble-topped nightstand on either side, an antique armoire, and bookcases with lots of dolls. In the corner, beneath a white plantation shuttered window, was a luggage rack with an open suitcase on top. From the looks of things, Crystal was still unpacking.

"It's in there." Crystal motioned with her head to a large walk-in closet where a life-size baby doll sat slumped on top of a vintage storage trunk. Its glass eyes stared back at us blankly, with its little mouth open in a perpetual "o" waiting for its next bottle. The doll looked like she had been trashed, its face scratched and dirty. The back of her head bashed in. Her pink ruffled dress, bloodstained and torn, revealed an open hole in the back of the doll's plastic chest where something—perhaps the doll's cry box—had been removed. "Somebody put it there."

"Do you know who?" Romero walked into the closet and looked around.

"Why don't you ask her?" Crystal jerked her head in my direction. "She'd love to frame me for Lacey's murder. All because I don't believe in her little charade about haunted houses and ghosts."

Romero put his hand up. "Ladies, please, let's do this one step at a time, okay? Misty, why don't you go take a seat on the bed while I talk to Crystal."

I backed out of the closet and sat on the edge of the bed where I could still see and hear Crystal and Romero.

"Just when did you first discover the doll in your closet?" Romero asked.

"This morning. Zoey left early for the studio. I told her I wanted to stay here and unpack some of my things. That's when I noticed it, and I can tell you, Detective, that doll wasn't here the night I moved in."

"Which was?" Romero asked.

"The night Zoey and Chad broke up." Crystal looked over her shoulder at me. "The night Misty did her séance. Zoey called and asked me to come over. She didn't want to stay alone."

"And everything else in the room is exactly as it was yesterday?"

"You mean after Misty came back to talk to Chad?" Crystal glared at me. "And you showed up with a search warrant?" Clearly, Crystal was bothered by the fact I had come back to the house after the séance. The fact I hadn't heeded her warning to *back off* and leave Zoey alone had unsettled her. I felt the girl was prepared to fight me like an alley cat.

"I don't remember," Crystal said. "I've had a lot on my mind. I assume if the doll was here, looking like she does now, you and your team would have seen it when you searched the house."

Romero swung the closet door open and shut, checking for its mobility, then returned it to its open position. "This door open all the time?"

"Since I've been here," Crystal said.

"Let me get this straight. You moved in the night Zoey and Chad broke up."

"Like I said, right after Misty did that séance where Lacey's ghost *supposedly* showed up." Crystal made air quotes around "supposedly" and leered at me.

"Okay," Romero said. "Zoey kicks Chad out and calls you to come over and stay the night."

"She didn't want to be alone," Crystal said

Romero cleared his throat, "Got that. And then the next day, Chad comes back to pack up his things, and you were where?"

"At the studio with Zoey."

"How did you know we searched the house again?"

"Chad called me. He wanted me to tell Zoey. He thought she should know right away."

"You and Chad close?"

"Not at all. Why?"

"Just asking," Romero said.

"Chad would have called Zoey himself, but he didn't think

she'd take his call."

"Chad ever talk to you about Lacey? Ever mentioned anything about the affair?"

"I told you, Chad and I weren't close, and I don't like the questions you're asking. I called you here because somebody put a bloody doll in my closet. And not that I should do your work for you, but I suspect it has something to do with Lacey's murder."

Romero walked out of the closet then back in and exhaled. "You're sure you've never seen this doll before?"

"I don't know. I suppose it's one of Zoey's. She has lots of dolls. But I can tell you, I didn't see that doll in this closet the night I moved in. And yesterday, we spent all day at the studio, so I didn't have time to finish unpacking." Crystal went to the suitcase sitting beneath the window. "It wasn't until this morning when I wanted to hang up a few things, that I went into the closet and saw the doll then called you."

Romero took out his cell phone and snapped a picture of the doll on top of the trunk. "I'm going to need you ladies to leave the room. I'm calling for a couple of crime scene techs to pick up the doll and dust for prints. In the meantime—"

"In the meantime, I assume I'm free to go?" Crystal locked her arms across her chest. "I have a busy day."

"Unless there's something else you want to tell me."

"Only that I think the person you should be talking to is sitting right there on the bed."

I was about to object when the doorbell rang followed by a quick knock and the sound of the front door opening.

"You expecting anybody?" Romero asked. "Maid maybe?"

Crystal looked at me then back at the detective and shook her head. "No. Not today."

"Stay here." Romero drew his gun from beneath his sports coat and tip-toed down the hall toward the front door.

Chapter 18

"Don't shoot!" Kelsey spotted Romero as soon as she entered the house and held her hands up. From behind Romero's back, I could see the color drain from her face as she struggled to catch her breath. "Please, please...don't...don't shoot."

"What are you doing here?" Romero holstered his gun.

"I forgot my jacket." With her hands still above her head, Kelsey pointed a finger at the big picture window facing out onto the patio where a jacket lay on the chaise lounge. "It's out there."

"You in the habit of coming by and letting yourself in?" Romero grabbed Kelsey's hands above her head, patted her down, then released her and stepped back.

"I have a key if that's what you mean." Kelsey's voice shook.

"You didn't notice my car out front?"

"You mean the sedan in the drive?" Kelsey pointed her thumb toward the door. "It doesn't exactly look like a car a cop would drive. Believe me if it did, I wouldn't have come in."

"Let this be a lesson to you. Detectives don't always drive around in identifiable, unmarked police cars. Sometimes they just look like any other car."

"Yeah, which is why I thought maybe it belonged to Zoey's housekeeper. I rang the bell and knocked, and when nobody answered, I figured the maid must be out back or something. Why, you going to arrest me?"

"He would if he could connect you to Lacey's murder." Crystal came from the hall with her bag and cell phone in her hand. "Somebody put a bloody doll in my closet, and it looks like it was used to knock Lacey out."

"We don't know that for certain," Romero said.

"Well, then, Detective, you don't mind if I leave the three of you to hash things out." Crystal pushed by Romero. "I promised Zoey I'd meet her at the studio in time for lunch."

Romero took a step back and raised his hands dismissively. "As long as you don't care if I wait around for my print guys to show up. Though it doesn't really matter to me if you do, Crystal. We still need to pick up the doll and dust for prints, and you and I, we'll be in touch."

Crystal paused at the door and smiled. Her sparkling whites as genuine as her bleached hair. "Be my guest. Just be sure to lock up, will you? There's a spare key on the rack in the kitchen by the back door. You can leave it under the mat."

I couldn't resist. "Don't let the door hit you on the way out."

Crystal flashed me the finger and stalked out.

"Not really a fan of yours, I see." Romero locked the door and looked back at Kelsey. "You mind answering a few questions."

"I don't have a lot of time, Detective." Kelsey looked small framed in the archway of the hall's grand entrance.

"Won't take but a few minutes." Romero gestured to the oversized stuffed sofa in the great room.

Kelsey glanced back at me. "She got to be here?"

"Why? Psychics worry you?"

"No," Kelsey answered. "I just don't like what she's done to Zoey, and it's not like I was close with Lacey. 'Sides, Zoey and I don't have much in common."

Kelsey sat down on the couch and Romero nodded for me to take a seat in one of the swivel rockers.

"You mean other than what you had in common with Chad and the band?" Romero asked.

"Yeah, I guess so." Kelsey looked down at her feet. She could barely sit still.

"So, you're more or less along for the ride. That how you describe it?"

"Excuse me?" Kelsey narrowed her eyes at the detective. "I don't know what you mean."

"I think you do. Zoey finances the band, Chad's happy, he's got money to spend, and so do you."

"I don't know anything about who finances what. I write music. And sometimes I sing a little. That's all."

"You didn't know anything about Lacey and Chad. That they were involved?"

"Like I said, I wasn't friends with Lacey, and Zoey and I, we barely speak. She's not usually around when I'm here."

"But if you did know about Lacey's affair with Chad, I would think you wouldn't like it. You might be afraid it'd break up the band. And where would you be if that happened? Not like you had a big career going before you and your boyfriend signed on with Chad."

"I don't know what you're talking about. Zac and I weren't here the night Lacey was murdered, and we weren't part of Zoey's inner circle. I don't know anything about Zoey and Lacey or Chad and Lacey for that matter. And unless you're going to charge me with something, I think it's time for me to go." Kelsey got up off the couch and started to head for the front door.

"Hey, didn't you forget something?" Romero asked.

"What?" Kelsey stopped and looked back at the detective.

"Your jacket. Isn't that what you came for?" Romero pointed to the window.

"Yeah, right." Kelsey turned around and headed toward the back door. "If you don't mind, I'll let myself out the back gate."

"The one by the side of the yard or on the hill leading into the park?"

"Shove it, Detective."

"You think she's guilty?" Detective Romero sat down in the swivel rocker next to me, and we watched Kelsey pick her jacket up off the chaise and throw it over her shoulder, then head out the side gate.

"I don't know," I said, "but from the way you talked to her, I suspect you do."

"I talk to a lot of people a lot of ways. Doesn't mean I think they're guilty."

"I should hope not." I couldn't shake the thought of my conversation with him yesterday. "And if that means you no longer think of me as a suspect, then I—"

"You can stop right there, Misty. If my questions about Lacey's murder bothered you yesterday, I apologize. Far as I'm concerned, you're not a suspect. You don't appear to have a motive. You didn't know Lacey, and the night of the murder you and your landlady were out to dinner together. Petite Trois. New restaurant in the valley. Have to try it myself sometime. It any good?"

I was stunned. "How did you know that?"

"I'm a detective. I wouldn't be doing my job if I didn't. But if it will make you feel any better, Denise told me. After you kicked us out yesterday we had coffee. The woman likes to chat."

Of course, Denise would tell him. She probably would have given him her life story if asked. And with the least little bit of prodding, shared enough information about me to make him wonder. Goodness knows I had enough.

"Is there anything else you've discovered about me that you've found interesting?" I asked.

If Romero knew anything, he knew Misty Dawn was an alias, that my real name was Agnes Butters, and I'd come to the Golden State back in the sixties in my VW Van, selling love potions that didn't exactly mesh with the laws of the land back then.

"Not that I'm willing to share." Romero winked. "'Least not now. But the restaurant? Any good?"

"Yes, Detective, it was good. Excellent in fact."

"Good to know," Romero said.

"Now that I'm no longer a suspect, what's next? Do you plan to ask for my help?"

"I do. I'll admit it's a stretch for me, since I'm a skeptic when it comes to all this psychic stuff. But, be that as it may, you appear to know these people. Zoey seems to trust you, and I could benefit from whatever it is you want to call it, your insight, maybe."

"What is it you'd like to know?"

"Let's start with Kelsey. You get any kind of read on her?"

"If you're wondering if I think Kelsey killed Lacey, I couldn't tell you. She was nervous and frightened when she saw you. But then why wouldn't she be? She didn't expect to find you here. As a psychic, I can sense if someone's upset or nervous, but anything more I'd have to have time alone to read them. Otherwise, it's just too general. And I couldn't read her if she didn't want me to. No psychic could. It's impossible to read someone who doesn't want to be read. They have to be open to it."

"Alright, then if you couldn't read her, let's start with what we do know." Romero took out his notepad and began checking off the facts. "Kelsey had a key to the house. Which means she had access. She could come and go as she pleased. She might have come back here after we searched the place the other day, put the doll in the closet, and left without her jacket. Maybe to frame Crystal or..." Romero clenched his jaw and looked up at the ceiling. "Maybe even your ghost. I don't know, but I can tell you this, her jacket wasn't in the backyard last time we checked the house."

"You might have missed it," I said. "With everything going on, it'd be easy to overlook."

"Not for my men," Romero said.

I couldn't sit silently by and let Detective Romero think Kelsey had put the doll in the closet when I knew better.

"Could have been anybody," I said.

"But who?"

I looked down at my lap. How could I begin to tell Detective Romero about Wilson? That I knew Wilson had moved the doll? Explaining one ghost was hard enough, but two?

Romero put the notepad down and crossed his arms. "Alright, so tell me this. If you can't read Kelsey, how is it you were able to read me yesterday? You knew about my wife. How she died. When. You even said a few things that made me think you knew what she'd be thinking if she were still here."

"That's different, Detective. I wasn't reading you. I was observing your wife. You brought her into the room with you when you came to see me. She goes everywhere with you. You've been hanging onto her since her passing. It's exhausting. For her too. It's time to let go."

Romero flushed. "You're quite the mystic."

"Perhaps it would be easier if you thought of what I do as more like what you do. Observing people, only with a little bit of a third eye."

"Where you going with this?"

"You talk to people all day long. Make observations. You probably even get a read off of them because of the way they're dressed. The way they walk. The way they talk. What they do for a living."

"I'm a detective. Talking to people, listening to them, following up on hunches, it's what we do."

"Exactly, and when you talk to people long enough, you begin to understand what makes them tick. What they like, what they fear, what baggage they carry with them."

"I'll agree with that."

"Well, I do the same thing. Only in addition to hearing what they say, I frequently see their loved ones or spirits around them as well. Usually, they're trying to lift the burdens of the person I'm reading because that person's been carrying around a lot of stuff they don't need to hold onto anymore. Mostly it's guilt. We all carry a lot with us."

The detective arched his brows. "That what you see with me? Guilt?"

"Your wife loved you. Still does. She doesn't blame you because you weren't home as much as she would've liked or that you forgot your anniversary the last year you were together. She doesn't let it burden her. Not like you do."

"People really pay you for this stuff, huh?" Romero drew his lips in a firm closed smile.

"Yes. And sometimes, I offer my advice for free. Like when I think someone's open to it and ready. Her death wasn't your fault. It was her time."

Chapter 19

I left Detective Romero in the house and returned to the car. Wilson sat behind the wheel with a very pasted, smug grin on his face. While I had been inside talking with Crystal and Detective Romero, Wilson had been in the backyard sipping tea with Alicia Mae and was bursting with news.

"I don't know about you, Old Gal, but I found out a few things that blonde ice queen of a personal assistant wouldn't want anyone to know."

"Crystal?" I asked. "Like what?"

"Like Lacey wasn't the only one carrying on with Chad."

"C-C-Crystal and Ch-Chad?" I choked on the names. "They had a relationship? A physical relationship? How did you find that out?"

"Alicia Mae."

"Alicia Mae? How could she..."

"According to her, when Zoey traveled, which has been a lot lately, Crystal kept Zoey's bed warm with her fiancé."

"Alicia told you this?"

"Not in those exact words, but when a four-year-old sees two people sleeping in the same bed together, she understands something's going on."

I laughed. "No wonder Crystal doesn't want me around. She was afraid I might pick up on her extracurricular activities."

"And that's not all. It gets better. So much better."

"Go on," I said.

"It appears our little Alicia's a bit of a pickpocket. Evidently, when Zoey was away, and Crystal would come over, Alicia would go through her purse and take things."

"Like what?"

"Like this." Wilson reached into his pocket and took out a small, round, plastic pink caddy. She thought it was candy, but turns out, it's—"

"Birth control pills?" I grabbed the pill caddy from Wilson's hand and opened it to see how many pills remained. The caddy was half full.

"She thought they were bitter, and don't worry she didn't take any, but she gave them to Mariposa."

"Mariposa?" The name was familiar, but why?

"Her doll. The one she and Heather used to have tea parties with. Alicia keeps the doll in the playhouse. It was a gift from her mother. But wait, it gets even better."

"What?"

"Right after Crystal moved into her room, Alicia Mae went through the trash, and she found this." Wilson took a blue and white pregnancy test tube from his pocket and held it out for me to see. "It's positive."

I grabbed the stick and stared at the positive plus sign. "You've got to be kidding. Crystal and Lacey were both having affairs with Chad, and they're both pregnant?"

"Or one of them is anyway, considering Lacey's no longer in the picture."

We rode in silence, Wilson driving much slower than his usual breakneck speed, the both of us wondering who killed Lacey.

Finally, it was Wilson who spoke. "My bet's on Crystal. I think she found out Lacey was pregnant and figured if Zoey knew about the baby it'd mess up Zoey big time. So Crystal killed Lacey."

"Which takes care of one mommy-to-be, but what about the fact Crystal's also got a bun in the oven?"

"I doubt Crystal plans to tell Chad or Zoey for that matter. Unlike Lacey, I don't see the Ice Queen settling for a home and marriage. For Crystal, I think the pregnancy had to come as a big surprise, and something she may intend to take care of. But Crystal knew Lacey was out for more than just Chad's baby, and she needed to stop her."

Wilson had a point. Crystal had admitted she was at the Pink Mansion for dinner the night Lacey and Zoey were running lines, and had made it very clear to Detective Romero that she left early. But what if she hadn't? What if that was all a lie?

"You think Crystal took the doll from the house, and instead of going home snuck into the backyard, then waited until it got late and she heard Zoey and Lacey say goodnight? And then she triggered the doll's cry box to make a whining sound and waited for Lacey to come out of the house and hit her over the head with the doll and killed her?"

"Exactly. Crystal knew Zoey had to be up early the next morning. All she had to do was wait until Zoey went to bed and Lacey came outside. I wouldn't even be surprised if Crystal slipped Zoey an extra sleeping pill, put it in her food to ensure she got tired early. Once Zoey heard what she thought was a cat-like sound, Crystal turned on the spa's bubblers to attract Lacey's attention, then snuck up behind her and hit her over the head with the doll. The perfect crime. Even Lacey didn't know who killed her."

"Except Crystal didn't take the doll, and she's too detailed to have left it behind."

"She might have panicked."

"Not Crystal. She's cool under pressure. She would have

picked up the doll, and she wouldn't have dropped the squawk box on the trail."

"Then who?" Wilson asked.

"Kelsey maybe. I get the feeling Detective Romero likes her for the murder. If she suspected Lacey was trying to break up Chad and Zoey, unlike Crystal whose ticket to success is Zoey and would do anything to protect her employer, Kelsey may have thought the future of the band was threatened by Lacey, and killed Lacey herself."

"Why not Chad?" Wilson asked. "He had everything to lose if Zoey found out."

"Chad has an alibi. He claims he was at a recording studio that night, and until Romero finds out differently, Chad's off the hook."

Wilson pulled the Jag into the drive. "Of course, there's always the possibility its none of them. Much as I hate to agree with my sister, it could be some random stalker looking to make a name for himself. Maybe someone followed Zoey home one day or bought one of those Hollywood Star Maps for sale on every corner. It'd be easy enough to locate her home, notice it backed up to the park, hike up the trail, and come in through the back gate. At that hour, anyone stalking Zoey would have seen Lacey in the backyard, thought it was Zoey, and killed Lacey by mistake. They did look a lot alike."

"But what about the doll and the cry box?" I asked. "A stalker's not going to have access to Zoey's dolls."

"Not unless somebody gave it to them," Wilson said.

Chapter 20

Zoey called the following afternoon on the verge of tears and said she needed to talk to someone. Through controlled sobs, I got that she couldn't talk to Chad, not after what he had done, and Lacey was...well...*Lacey was dead.* I tried to bolster Zoey the best I could through the phone and quickly realized it was a losing proposition.

"I miss her, Misty," Zoey's voice cracked, "I can't believe my best friend would betray me like that. And...and, I can't talk to Crystal. Not about Chad anyway. Besides, she's out shopping for a few things I need around the house."

Superstars like Zoey, particularly one in the middle of a murder investigation, didn't go out shopping like everyday people. Too many paparazzi with cameras and overly curious fans who wouldn't respect boundaries and wanted selfies with the star.

"At times like these, I miss my mom." Zoey paused. I pictured her, the phone in her hand, her eyes welled with tears, alone in the house without anyone to talk to. "I know it's been a long time. My mother died years ago when I was just a little girl. But I really wish I could talk to her. Can I talk to you instead?"

"Of course you can talk to me, but not on the phone. I think this is more of a person-to-person type of thing." I promised I'd be right over and roused Wilson from the study. "Zoey called.

She needs me to come by."

"Is she okay?" The quick response and concern in Wilson's voice surprised me. Since the night of the séance, I was beginning to see a new, softer side to Wilson, one despite his snooty airs, I was starting to like.

"She's fine. She needs someone to talk to, that's all."

"We'll take the Jag." Wilson grabbed the keys and, once again like a man who no longer feared his mortality, we raced from our house to Zoey's in record time.

Zoey was on the front patio, sitting by the koi pond as I came up the steps. She was still in her robe with her hair pulled back in a messy ponytail and wasn't wearing any makeup.

"Thank you for coming." Zoey wiped her eyes with a tissue, put her arms around me, and bent her forehead to mine. "I didn't know who else to call."

I wiped a few tears from her eyes. "I'm a good listener, Zoey."

"I should probably pay you."

"This isn't a reading. This is me being a friend, and I won't allow it. Now suppose we go inside and you tell me what it is you want to talk about."

Zoey took my hand and we walked inside where she curled up on the couch in the great room. "I feel so alone, Misty. This is all my fault. I should have realized what was going on."

"Zoey, you can't blame yourself."

"Maybe not. But I was hoping you could tell me if Alicia Mae's still here. I haven't felt her presence since the séance. I'd feel so much better if I knew she was."

"You want her to be?" I asked.

"I do. I really do. I woke up last night and I heard the piano playing. I thought maybe it was her and I came rushing in here to see. But when I came in the room, there was nothing. The room was cold and empty, and the piano..." Zoey shook her head. "There wasn't anyone there. I'm beginning to think Chad's right. I am going crazy."

"But you thought it was Alicia, and you still think so, don't you?"

"I want it to be. Unless you think I've got another ghost." Zoey looked at the piano, her eyes wide.

Wilson hadn't mentioned the presence of any other spirits in the house, and I had my doubts Lacey would dare come back to haunt Zoey. Or revisit the scene of the crime. There was always the possibility another presence might have visited the house. Perhaps another ghost that felt a connection to the Pink Mansion or maybe Zoey.

I looked back at the piano and took Zoey's hand. I had no sense of a spirit in the house with us. "If there was another ghost in the house, I'm afraid it's gone now."

Zoey looked disappointed. "It's just, ever since I moved in, sometimes at night I wake up and hear the piano. At first, I thought I was dreaming. The music reminded me of when I was a little girl. I think I told you my mother used to play. I remember falling asleep to the sound of her playing. But later, after we met and you told me about Alicia, I just assumed it had been her."

In my mind's eye, I didn't see Alicia playing the piano. It didn't feel right. It felt more like a second presence in the house. Someone with a reason for being there. Someone who played the piano because of the emotional connection Zoey had to it.

"Do you remember what tune you heard?"

"I'm not sure. "Clair de Lune," maybe? My mother used to play that. It was her favorite. I can't hear that song without thinking of her."

"And do you recall what tune you heard when you woke up last night?"

"Not really. I just remember hearing the sound of the piano

playing. My first thought was that it was Alicia. But now that Lacey died, I'm afraid I've done something to anger Alicia. That I've frightened her away."

I filed the thought about Zoey's mother away in the back of my mind and looked out the big picture window at the backyard. A lighter-hearted scene played out in front of me. Wilson was sitting at the little picnic table beneath the big weeping willow. Alicia was playing hide-and-seek, peeking out the door of the playhouse with her doll Mariposa in her arms. But Zoey could see none of this.

"You really think Alicia would run away?" I asked.

"I don't know what to think or why it's even important anymore. Yet somehow the idea she's still here makes me feel less alone, and I want to believe she is. Do you think she's still here, Misty?"

I pointed to the window. "There used to be a little playhouse out there. Just beyond the pool beneath that old weeping willow in the backyard. I know you can't see it now, but if I told you it was still there, would you believe me?"

Zoey looked at me, her eyes moist with tears. "Was it Alicia Mae's?"

"It was, and it still is. When she's not here in the house with you, she's out there playing with her doll. She considers it her safe place. Her father built it for her, just like he built this house. And near as I can tell, her parents loved her very much."

"What happened to her? Why is she still here?"

"There was an accident. It was Alicia's birthday, and the Manns had invited friends to celebrate. Something happened. Her parents weren't watching. Alicia Mae fell into the pool and drowned."

Zoey put her hand to her heart. "But that must have been years ago."

"September 9, 1943, to be exact. Her parents couldn't bear

to be here after that. They put the house up for sale and left. Moved far away. I suspect it was too emotional for them to stay anywhere near here."

"But Alicia Mae came back."

"She did, as ghosts sometimes do. I believe she was looking for them, but they were gone. Alicia's been here ever since. I don't know about the previous owners, but Heather, the lady you met the night of the séance, knew her. Alicia was her imaginary friend. Heather's family lived here in the late nineties and said she and Alicia shared a bedroom."

"The front guest room, where Crystal's staying?"

"Alicia still thinks of the room as hers, and in her world, the playhouse is still here too. It's where she went the night she heard you rehearsing with Lacey. She was frightened by the yelling and went and hid there."

"But she knows I wasn't really arguing with Lacey. That I didn't kill my best friend. I tried to tell her at the séance. Do you think she heard me?"

"I don't think Alicia knows who killed Lacey, but I'm quite sure she knows it wasn't you."

"Then why haven't I felt her here the last couple of days? The house feels so empty. And I'm so alone. Can you bring her back?"

I put my hand on the back of Zoey's head and stroked her hair. I wanted to help her. To bring some kind of peace into her life. "I believe I can put your mind at ease about Alicia if that's what you want. I doubt you'll be able to see her. That will come with time. As you both learn to trust one another. But first, there's something I need to know before I can assure you Alicia's still here."

"Whatever you want."

"Did Crystal tell you about the doll she found in the guest bedroom closet?"

"Ugh." Zoey shook her head. "That's the other thing that kept me up all last night. I don't know how my doll ended up in the closet like that. All beat up and bloodied. Now the police are looking at me like I'm a suspect. And Detective Romero's called my attorney and told him I shouldn't be thinking of leaving town any time soon. Even worse, my commercial agent's threatened to drop me, and the studio's freaked. The final shoots are scheduled in Italy in two weeks, and there's no way they can shoot around me. 'Cause guess what?" Zoey looked up at the ceiling, her eyes filled with tears. "My double's dead. My best friend. And everybody thinks I did it." Zoey bowed her head, and the tears started to flow again. "I didn't kill Lacey, I swear. This is all a terrible nightmare."

I handed Zoey a tissue. "I don't think you killed Lacey, not for a second. There's only so much you can do while Detective Romero searches through the facts. Let's not borrow trouble from tomorrow that may or may not ever materialize. Instead, I think maybe I can help you find something that will make you feel better."

"Anything."

"You asked me if Alicia Mae's still here. You wanted proof, so let's play a little game again, shall we? Last time, I asked you to leave the little plastic ring Detective Romero found in the spa on your dressing table for her, so that she might find it. And she did, right?"

"It was missing in the morning, so I think so."

"Then let's do it again. Do you have something else, something that was yours from when you were a child? Something you adored. Perhaps something your mother gave you?"

"I have a box of things somewhere that still needs unpacking. I'd have to look, but...wait. I know something. It'd be perfect. I have a pair of ponytail clips with little unicorns on them. My mother used to take me to the pony rides in Griffith Park when I was little. One day there was this street merchant selling things. Plastic combs, barrettes, little mirrors and such. I wouldn't let my mother leave until she had bought these cute little pink clips with unicorns on them. I still have them in a box on my dresser."

"Good. Get them, put them out on your dressing table tonight. Exactly like you did with the ring."

"You think she'll come back for them?"

"I do. But there's something else I think you need to do as well."

"What's that?"

"It concerns Crystal. I don't believe Alicia Mae likes her, and Crystal's been sleeping in that front bedroom. Alicia's old room. If you want her to come back, you need to ask Crystal to move into another bedroom. This is a large house, there must be another room she could use."

"I've got five big bedrooms, not counting my own. If you think Alicia would return, I'll ask Crystal to take another."

"I think that's a good idea," I said. "At least for the time being."

I heard the sound of someone coming into the house through the kitchen. A moment later, Crystal's voice rang through the hallway and into the great room where Zoey and I were sitting.

"Zoe, I'm back." Crystal stopped as she entered and spotted me on the sofa. "Oh, I didn't realize you had company. I came in the back 'cause I had groceries. I'll take the dry cleaning and put it in your bedroom." In her hands, Crystal held several freshly laundered garments in clear plastic bags and a small vase of flowers in the other. Without saying anything more, she proceeded down the hall toward Zoey's bedroom.

"Crystal, wait. I've been talking with Misty about Alicia Mae. You know she used to live here. Her father built this house, and the room you're in? It used to be hers and I'd like for Alicia to have it again. Misty thinks Alicia might come back to it if you moved out. Why don't you take the second guestroom down the hall? It's not quite as big, but you should be fine there."

"Misty thought it'd be a good idea?" Crystal shot me a look that could have melted ice.

"Just for a while," Zoey said. "I need to get my head straight. It'd really help me if you would."

Crystal bit her lips together. I sensed she was biting back a response. Thinking better of it, she smiled. "Not a problem."

"I really appreciate it," Zoey said.

"Oh, and somebody left these on the front porch." Crystal put the vase of flowers on the coffee table. "They were there when I came in."

"Who are they from?" Zoey asked.

"I don't know. I suppose you'll have to read the card for yourself." Crystal snapped and did an abrupt about-face and left the room.

Zoey squelched a smile. The first I'd seen all morning. "You think she's upset?"

"The Ice Queen?" I said.

Zoey laughed then reached for the card with the flowers. As she read, her expression darkened, and she threw the card on the table. "Oh, my God. Crystal! Come back here. Quick. I need you."

"What's the matter?" Crystal came running back.

"The card on the flowers. It's—read it. They're from AJ."

Crystal picked up the card and stared at it.

"Who's AJ?" I asked.

"He's a stalker." Crystal handed me the card. "The police arrested him a couple years ago for attempted kidnapping. We thought he was in jail, but obviously, he's not."

"Call Detective Romero." Zoey put her hand to her heart and leaned back against the couch. "Tell him he needs to come out here, right away. I need to talk to him. Now!"

While Crystal called LAPD, Zoey filled me in on AJ, Adam Johnson, a drifter who had worked as an extra on a movie Zoey had filmed. She immediately pegged him as trouble and the director finally kicked him off the set. But that didn't stop AJ's attempt to follow Zoey, and, eventually, he tried to break into her former residence. Chad found him hiding in the garden outside her house and called the police. Since Johnson hadn't broken in and wasn't carrying a gun, he was sentenced for trespassing on private property and stalking. The judge gave him three to five years in the state penitentiary, but with today's overcrowding, Zoey feared he had qualified for early release and was coming after her again.

Detective Romero arrived thirty minutes later. Crystal met him at the front door and invited him in. Upon seeing me seated on the sofa, he nodded to Zoey and asked if I'd moved in. "Seems like every time I show up, you're here, Misty."

"Zoey wanted to talk. The flowers arrived after I did."

Romero looked at the flowers on the table. "This them?" he asked.

Zoey pushed the vase across the table with the tip of her toe. "Crystal brought them in. She found them on the front patio."

"That right, Ms. Martini? That where you found them?" Romero asked.

"That's where they were," Crystal said. "Next to the koi pond."

"And when you picked them up and brought them in, did you happen to see a delivery van or anybody hanging around like they'd dropped them off?"

"No, and I don't know how anyone got through the security gate unless they scaled the bushes."

"The card's signed by AJ," Zoey said. "I thought he was in jail. He was arrested for stalking me two years ago. He's crazy. For a while, I was scared he was going to kill me. Please tell me there's some mistake. I can't go through this again."

Romero took a pair of latex gloves from his pocket and slid the card off the table, careful not to disturb any prints that might remain. The writing on the card was distinctive. The letters were capped and blocked, equally as wide as they were high, with a slight upward tilt. The message read, *SORRY FOR YOUR LOSS. MAYBE WE CAN BEGIN AGAIN. LOVE, AJ.*

"You recognize the writing? It's pretty distinctive," Romero said.

I glanced at the card. I had seen enough designs around Wilson's home to recognize the writing as the type used on architectural or stage designs. "It looks like the type of printing an architect might do."

"Or a draftsman," Zoey said. "According to the police, AJ had been studying to be a draftsman before deciding he wanted to be an actor. He sent all his letters to me in the same strange handwriting."

"It's going to be okay, Zoe." Crystal put her hand on Zoey's shoulder. "Detective, you have to find out if AJ's been released. If he has, maybe he's responsible for Lacey. Wouldn't surprise me. We all worried he would have killed Zoey if he'd ever gotten close to her. It's easy enough to think he might have mistaken Lacey for Zoey. The man's nuts."

"I'll make a few calls," Romero said. "If AJ qualified for early release you should have been notified. I'm surprised you didn't hear anything."

"You'd think somebody might have said something," Zoey said. "Did anyone contact you, Crystal?"

Crystal shook her head. "No. I never heard anything."

I didn't believe Crystal. But I knew she wasn't about to sit around with me in the room. She put her hand on Detective Romero's arm and excused herself. Then looked at me like she could have spit bullets and said she'd be in the guest room, packing.

Chapter 21

"Just got off the phone with AJ's parole officer. He's been released alright." Romero walked in from Zoey's kitchen where he had gone to make his calls. "But don't worry, Zoey. If AJ sent the flowers, he'll be in jail for violating his parole before sunset. The District Attorney takes stalking very seriously."

"And if AJ killed Lacey?" Zoey asked.

"We'll find that out too." Romero put his phone in his pocket. "Meanwhile, Misty, you got a minute?" Romero tilted his head toward the courtyard.

I followed him outside. Wilson close behind me. "Something you need, Detective?"

"You said you didn't see the flowers when you arrived. I was curious if maybe—"

"What?" I asked. "That I sensed something else was going on here? If I didn't think you'd tell me different, I'd suspect you were beginning to trust me."

Romero put his hand to his head. I noticed he wasn't wearing his wedding ring.

"Take me with you," I said. "You know you want to."

"What, bring you along to question AJ? A former felon?"

"The only way I can help is if I meet the man. Come on, Detective, why not? What's it going to hurt?"

"You really think you're going to get a read on him?"

"Probably not. But if we hurry, I could get a sense of him. Tell you if he's hiding something. But we need to leave now, before the trail goes cold."

"There is a certain risk, Misty. This wouldn't be just a ride along. Things could happen."

"I'm quite capable." I glanced at Wilson. Together we could handle whatever came our way. "You needn't worry."

Romero shook his head. "One condition."

"What?" I asked.

I knew Romero had been debating the wisdom of asking me to come with him. But somewhere in the back of his mind, it was something more. I had struck a nerve. It wasn't just me pushing him to open himself up. His wife was there too. Telling him to let go.

"I drive." Romero skipped down the steps ahead of me.

Wilson whispered. "I do hope he means his car."

"You and me both," I said under my breath. I hollered to Romero. "I assume you mean your car?"

Romero stopped in front of the sedan and opened the passenger door. "This is official police business, Misty. Much as I'd love to get behind the wheel of that beautiful Jag of yours, I doubt it'd be appropriate for me to be driving you around in anything but my own car."

I hobbled down the steps. "Since this is official police business, I'd like to add one stipulation."

"Which is?" Romero asked.

"You start by sharing with me everything you know about Lacey's murder, including what you have on Zoey."

If Zoey was convinced Romero thought she was a suspect, I wanted to know why, and what he had on her. With a little inside police knowledge, I felt I could better direct and expedite the case. Maybe even help Zoey meet her deadlines in time for her to make her trip to Italy. "I can be much more helpful that way. And when the case is solved, which it will be, I'll be happy to hand you the keys to the Jag, and you can take it out for a spin."

"Deal." The detective shook my hand, and before he could help me into the car, Wilson slid behind me and took the middle seat. Romero, totally unaware of our passenger, shut the door and walked around the driver's side of the car.

"You really plan to sit *there*?" I whispered as I struggled to make enough room for myself next to Wilson. Despite the fact Wilson couldn't be seen, I didn't want to be sitting in his lap, and cozied up close as I could next to the door.

"You really plan to give the keys to my Jag away?" Wilson elbowed me. "How dare you."

"What else would you have me do? You've seen the way Romero looks at the Jag. He's got mid-life crisis written all over him."

"Whose fault is that? Introducing him to my sister like you did."

"It wasn't like that. I—"

Romero opened the door. "Are you talking to yourself again?"

"Am I?" I placed my hands on the dashboard and ran my fingers across the paneled instruments. "It's just, it's been so long since I've been in a car with the steering wheel on the left it seems a little odd to me, that's all."

On the drive over to AJ's, Romero filled me in on what he knew about Lacey's case. Which wasn't any more than what I already knew. Except for the fact forensics had made a positive ID from the doll Crystal had found in the guest closet. The blood on the doll's hair was a positive match to Lacey. Add in the fact the doll belonged to Zoey, not Crystal, and Zoey had moved up Romero's chain of suspects.

"So for now," Romero said, "I think Zoey looks just as good, maybe even better, for the murder than does her fiancé, Chad."

"And Crystal and Kelsey?" I asked.

"They're still a possibility. Cases like this, it's usually someone close to the victim, but not always."

"So maybe it is AJ then?" I asked.

"We'll see," Romero said. "Over my years of investigating murders, I've learned one day you like one suspect for the crime, the next day it's the other. Best to keep an open mind and follow the facts."

AJ's house was what Denise would have called a teardown. A small, 1960's, single bath, two-bedroom in Van Nuys, sandwiched between two three-story apartment buildings. It looked like the owner, whether it was AJ or not, had lost out on negotiations with a developer and was paying for it dearly. The front lawn was overgrown with weeds and cluttered with lawn furniture. A fat-tire bike, a trike, and a dusty two-door Honda with a dented front fender were in the drive.

From the outside, it looked like nobody was home. Romero checked the address on his cell phone and suggested I wait in the car while he went up to the door.

Never to be one for following orders, I signaled Wilson to check the house, then waited until Romero's back was to me and got out of the car. While the detective knocked on the door, I checked the Honda. I hoped to find the engine was still warm or any indication the car had recently been driven. Perhaps to make a floral delivery. I put my hand on the hood. It was dusty, covered with leaves, and dead cold. From the looks of it, I doubted the car had been moved from where it had been parked in months.

Romero came back to his sedan, his cell phone in his hand. "Doesn't look like anybody's home. Nobody's answering the phone."

"Now what?" I asked. "We just leave?"

"Not much else we can do. I don't have a search warrant, and I can't just go barging in. I can call his parole officer again. Don't worry, one way or the other we're going to talk to this boy. Sooner or later."

Later wasn't the answer I wanted. I needed to meet with AJ soon as possible. If he had delivered the flowers, I'd sense his excitement of his sneaking onto Zoey's property and being so close to his once intended victim. If I waited too long, all that anxious energy would be gone. I'd have no sense of what he had done or where he had been. I looked back at the house. Wilson was on the porch with a big thumbs up.

"You mind if I try?" I asked.

"You think he's home?"

"Detective, I know he's home. He's not going to just answer the door for someone like yourself. But I doubt he's seen me. If you move your car, and I was to show up fifteen minutes from now, I'm not nearly so threatening."

I was certain if AJ had seen Romero it was before I had gotten out of the car. AJ had no reason to think Romero wasn't traveling solo. My guess was, if I knocked on his door AJ wouldn't be nearly as suspicious of an old lady on his porch in the middle of the day as he was an obvious plain-clothed detective.

"That's highly irregular. Not at all how the department would handle it."

"I'm irregular, Detective. And if I'm right, we won't have to wait for a court order or AJ's parole officer to show up. Really, there's nothing to this. I'll chat with him. See if I can get inside the house. Look around. If I find anything or feel as if he's our man, I should know pretty quickly. Then you can come back and arrest him or pick him up for questioning or whatever you think necessary. Meanwhile, if anything doesn't look right, you can come get me. Guns blazing. But believe me, you're not going to need to do that."

Romero sighed. "Fine. We'll try it your way. But the minute things go south, you're out of there."

I promised. We drove around the block and parked in front of the apartment building adjacent to the left of AJ's house. I left Romero standing beside his car with a clear view of the front porch. Wilson waved as I approached and took a seat on a patio chair.

Over the years, I've found two things that work well for me when I need to elicit help: The first, is my gray hair. It's a door opener. People love to help old ladies; makes them feel good. And second is my cat. Bossypants.

Feeling like I had both going for me, I pulled up a photo of Bossy on my cell phone and knocked on the door. "Hello?" There was no answer. I knocked again. This time trying to sound a bit distressed. "Hello? I'm your neighbor. From the apartment building next door? I'm looking for my cat. Hello? Anybody home?"

Moments later, a woman holding her hands beneath a pumpkin-sized belly that could have won first prize at the state fair, answered the door. She was pregnant, and dressed in a short, sleeveless, cotton maternity dress, and wearing a pair of cowboy boots. A toddler wrapped himself around one of her bare legs and peered up at me.

"I'm so sorry to bother you. My cat's missing." I pulled open the screen door and held out my phone for her to see. "I think she might have jumped from my balcony into your backyard." I pointed back to the apartment building next door. "She's white with orange and black markings. A calico. 'Bout eight pounds." I patted the youngster on the head. "Have you seen her?"

The woman took my phone and stared at Bossy's picture. From her smile, I could see she was an animal lover, and busy as she was with the toddler and babies on the way, I suspected she knew nothing about Zoey or the flowers. From behind her, a husky voice interrupted.

"Who's there, Babe?" I peered into the living room. A man was huddled over a drafting table, his head in his hands.

"Just some lady looking for her lost cat," she said.

"Tell her to go away. We don't have any cats here."

"I'm sorry." The woman handed me back my phone and started to close the door. "I hope you find her."

I put my hand to my throat. "Do you mind? I'm thirsty. I could use a glass of water."

The detective might have put his foot in the door, but for someone like myself, much frailer, the act of asking for a glass of water was just as effective. While Babe went back to the kitchen, I poked my head inside and started chatting with the man of the house.

"You a draftsman?" I asked.

"Who wants to know?" AJ didn't bother to look up. I stepped further into the room with one hand behind me, holding the door open.

"Just me," I said. "My late husband did the same thing. All the work and none of the glory, right?"

AJ looked up from the table. I noticed several tabloid newspapers on the coffee table, and a vase of flowers next to them. Surprisingly similar to those delivered to Zoey.

"Are those peonies?" I pointed to the flowers. "They're my favorite."

AJ got up from the table. He was big. Paul Bunyan big. With dark eyes and a full beard. He went to the table and took a flower from the vase.

"You like these?" he asked.

The man sounded irritated. I backed out the door. He was twice my size. Out of the corner of my eye, I saw Wilson get up. Ready to spring to my defense should I need it. With one hand behind me, I waved him off.

"I love them," I said.

"Here take one." AJ handed me the flower and held the door open while we waited for Babe to return with the water.

"Lived here long?" I asked.

AJ was about to answer, when from behind me, Romero bolted for the patio. He must have suspected the flower was some kind of signal and came rushing up the walk, flashing his ID.

"Your name Adam Johnson?" Romero pushed me aside. His voice gruff.

"Yeah. Why you askin'?" AJ rubbed his hands down the outside of his pant legs. The man was nervous. I could feel it like an electrical charge in the air between us, cancelling out any chance I had of getting a sense of him. "I ain't done nothin'. What you want?"

"Why don't you answer your door?" Romero barked.

"What's this about?" AJ looked from me to the detective. His eyes weary. He looked like he had pulled an all-nighter.

"I knocked on your door ten minutes ago," Romero asked. "Where were you?"

"In the backyard. Fixing the kid's swing. Why? That against the law?"

Romero ignored the question. "You sure you weren't just getting back from Zoey's, where you'd delivered some flowers?"

"What's this all about?" AJ asked.

Romero continued. "I understand you got an early release from the state pen."

"So what?" AJ jutted his jaw. "That the reason you and this

woman are standing on my doorstep?"

"Record showed you served fifteen months for a three- to five-year sentence for stalking."

The color in AJ's face went from a ruddy red to a pale salmon. The realization this was not some ordinary, unannounced parole visit was beginning to sink in.

Romero continued. "And being that you were in jail because you're a big fan of Zoey, I imagine that you must have heard about her best friend Lacey being murdered?"

AJ took a step back. "I didn't have nothin' to do with that."

"You mind telling me where you were a week ago, last night?"

"A week ago?" AJ scratched his head. "Man, I hardly remember where I was yesterday. You accusing me of somthin'?"

AJ's wife joined us at the door. "What's going on?"

"This cop's here about Zoey. He wants to know where we were a week ago. Specifically, the night Zoey's best friend got murdered."

"You're not serious?" The woman looked back at Romero. "AJ's been here. And a week ago today? We were in the ER. We were there three times last week." The woman put her hands on her stomach. "You can check the record if you like. I've been having cramps. The doctor thinks the babies might come early."

"Local ER, right?" Romero took out a small notepad and scribbled a note.

"Providence St. Joe's in Burbank," she said.

AJ held his hands up. "Look, I don't know what you think. And I don't know nothin' about any flowers or Zoey's friend getting herself killed. That stuff that happened 'tween Zoey and me? That's in the past. It was bad news. Chick blew it all out of proportion. But it's behind me now, okay?"

"You're sure you didn't take a little break, maybe? Drive

over to Zoey's just for the fun of it this morning?'

"Yeah, right. You seen my car?" AJ pointed to the gray Honda. "Battery's dead. Haven't had money to fix it."

"Really?" Romero sounded skeptical. "Then how'd you get your wife to the doctors?"

"Ever hear of Uber?"

"What about the bike in the drive?"

"What about it?" AJ asked.

"Looks like you've ridden that recently. Unless you're in the habit of leaving it out front."

"I took a ride to Trader Joe's, okay? Got milk for the kid. Eggs for breakfast and flowers for my wife. What do you think I'm training for, the Tour de France? Zoey's place gotta be at least fifteen miles from here."

"Ten," Romero said. "Easy ride if you use the bike lanes."

"You guys never give up do you?"

"Not 'til we have answers." Romero reached back into his pocket, took out the plastic bag with the small card that had come with Zoey's flowers, and held it up for AJ to see.

"This isn't your writing then? And if I run this card by my forensics guys they're not going to find your prints on it?"

AJ looked at the card and laughed. "You think that's my writing? Give me a break."

"Odd though, don't you think? You being a draftsman and all. You ask me, this note looks exactly like the type of lettering a draftsman might use. The same type of lettering you used the last time you sent notes to Zoey."

"Yeah, well I didn't write that note. And I sure as hell didn't send Zoey any flowers. Look around. I got my hands full. Pregnant wife, a drawing board full of plans that are past due, and a house that's falling apart."

"Sounds tough, son." Romero took out a business card and stuffed it into AJ's shirt pocket, patting him on the chest. "Just in case you want to talk."

I could feel AJ's anger rising. I stepped between the men. Another second and I felt the two would come to blows.

"I think we're done here, Detective. I've got everything I need." I put my hand on Romero's arm.

AJ took the card from his pocket. Looked at it, then jutted his jaw again in my direction. "Who are you? Some social worker? Come to check on the kid?"

"I take it that's not your son?" I asked.

"No, but he might as well be. He belongs to my wife. The two in the oven, them two's mine."

"Three," I said.

"Three?" AJ's head jerked back. "You're kiddin' me, right? How you know that?"

"Tell the doctor to check the sonogram again," I said. "The third baby's small. He missed her. She'll be fine, but you might want to buy another crib. They're coming early."

Chapter 22

"That some kind of trick you were doing back there or were you just trying to unsettle the kid?" Romero buckled himself in behind the sedan's steering wheel. "Telling him his wife's pregnant with triplets?"

"That's what you want to know?" I couldn't believe Romero was more concerned about how I could predict the number of babies AJ's girlfriend was carrying than whether or not I thought the man might be guilty of murder.

"Yeah, that's what I want to know. How do you do it?" Romero put the car in gear and pulled away from the curb.

Wilson elbowed me. "Me too, Misty. Go ahead, explain that one. I'm curious,"

"Stop." I put my hand out to the side of my head, in front of Wilson's face. I couldn't deal with him, not now.

Romero braked. "Something wrong?"

"No." I shook my head. "Not you, Detective. Please, I don't mean for you to stop. Just go."

Romero put his foot back on the gas and continued pulling away from the curb. "Misty, I'm beginning to think in addition to talking to spirits, you talk to yourself."

"You have to understand, if I wanted to unsettle AJ I could have found easier ways."

"Like what? Bang a few doors? Flip the lights off and on?"

"That's not what I do. I'm a psychic, not a magician. An intuitive medium, if that makes it any easier for you.

"An intuitive medium is it now. And exactly what is that?"

"Same thing as a psychic," I said. "I sense things. See things others don't, but that doesn't mean they're not there or that you couldn't see them just as easily."

Romero grunted. "I don't know about that."

"You don't have to see something to believe in it. You do it every day."

"Like what? Help me to understand. 'Cause I really don't get what it is you do. Something about it unsettles me, and I'd like to know why."

"Okay. I'll give you an example. When one of your patrol officers sees a speeding car, he can't detect how fast it's going. He simply knows it's a car and it's traveling faster than some of the others around it. It's not until the officer points a speed gun in the direction of the target and clocks the speed that he can get a read on it."

"That's supposed to explain how you know how many babies AJ's wife's got in her belly?"

"We both know she's pregnant. She's big as a balloon and about to pop. The only difference is, in the cop's case, he points a radar gun at a moving target, and sonar scans the target and bounces back with a number. Telling you how fast the target's moving. In my case, I focused on the target's energy, the girl's belly, and come back with the number of souls on board. It all amounts to the same thing. We both just use different tools to learn something we can't see."

We rode along in silence. Me aware Romero's mind wasn't only on AJ and the Q&A he had just had on his doorstep, but the conversation the detective and I had the day before about his wife.

"Sometimes you just have to sit with the idea for a while.

Get comfortable with knowing we all have other energies around us."

"Like sonar waves?"

"If that's how you like to think of it, yes, that's one form of energy. There are lots of invisible energy forms around us all the time. Just because you can't see them, doesn't mean they don't exist."

"Maybe," Romero said, "but if AJ's wife has three babies and we don't find him guilty of murder or delivering the flowers to Zoey, I'll be the first to buy the guy a cigar, and you too."

"You won't have to wait long to know, Detective. My guess is AJ's going to be busy sooner than he expects. Probably before the end of the month."

"What about AJ? Do you think he sent the flowers or dropped them off?"

"I don't know. You interrupted me before I had a chance to go inside the house or get a feel for what was going on with him. The man's stressed. That's for sure. He looked like he hadn't slept. But I got the feeling it had more to do with money issues. As for the flowers? Something about them bothers me. It's a little too obvious, don't you think? The card. The handwriting. The block lettering. If AJ really wanted to reach out to Zoey, particularly knowing he'd go back to jail if he was caught, I don't think he'd be foolish and use the same approach as he'd done before. And why now? His wife's pregnant, and unless we're missing something, he hasn't made any attempt to see Zoey until today. It just doesn't make sense to me."

"You think someone else sent the flowers and made it look like AJ sent them?"

"I think someone else knew AJ got a get-out-of-jail-early card and used it to their advantage."

"Any ideas?"

I had lots of ideas, some I was willing to share with

Romero, but my cell phone rang before he could press me for answers.

I pulled the phone from my bag and glanced at the caller ID. Wilson leaned over my shoulder and looked at the screen.

"Don't answer," Wilson said.

I scowled at him. "Hello?"

"I'm in jail!" Denise wailed.

"What for?" My jaw dropped.

"I'll explain later, but I need you to come and get me."

"Leave her there," Wilson said.

"I can't do that." I gave Wilson a dirty look.

"What do you mean you can't?" Denise was hysterical. "Please, you can't leave me here."

"Not you," I said to Denise.

"What's wrong?" Romero looked at me. "What's going on?"

"It's Denise," I said. "She's been arrested."

"For what?" Romero asked. "What did she do?"

Wilson moaned. "Oh my God, look at him. The man's smitten."

"Wils—" I cut myself short and shot Wilson a terse look.

"What?" Romero looked at me. "Misty, what's going on?"

"Wil—I mean, will you or could you drive me to the jail? I need to pick her up. She needs my help."

Chapter 23

On the way over to the LA County Jail, I tried to explain Denise to Detective Romero as best I could, and that I suspected she had been arrested for impersonating a reporter.

"A reporter?" Romero tsked. "I don't think we have a criminal code for that on the books. FBI agent. Cop. Doctor, yes. But reporter? No. It's not like we arrest people for fake news or bad grammar. Too bad, huh?" Romero laughed at his own joke.

Wilson buried his head in his hands. "Not only does the man have no taste, he thinks he's funny."

"I appreciate the humor, Detective, but if I'm right, Denise may have been impersonating a reporter so that she can get close to Hugh Jackman."

"The actor?" Romero's brow wrinkled.

"I'm afraid so. You see Denise is also an actress of sorts, and—"

"I thought she was your landlady."

"She is, but she fancies herself an actress. Song and dance mostly. Small productions, musical theater. That type of thing. And for reasons that defy logic, she has this kind of teenage-girl crush on Hugh Jackman. She's convinced they're soul mates, and I'm afraid things may have gotten out of hand."

Romero bit back a smile. I could see he didn't think Denise was much of a threat. "You mean she's been stalking him?"

"Not in her mind, but yes," I said.

"You realize if Denise's been arrested for stalking, it's likely Jackman, or his manager anyway, may have filed a restraining order against her. Bailing her out not only won't be easy but it won't be cheap either."

I wasn't familiar with the process. Fortunately, most of my clients were good, law-abiding citizens. While I had worked with the police before, this was the first time I'd worked with someone whom the police had arrested and was likely to spend the night in jail.

"What is it I need to do?" I asked.

"To start with, you'll have to post bail. For stalking you're looking at about a half-million dollars."

"A half a million dollars?" I choked. "You're not serious?"

"Like I told Zoey, stalking's a serious charge. But the good news is, there's plenty of bail bondsman around, and one of them can help you out with the money. If Denise owns a home and is willing to put a lien on it to guarantee she'll show up for trial, the bondsman will issue a bond. Beyond that, I'm afraid, you'll still have to come up with about fifty-thousand dollars."

"Cash?" My personal checking account never had more than a couple thousand dollars in it. And my savings wasn't much better. How could I possibly come up with a sum like that?

"But I may have another idea, provided you're convinced Denise isn't a real threat to Mr. Jackman or herself."

"I'm listening," I said.

"Denise could be released into my custody. If I were to tell the sheriff she's a principal witness in a criminal investigation, the sheriff could be convinced to release her to me."

Wilson put his hands to his head again and began rapidly shaking his head from side to side, the words coming out of his mouth like rapid gunfire. "No, no, no, no. No, no. Please, Misty, tell him not to do that."

"I can't—" I was about to tell Wilson I couldn't leave Denise in jail when Romero reached over and put his hand on top of mine.

"It's not a lie. Denise was in your house the night of the séance. In a sense, that makes her a material witness. Someone I still need to talk to. And, just so you know, she's someone I wouldn't mind spending more time with."

Romero's idea worked like WD-40 on a stubborn lock. He flashed his detective's ID at the Sheriff's senior administrator. Words were said. Papers crossed the desk. Signatures were scrawled on dotted lines. And suddenly, Denise was a free woman. Marched out from behind the jail's heavy metal security doors and back out onto the streets. Holding her purse in front of her face to hide her identity, just in case of paparazzi—there were none—Denise jogged from the jailhouse to Romero's car. When Wilson realized his sister was about to sit next to him, he slipped over the front seat like a seal diving for cover and joined me in the back of the car.

Romero hadn't even put the key in the ignition when Denise turned to me. "I don't believe you didn't see this coming. If you'd warned me, I never would have been arrested or humiliated myself. How could this happen? How could you let me do this?"

Denise hung her head and tears ran down her face as she poked into her handbag for a tissue. I reached for one in my bag, but the detective was faster. From within his coat pocket, Romero took out a handkerchief and offered it to her.

Wilson moaned. "There is no justice. Look at him. He's falling for her."

I spoke up. "Perhaps, Denise, the universe is trying to tell you something."

"Well if the universe is trying to tell me something why didn't you tell me first?" Denise sniffed and wiped her eyes.

"Ladies," Detective Romero glanced back at me in the rearview mirror. He had this. "Perhaps it might be better if we let Denise explain what happened."

"What happened is I'm ruined." Denise blew her nose. "Oh, I know it sounds terrible. The police think I broke into Hugh's hotel suite, but that's not entirely true."

"What do you mean not entirely?" I couldn't believe what Denise had just said. "How could you do such a thing?"

"Misty." Romero's eyes caught mine in the mirror. A warning shot.

Denise batted her wet eyelashes at Romero and continued. "Well, first, you must remember I was there for an interview. Hugh and I were supposed to meet in the lobby, at least that's what his assistant had told me. But when Hugh didn't show up, and I realized time was getting short and he'd probably not have time for the interview, I decided to go to his room and wait for him there."

"His room?" Romero's jaw tightened. "Just how did you manage to get the key to his room?"

It was well known most of the celebrities in town for the awards shows stayed at the Four Seasons in Beverly Hills. Security around the hotel was as good as it gets, so how Denise managed to get a key to Hugh Jackman's room was beyond even my imagining.

"I took it," Denise said.

"You took it?" This went far beyond Denise impersonating a reporter or printing up fake business cards. "How?" I asked.

Denise looked over her shoulder at me and bit her lip. "It's like I told you, Misty, the other day. I went to the hotel for a fan meeting, and when it was clear I wasn't going to get any one-on-

one time with Hugh, I was very disappointed. Then today, when I went back for what I thought was going to be a scheduled interview, I could see I was never going to get any one-on-one time with him. I knew I had to get creative, which isn't hard when you've been acting as long as I have."

"Ugh!" Wilson clawed the air like a wild cat. "Here she goes."

"You see, years ago I played the role of Fagan for a local production of *Oliver* at the Pasadena Playhouse. Maybe you saw it?" Romero shook his head. "Fagan was a pickpocket, wonderful role, and I had to learn a few tricks of the trade so to speak."

"You learned to pick pockets for a role?" Romero asked.

"You know the song 'You've Got to Pick a Pocket or Two'? I could sing it for you if you like."

"Pleeeeeeeeeeease." Wilson pleaded. "Don't encourage her."

"Another time," Romero said, "but I'm getting the idea. You played this role, and because of that, you were able to pick Jackman's pocket?"

"Yes, but in my defense, all I took was the key. I wasn't after his wallet or anything like that. I assure you, it was all very innocent. Hugh was at the bar, right where I was scheduled to meet him. But he was surrounded by fans. I realized very quickly this interview was never going to happen. Not like I wanted anyway. So I sidled up to the bar, ordered myself a ginger beer, 'cause that's what he was drinking, slipped my hand in his pocket, and took his room key. I couldn't help myself."

"And then you went to his room and waited for him there?"

I could hear the disbelief in Romero's voice. It was laced with a myriad of emotions: surprise, humor, conflict, frustration. The surprise was no greater than my own. How quickly Denise has lassoed the detective's interest. Albeit, not without the blessings of the detective's former wife. Sometimes spirits give us a little shove.

"I knew he'd have to come back to his room, and I didn't think of it as breaking in. I wasn't there to harm him. I know it sounds awful, but I knew if I didn't do it now, he'd be gone. He leaves in a couple of days, and who knows if we'll ever meet again?"

"All you really wanted to do was meet Hugh Jackman, face to face?"

"Is that so bad? Honestly, Detective, I'd do anything. I'm convinced if we could just talk he'd know I'm a talented actress and not just some crazed fan. That we have a lot in common, and maybe, who knows, we'd click. You know what it means to really click with someone? To look across a crowded room and know—"

"That somewhere you'll see her again and again?" When Romero quoted the line from Rogers and Hammerstein's *Some Enchanted Evening,* Denise flushed.

"Why, Detective, I didn't realize you were a theater buff."

"Musicals mostly," Romero said. "Did a little theater myself back in high school. Anything Rogers and Hammerstein I could recite line for line."

Wilson collapsed against me. "There's no justice."

We turned onto Fryman Canyon, just a block from Zoey's house where Wilson and I had left the Jag. Romero asked Denise if she'd like to join him for coffee. The two of them had a lot to talk about.

Chapter 24

Thursday morning I found another breadcrumb on my doorstep. This time in the form of Heather Jefferies. She had stopped by to visit, and in her hands she had Wilson's book, *Historic Hollywood Homes*.

"I hope I'm not disturbing you. I woke up this morning and had the oddest feeling I should see you. I realized I still had the book Denise lent me the night we first met, I thought it was a good excuse." Heather held the book up and smiled apologetically. "Plus, I wanted to tell you. My husband and I have decided to buy the house down the street. We're going to be neighbors."

I welcomed Heather inside. "I had a feeling you'd buy the house. Just so you know, now that we're going to be neighbors, you don't need an excuse to stop by. In fact, I've been thinking about you too." I took the book from Heather and placed it on the entry table in front of the study.

"You think that means I might be psychic?" Heather stepped into the living room and looked about anxiously. "I've had the strongest feeling, ever since the night of the séance, that I should call. I feel like there's so much more for us to talk about."

"So do I. In fact, I've had a few questions myself, and I suspect you may have the answers." I waited for Heather to take a seat on the couch.

Bossypants joined us from beneath the stairs and curled up on my lap as soon as I sat down.

"You have a cat," Heather said.

"I do. At least when she makes herself available. Lately though, she's done a good job of hiding."

"May I?" Heather gently picked up the cat, put her in her lap and began to stroke her. Bossy purred contentedly.

"I think she's found a friend," I said.

"I'm an animal lover." Heather scratched Bossy behind her ears, and Bossy continued to purr. "My mother never allowed animals in the house growing up. I wished she had, but she was very particular."

"That's interesting," I said. "In fact, it's one the things I wanted to chat with you about. When you were a child and lived in the Pink Mansion, did you have a piano?"

"Yes. Why? Is it important?"

"Maybe," I said. "Did you play?"

"Not then. I was too young. But my mother did. Every afternoon. I remember Alicia and I used to sit on the floor in front of the piano and play with our dolls while my mother practiced. She was quite an accomplished pianist."

"By any chance do you recall what she played?"

"A lot of different things, but my favorite was 'Clair de Lune.'"

I stopped Heather before she could go on. "'Clair de Lune'? You're sure?"

"Yes, I'm positive. It's kind of slow and haunting. Years later, when I was in college, I took piano lessons and tried to learn to play it myself. I'm afraid I didn't get my mother's gift for music."

"Your mother never taught you to play as a child? Even simple melodies on the keyboard? Perhaps something like

'Chopsticks' that you and Alicia may have played together?"

Heather shook her head. "I never touched the piano as a little girl, and Alicia Mae didn't either. It was my mother's instrument. But Alicia loved to listen to my mother play. She said it reminded her of her mother, because she used to play the piano too."

"Do you remember anything else Alicia said about her mother?"

Heather continued to stroke the cat. "Only that her mother would come for her one day, and they would go home together."

"Did she say when?"

"I don't remember. I was very young, and when I was about six or seven, we moved. I grew up, put my dolls away, and forgot all about Alicia Mae until my husband and I started looking for homes in the area. Why?"

"When Zoey first came to see me, it was because she thought the Pink Mansion was haunted. She said several times she was awakened in the middle of the night by the sound of the piano playing. She described the music she heard as 'Clair de Lune,' a tune her mother used to play. Chad tried to tell her she imagined the whole thing, but I'm wondering if there might be another ghost in the house who's been playing the piano."

"You think it might have been Zoey's mother? Or maybe Alicia's?"

"I take it your mother's still alive?"

"Oh, very much so. Although I happen to know Alicia's mother's not."

"I'd be surprised if she was," I said. It hadn't occurred to me Margaret Mann might still be living. The woman would have to be well into her mid to late nineties.

"No, really, Misty. I happen to know because my mother was in the same retirement home as Margaret Mann. I probably wouldn't have thought anything about it, except the last time I visited I noticed a memorial sign for Margaret Mann in the lobby. At first, I didn't much pay attention. Older people are always passing away in places like that, but something about her felt familiar. Maybe it was her name, I don't know. When I read the small memorial card on the table, I realized it was the same Margaret Mann who lived in the Pink Mansion. The card said she had been married to Clayton Mann and was the mother of Alicia Mae Mann, both deceased."

There it was, another breadcrumb. Along with the idea Alicia Mae may not be the only ghost in Zoey's house. Perhaps both Zoey's mother and Margaret Mann had been recent visitors to the Pink Mansion. It was a thought I needed to flush out with Wilson. If there were other spirits in the house, he must have some idea.

Bossypants jumped down from Heather's lap and disappeared beneath the stairs. Heather tented her fingers and looked at me.

"You've a question," I said.

"I'm curious. I haven't seen or heard anything in the news, but maybe you know. Are the police close to an arrest for Lacey's murder?"

"They're getting there," I said. "I believe we'll hear something in the news very soon. But I sense something wrong with the report. They don't have all the facts yet."

"Was it Zoey?"

"No. I'm quite sure of that."

Heather's eyes opened wider. "Chad then?"

"Now I'm going to have to disappoint you. I can't talk with you about Lacey's death. Not now. I've been working on the case with Detective Romero, and I really shouldn't be discussing it. But I can thank you for coming by today and chatting with me about Alicia and her mother. You've been more helpful than you might imagine. I think I'm beginning to get a better idea of who

Alicia Mae is and what it is she wants."

"I hope so. I don't know what I expected when I came by this morning, I just knew I had to come."

"I'm glad you did."

"It's somehow freeing to know, even all these years later, I wasn't just imagining Alicia. That she's real and that we aren't so alone."

"We're never alone, Heather." I got to my feet and walked Heather to the door. I stopped short of opening it. I sensed Heather had one more question. "There's something else on your mind. You didn't finish asking me everything you came to ask."

"It's really not all that important," Heather said. "I shouldn't bother you any more than I already have."

"You're not a bother. It's about the new house isn't it, and the move. You're concerned?"

"It's just—" Heather exhaled and looked up at the ceiling.

"You're going to love the neighborhood. You'll make a lot of friends here. And..." I paused. The real question on her mind was far more personal and of a growing nature. "There are lots of young families, and while it's a little early to be planning for schools, the grade school down the street, is excellent."

"So you know then?" Heather searched my eyes.

"That you're pregnant?" I smiled. It seemed there was a lot of that going around lately. "Yes, and congratulations. You're going to be very happy. Any doubts you had about the house being big enough will disappear the moment you move in."

As soon as I said goodbye to Heather and shut the door, Wilson appeared from the study.

"I see she's returned my book," he said. Then picking the book up off the entry table, Wilson hugged it to his chest.

"She's also posed an interesting possibility. I assume you heard?"

"That there may be another spirit in the house?" Wilson opened the book to the page with the picture of the Pink Mansion. "Yes, I was listening."

"You think she's right?" I explained to Wilson what Zoey had shared with me about being awakened in the middle of the night to the sound of the piano, thinking it must be Alicia. "But it couldn't have been. Because according to Heather, Alicia didn't play the piano. If it wasn't Alicia playing the piano, who was it?"

Wilson cradled the open book to his chest. "What if it's Alicia's mother? What if she's finally come back for her?"

"It could be," I said. "Alicia admitted she's been waiting for her mother. And if Heather's right, Alicia's mother just recently passed. In such a case, the time is right. It's often the mother spirit that arrives to carry us to the next world."

"And what if you're wrong? What if it's Zoey's mother?" Wilson put the book down on the entry table.

I felt a chill down my back. "Then we need to get back to the mansion. If it's Alicia's mother, you need to be there to say goodbye."

"And if it's Zoey's mother?" Wilson asked.

"I don't know."

Wilson went back into the study and shut the door behind him. My mind was awash with the possibility of two mother spirits inside the Pink Mansion. I wasn't sure what it all meant. Only that I knew change was coming.

Chapter 25

The following morning I was meditating in the living room, drifting in and out of a semi-conscious state, trying to decipher what it was the universe wanted to tell me. Alicia, Zoey, Lacey? The Pink Mansion? The two mother ghosts? All of it mixed together with a sense of unease like a storm brewing. I was about to get up and suggest Wilson and I hash it out, when the front bell rang.

I shuffled to the front door, hoping I wasn't about to face a new consult, and found Detective Romero on the porch. He looked like he hadn't slept nor shaved, was dressed in the same khakis, wrinkled sports shirt and tweed blazer he had worn when I had last seen him two days ago.

"Good. You're home." Romero opened the screen and stepped inside. "I'm afraid I've bad news, and I wanted to deliver it in person."

My first thought was that something terrible had happened to Denise, and because of my concentrated efforts on Lacey and Alicia, I'd missed the universe's warning. "Is it Denise? Is she back in jail?"

"Denise is fine. Better than fine in fact. I took her back to her place after we had coffee. Told her I was releasing her on her own recognizance provided she promise not to try to make contact with Hugh Jackman again."

"Did she promise?" Denise was never one to give up so easily.

"She did." Romero grinned.

"And you believed her?" I was dubious.

"I bribed her. Told her if she promised not to go back to Hugh's hotel or try to follow him, I'd fix it so she could meet him before he left to go back to New York. If she does that, there's a good chance Jackman will drop the charges against her."

"How do you know that?"

"I have a brother-in-law on the force who works transport for the studios. Just so happens he's been driving Jackman around while he's in town. I told him about Denise and asked for a little help. Suggested he let Jackman know the lady who broke into his hotel room wasn't really a threat, just an overeager fan. Jackman said as long as she agreed not to bother him the rest of the time he's in town, he'd be happy to meet with her. In fact, she can drive with Hugh and his wife to the airport when they leave."

"That's very nice of you." It occurred to me as I listened to Romero that whoever the psychic was Denise had two-timed me with—and predicted she would meet a man under unusual circumstances, and that they would have a lot in common—was right. Only the man Denise was destined to meet wasn't Jackman, it was Romero. I tabled the thought and planned to share it with Denise later.

"That's not what I came to talk to you about, and I'm afraid you're not going to like what I have to say."

I suggested bad news was best delivered over a pot of hot tea and invited Romero into the kitchen where I brewed some chamomile peppermint tea. A favorite of mine for soothing jangled nerves.

"What is it you felt was so important you had to race over here to share it with me, Detective?"

I felt I already knew. A great black cloud was about to burst and rain down on our investigation.

"The DA issued a warrant for Zoey's arrest. It's being served as we speak. Since I promised I'd keep you posted, I wanted to stop by before Zoey called or you heard about it on the news."

I finished pouring our tea and calmly put a cup down in front of the detective. This wasn't unexpected.

"You won't mind if I tell you I think you're wrong. That I don't believe she's guilty."

"Either way, she's being charged. Her attorney will no doubt negotiate bail. The judge will grant it and request Zoey surrender her passport."

"I see." I sat down at the table and took a sip of my tea. If Zoey had to surrender her passport, she couldn't finish the movie and she'd be done. It didn't matter if the courts would later find her guilty or not. Pulling her passport now would kill her career. "But until her trial, she'll be free to go home and go about her daily activities?"

"Long as she doesn't try to leave the country."

"And you, Detective? What's your next move?"

"The DA's going to want me to provide more evidence to prove his case against Zoey."

"Which means the real killer could go free?"

"Look, Misty, I know you don't like this, but let's face the facts."

Romero started with AJ. The department's forensics team couldn't determine if there was a match to AJ's writing and what they had on file from his prison record. And detectives had verified AJ was with his wife in the ER the night Lacey was murdered.

"Just like he said. She had those Braxton Kicks something or other."

"Braxton Hicks," I said. "Pre-labor cramps."

"Call it whatever you like, the nurse in the ER said AJ came in with his wife and never left her side. And you're right about those babies coming early, the attending physician said they could be any day. So unless we uncover something new, we got nothing to pin AJ to Lacey's murder, much less harassing Zoey."

"I'm sorry, but I don't see how all this puts Zoey back as your number one suspect."

"I know you think she's innocent, but let's face it. The girl's an actress. Her best friend was fooling around with her fiancé. You ask me, she set you up. Planned the whole thing out, then pulled you in to act as a kind of character witness. She knew you had worked with the cops before, so she comes to you with a story that was bound to make headlines. 'Star's Home is Haunted.' Must have been on the front page of every tabloid in the county, including how Zoey had solicited your help to do a ghost hunt or whatever you want to call it. Meanwhile, before you arrive, Zoey kills Lacey. Then you show up and she comes running down the drive to you, all panicked that her best friend has drowned in the pool. You ask me, the ghost was the perfect backup plan in case the coroner discovered Lacey's death wasn't an accident. Fits right into the whole Chamberlain Curse of mysterious, untimely deaths."

"You'll pardon me if I tell you I'm just not feeling it."

"Misty, I know you're close to this girl. But, look at the facts. Number one, Zoey was the last person to claim to see Lacey alive. That's frequently a tip-off. Number two, and this is a biggie, we got physical evidence. Zoey's prints on the doll the coroner believes was used to kill Lacey, and again on the cigarette butt we found in the backyard. Which the DA will say proves Zoey wasn't just in the house the night Lacey drowned but in the yard. And three? We know Chad was having an affair with Lacey, that she was pregnant with his child."

"Which in my mind makes Chad the more likely suspect."

"Except Chad has an alibi. Michael Stevens, the fella who owns the sound studio where Chad was recording the night Lacey was murdered, confirmed Chad was there until two a.m. He even has the tracks set down on tape, and they're all time stamped."

"What about Zac and Kelsey?"

"According to Stevens, the two of them were in the studio with Chad and left 'round ten p.m. Kelsey said she had an upset stomach. I did a surprise visit and spoke with them this morning. Zac confirmed Kelsey hadn't been feeling well and they stopped by a drug store on the way home to get some Pepto. They even had the receipt."

"Which I assume was also time stamped." Another convenient clue I thought. Who saves sales receipts from drug stores these days?

"It was. They claim after they visited the pharmacy they went home and went directly to bed. I pulled the video from the pharmacy. It backs up their visit."

"You've nothing to prove they actually went home from there, right? I mean they could have just as easily gone back to Zoey's and waited in the backyard for Lacey. They certainly knew how to get in from the park."

"What's their motive? Why would Zac or Kelsey want Lacey dead? What was she to them? Nothing."

I took another sip of my tea. Romero had zeroed in on Zoey, and I had nothing other than a feeling that he was wrong. No hard evidence Romero could carry into court to dispute their findings. I did a mental check list of everyone I had met since meeting Zoey.

"What about Lacey's cousin, Joel? He was at the house with his girlfriend the day after Lacey's body was found in the spa. Maybe there was bad blood between them?"

"I spoke with him. He and his girlfriend Nora were in Santa

Barbara for a horse show the night Lacey was killed. He said he didn't think Zoey and Lacey were running lines the night she was murdered. In fact, he thinks they were arguing. That Lacey told Zoey about her relationship with Chad and Zoey killed her."

"Sounds to me like the statement of a bereaved relative, not an eye witness."

"It's circumstantial, I'll admit. But it adds up."

"And Crystal? When you questioned her at Zoey's the other day, I thought you might have warmed to her for Lacey's murder. I'll admit she gives me pause."

Romero played with his cup, turning it with both hands. "The night of the murder, we have her on Zoey's security camera at the front gate. She left 'round ten p.m. Before Lacey was murdered."

"Did you know Crystal's pregnant? And that it's likely to be Chad's baby."

Romero stopped playing with his cup. "How do you know that?"

"Circumstantial evidence, Detective." Where could I begin? There was no point in explaining to Detective Romero about Wilson. Romero didn't believe in ghosts. He would never believe I had a recalcitrant spirit guide living in the house—Denise's brother no less—who had developed an almost paternal relationship with Alicia Mae. And that Alicia had stolen Crystal's birth control pills thinking they were candy.

"Are we talking the type of circumstantial evidence I can drag into court or your psychic-ghost type of stuff?"

"Call it whatever you want to, but if you'd allow me to, I'd like to make a psychic prediction."

Romero smirked. "Go ahead."

I put my hand on top of Romero's. "You may have made your arrest, but there's more information yet to come. And as it unravels I have a feeling you're going to be surprised. In fact, I'd go so far as to say, not only will you be surprised, but you will agree to some rather unconventional police practices to bring our killer to justice."

Chapter 26

I didn't have to wait long for more breadcrumbs to drop. In fact, it wasn't just bits of breadcrumbs the Universe rewarded me with, but a visit from Zac and Kelsey later that afternoon, and what they had to say hit me over the head like an entire loaf of bread.

Zac rang the bell, and when I answered, I found the two of them on the porch with Kelsey standing slightly behind him. Per usual, the two were dressed similarly in dark pants, t-shirts, hoodies and military-style black boots with buckles. In Zac's hands, he held a partially opened, brown packing box.

"I'm sorry to bother you, but Kels and I, we didn't know what else to do." Zac nodded at the box. "This here's Zoey's. It was in one of the guest room closets, and we accidentally packed it up when we were helping Chad move out. We were hoping maybe you might take it back to her."

I held the door open and pointed toward the coffee table in the living room.

Kelsey waited in the foyer while Zac lumbered into the room with the box and set it on the coffee table.

I stepped closer to the table and peeked inside. On top were several vintage looking, silver-framed photos and, beneath them, something soft and pink, a blanket maybe or perhaps a baby's sweater.

"You didn't want to take it back yourself?" I asked. "Or perhaps you thought you shouldn't?" I directed my question to Kelsey. After her run-in with Detective Romero at Zoey's, I doubted she would want to go back to the Pink Mansion again without an invite.

Kelsey stomped her foot. "I told you this wasn't going to work."

"What's going on?" I asked.

"Chad's a mess." Zac sat down on the chair opposite me, took a deep breath and dropped his shoulders. "Ever since he and Zoey broke up, he hasn't been able to sleep. He's talking to himself, and he's canceled all our recording sessions. Out of loyalty, I didn't think we should take the box back to Zoey's place. What if we ran into her and she wanted to talk?"

I looked back at Kelsey. "Would you like to join us?"

Kelsey folded her arms. "No offense, but I'm not into psychics. I don't trust them."

I sat down on the couch and patted the empty spot next to me. "I don't bite. And if you're worried I'll try to read you, don't be. I can't read anyone who doesn't want me to."

"Come on, Kels." Zac tilted his head in my direction. "It's like I told you. Misty's harmless. It's all a magic act anyway, and we did agree we needed to talk to her."

I winced at Zac's reference to my talents as like that of a magic act, but let it go. No point in trying to convince non-believers.

"Fine," Kelsey exhaled, then stepped into the room and took a seat at the end of the couch, as far away from me as possible.

"So you came to talk, did you? Not just to return some of Zoey's items. Because you could have given them to Crystal."

"Yea, well, that wasn't going to happen." Kelsey shook her head.

"No?" I asked.

"I wouldn't trust Crystal. She'd probably tell Zoey we stole them or something." Kelsey put her hands in her lap and twisted her fingers together.

"I take it Crystal's not a friend?"

"Are you kidding?" Zac interrupted. "Crystal doesn't have friends, she has business associates. I doubt she even knows the meaning of the word."

"She puts on a good show of it with Zoey. Fussing over her like she does. How about Chad? Is she friendly with him?" I already knew the answer to that but floated the question out to see what response I might get. Did either of them know about Crystal's affair with Chad? Or was it more covert than that?

Zac shot Kelsey a quick look. "I don't know. It's none of our business what they are. We didn't exactly socialize together if that's what you're asking."

"I see. You're friends with Chad and not so much with Zoey, is that it?"

"It's not like Zoey's not friendly. She's busy, and she's gone a lot. We work with Chad. And Crystal, well, when we're around the house, she kinda floats in-between as it suits her."

"You mean when Zoey's traveling and Crystal stays behind she finds excuses to hang out. Maybe to check on how things are with Chad."

Zac cleared his throat. "Yeah. More or less."

I decided to leave the conversation at more or less and moved on to Lacey. "And what about Lacey? Were Crystal and Lacey friends?"

There was an uncomfortable silence. Zac and Kelsey exchanged a look. Then Zac answered. "I don't know. Maybe. I mean, she was at the house for dinner with Zoey and Lacey the night Lacey drowned. I always thought Crystal might have been a little jealous of Lacey."

"Really?" I sensed unspoken energy between Zac and Kelsey, and began to wonder if that energy was an attempt to manipulate me. Did they want me to think Crystal had murdered Lacey?

"Crystal didn't like that Lacey spent so much time at the house," Kelsey said.

"How did you know that?" I asked. "Did she tell you?"

"She didn't have to say anything," Zac said. "You could feel it in the air when Crystal walked in the room and saw Lacey there. She hated the girl. She was too smart to ever say anything—at least in front of us—but you could see it in her face."

"And the police can't prove it," Kelsey added.

I stopped them both with a hand in the air. "I get that you're worried about Chad and the future of the band, and I know Crystal can be intimidating, but if you came here thinking I could convince the police Crystal murdered Lacey simply because you think so, I'm afraid you'll be sadly disappointed."

"Yes, but if you told them, because of who you are, they might believe you," Kelsey said.

"Because I'm psychic?" I wanted to laugh out loud. "Interesting thought coming from the two of you, considering neither of you claims to believe in what I do. The truth is, I don't know who killed Lacey, and trying to determine who did isn't all that easy. Even for a psychic. While I understand you think what I do is all trickery, Lacey's appearance the night of the séance was a total surprise. Even to me. The only thing she revealed that night was that she and Chad had been carrying on. In fact, I don't believe Lacey has any idea who hit her on the back of the head or how she drowned. Which, in my experience, isn't unusual. Some ghosts have a kind of amnesia about it all. A blessing I suppose."

Wilson had never been curious about the cause of his death.

All he remembered was that he had gone to bed one night with a headache and never woke up again. He had never pressed me for details.

Kelsey got up. "I think we should go, Zac."

I stood up and put my hand on the box. "You can leave the box. I'll be happy to take it back to Zoey." I was anxious to get back to Zoey's anyway, particularly since her arrest. "But before you go, I have a question for you both."

"What?" Zac stopped at the door, his hand on the knob.

"Where were you the night Lacey drowned?"

"The cops already asked," Zac said. "But just so you know, we were at the studio with Chad, recording a new song Kelsey wrote."

"And you left when Chad left?"

"No. We left early. Kelsey wasn't feeling well. She had a headache. Why?"

"No reason. I'm just trying to keep the timeline straight."

Their story didn't quite match up with the story they had given Romero, but close enough. Could be Zac had forgotten they had told the detective Kelsey had a stomachache.

I closed the door behind them, and Bossypants appeared from beneath the stairs and scampered to the sofa where she curled up in a ball. Wilson came out from the study.

"Visitors?" he asked.

"Several," I said. "Where've you been?"

"Meditating."

Shades, particularly those that have become self-aware, spend an inordinate amount of time meditating. In some ways it's an exercise of reflection, an opportunity to take inventory and focus on their new being and direction. It's also a sign they're evolving.

"Well, meditate on this. Zoey's been arrested."

"Arrested!"

"Yes, although she's not in jail. Not yet. But we need to step it up, Wilson. The clock's ticking"

"And the second caller?" Wilson went to the sofa, picked up the cat and cuddled her in his lap.

"Zac and Kelsey." I explained they had brought a box of Zoey's things they claimed to have accidentally packed up when helping Chad move out. "They wanted me to return it, but that's not the real reason they came."

"Oh?" Wilson glanced at the open box on the coffee table.

"No, I think what they really wanted was to know what I thought about Lacey's murder. It's too early for them to have heard about Zoey's arrest. I think the box was just an excuse to question me. To see if I thought Crystal might have done it."

"Aha! The Ice Queen?" Wilson pulled back one of the box's folding flaps and stared down at the contents. "That wouldn't surprise me."

"That's exactly what they wanted me to think," I said. "In fact, they went so far as to ask me to share that very thought with Detective Romero."

"Will you?" Wilson started to rummage through the box.

"No. Zac and Kelsey may be pushing me to talk with Romero about Crystal, but I feel like there's a little too much finger pointing going on for me to be comfortable with the idea. I'd like to hit the pause button as far as Detective Romero goes, and do a little more digging on my own before I share anything more with him."

"Well then, you're definitely not going to want to share this with him." From within the box, Wilson took a small silver baby's rattle and handed it to me. "This box isn't Zoey's, it's Alicia Mae's."

"What?" I took the rattle. It looked as though it had doubled as a teether with a round coral teething extension. The type of teether I had only seen in antique stores.

"Look at the handle. The initials inscribed on it. AMM. It's Alicia's." Wilson mindlessly stroked the cat as though it was an everyday occurrence.

I pulled the box closer to me. "That can't be."

Zoey had mentioned several boxes she had yet to unpack, things her aunt had stashed away for memories sake. Old family photos and keepsakes. Pictures and mementos from when she was little. When Zac had presented the box, I had assumed it was Zoey's. It hadn't even occurred to me it could be Alicia's.

"But it is." Wilson reached back inside the box, took out a silver-framed photo, and handed it to me.

"Is this who I think it is?"

Wilson nodded. It's Alicia with her mother, Margaret Mann. It must have been taken shortly before Alicia died. She looks about three or four years old."

I studied the photo of Alicia with her mother, sitting at the picnic table in front of the playhouse. I traced the outline of their faces with the tip of my finger, then placed the picture on the table and looked back in the box. What else would I find?

"But you're wrong, it's not just Alicia's things. Look at this." I pulled out another silver picture frame, less ornate than the first, with a black and white picture of Zoey and her mother, Cora Chamberlain. The two were sitting at a piano, very much like the one inside the Pink Mansion. "Zoey looks a lot like her mother doesn't she? She couldn't have been more than four or five years old when this was taken as well."

I put Zoey's photo down on the table next to Alicia's and started to pull the other items from the box. A silver baby's cup. A child's spoon and fork. A pacifier. Bracelet. Barrettes. Things a very young child might have, but nothing for a child beyond the age of four or five.

"These aren't keepsakes. This is a time capsule. A memorial. For every picture of Zoey, there's a photo of Alicia.

For every toy for one, a toy for the other. A silver rattle for Alicia. A silver cup for Zoey. A picture of Zoey with her mother, and a picture of Alicia with her mother. And all of them, either photos or items each girl had before the age of five."

"What's it mean?" Wilson cuddled the cat closer to his chest, his hand scratching behind Bossy's ear.

"It means things are changing." My eyes went from Wilson to the cat purring in his arms. "Everything. All around us. And you too."

Wilson's eyes widened. I had hit a nerve. He stood up and the cat jumped down from his lap and scurried back to her hiding place beneath the stairs. "You really think the universe is messing with me?"

"I do." I had witnessed the transformation of shades before. The graduation of spirit. The letting go of old habits and physical properties. It was obvious. Wilson had started to change. He no longer sneezed when the cat was in his presence. The cat no longer screeched when she saw Wilson. "I feel I need to warn you. Your time may be growing short. What you do with it and how you do it, is entirely up to you."

Chapter 27

I called Zoey later that same afternoon and was relieved to find her at home. She had returned from the courthouse where she had met with her attorney. And exactly as Romero had said, entered a not guilty plea, was allowed to post a bond and return home with Crystal on the proviso she surrender her passport and not leave town. The two had just walked back into the house.

"Did you know I was going to be charged?" Zoey asked.

"I had a feeling," I said. "I didn't want to worry you. But just so you know, I have an even stronger sense you're going to come through this just fine."

"I wish the studio felt the same way. Things are insane right now. They're threatening to cancel my contract. If I can't get to Italy by the end of the month, they may have to pull the entire project. It's not like I can finish filming from a jail cell."

"You're not going to go to jail, Zoey. Trust me."

"I hope you're right."

"Things can sometimes look pretty dark. My experience is, it's best not to put energy into worrying about something you can't do anything about. Not when there's something else in front of you that needs tending and may be just the thing to help lighten your mood." Whatever it was about the box, I knew it would divert her energy into something less stressful.

"And what's that?" Zoey asked.

"Zac and Kelsey stopped by this morning with a box they claim they accidentally packed up when they were helping Chad move out. They didn't want to return it themselves. Said they felt awkward, being so close to Chad and all. So they brought it to me. If you've time, I'd like to bring it by. Plus, there's something we need to talk about regarding your ghost."

"I'm free for the next couple hours," Zoey said. "Crystal scheduled me a massage. She thought I could use it."

I told Wilson to ready the Jag, and fifteen minutes later, with the box in my hands, the two of us stood in front of a newly installed wrought-iron security gate at the foot of the Pink Mansion. Bigger and more impressive than the previous gate.

I pressed the intercom button and watched the video cam above my head zoom-in and focus on my face. Crystal's shrill voice came at me through the speaker. "What do you want?"

I mustered my sweet little-old-lady voice. "I'm here to see Zoey. She's expecting me."

"Star. Three. One. Nine. Eight," Crystal barked the security code back at me, then abruptly hung up.

I entered the numbers exactly as Crystal had dictated and stood back as the gate swung open. I started up the steps and stopped to catch my breath before I got to the top. Zoey appeared in front of the atrium entrance, dressed in a colorful caftan robe with her hair down. Considering everything she had been through that morning, I thought she looked pretty calm.

"You replaced the security gate." I glanced back at the gate and then to Zoey.

"I thought it was about time," she said. "It's the one thing I hadn't tackled with the remodel, and with Chad out of the house and everything that's gone on, I feel safer knowing I've replaced it."

Zoey took my hand as I hobbled up the last of the steps.

"You're looking good," I said. "Better than I expected."

"Xanax," she said. "It's why I have a personal assistant."

Zoey pushed open the front door. Wilson slipped invisibly in behind me, and as he did, the door to the powder room slammed shut.

"Is that—"

"Crystal?" Zoey bit her lips and squelched a laugh. "You'll have to excuse her. She's not feeling well. Stomach bug or something. She's got a doctor's appointment this afternoon. She's on her way out now. You'd think she was dying."

From behind the bathroom door, I could hear Crystal wretching, then the flushing of the toilet and water running.

"Saltines," I said. "It does wonders for an upset stomach." I wanted to add "or a little morning sickness," but kept the thought to myself and handed the box to Zoey.

"Oh my God! I'd forgotten all about this." Zoey put her arms around the box and hugged it close. "I can't believe Chad took it. I haven't seen any of this stuff in years. I was planning on going through it once I finished the movie and had some time."

"I hope you don't mind," I said. "It was open when Zac and Kelsey delivered it, and I couldn't help but notice some of the things inside.'"

Zoey ran her hand across the top of the flapped lids. "It's nothing. Just a lot of old memorabilia. Not worth anything, but all the same, I'm glad to have it back. And you're right, it does take my mind off this morning's events."

"How about we sit out back? The fresh air will do you good, and there are some things in the box I think we should talk about."

Zoey looked over her shoulder toward the backyard and closed her eyes. I could see she was still struggling with the image of Lacey's death more than she let on. She probably hadn't been in the yard since Romero and his team had fished Lacey's body from the spa.

"It's okay," I said. I put my hand on her shoulder. "I'm here."

We settled ourselves on two cushioned patio chairs, and Zoey put the box on a round stone table in front of us.

"Before we begin," I said, "I need to tell you that not everything in the box may be yours."

"What do mean, not everything?" Zoey looked at me curiously.

"I believe most of what's inside are things from when you were a very little girl. Things from before your mother died. Before you were four or five." Zoey's fingers lightly rubbed the corner of the box. She closed her eyes as though she was touching a memory. "But there are also some things in the box that I don't believe are yours. Things that belonged to Alicia Mae. I think Zac and Kelsey picked up the box by accident, just like they said. But I don't believe for a second it was put there by accident. I think Alicia put it in your closet for a reason.

"Alicia? But why? This box was sealed when it was delivered from storage. If Chad took it, it was a mistake. It wouldn't have even been opened. I hadn't had time to go through it yet."

"Maybe so," I said. "Or maybe you never noticed it. But right now, I'm more concerned with why Alicia's things are in the box than how they got there."

I opened the box and handed Zoey the silver-framed photo of herself with her mother.

Zoey smiled and traced the line of her mother's face with the tips of her finger, like she was outlining a memory "I remember when this was taken. In a way it feels like it could have been yesterday. I was probably only four or five years old. We were in my mother's dressing room at the studio." Zoey hugged the photo to her breast. "I wish I could go back and hold her in my arms like I can this picture. She was so beautiful, and not in an actress kind of way, but as a mother. If only we had had more time together."

I thought so too, but before I said anything more about Zoey's mother, I took out the small, pink baby's sweater, no bigger than a newborn might wear, and handed it to her. "Do you recall your mother ever doing any knitting or crocheting?"

Zoey put the frame down and picked up the sweater, her fingers gently poking through the delicate crocheted pattern. "I don't think so. I doubt she ever had time. Why? Do you think this is Alicia's?"

I held the edge of the pink sweater between my thumb and index finger and rubbed it slightly. My sense of it was that it was quite old, and made long before either Alicia, or Zoey for that matter, was born. "I can only tell you, whoever made it, made it with love. That with each hook of the needle the maker thought of the baby who would wear this." I let go of the sweater and reached into the box and pulled out the second silver framed photo. Smaller and more ornate than the first.

"This," I said, "is Alicia." I handed the frame to Zoey. "Her full name was Alicia Mae Mann. AMM. Exactly like the initials you found on the tea towel with the cache of items she hid beneath the stairs. The woman in the photo with her is her mother. Her name was Margaret Mann, and, if I'm right, I believe this photo was taken shortly before Alicia's fifth birthday. Before she drowned in the pool."

Zoey wiped a tear from her eye. "That had to have been an awful day."

"For her parents, unimaginable. But for Alicia, even though parents had filled in the pool and sold the house, everything remained the same. Alicia came back here as though nothing had ever happened. You can't see it now, but the playhouse, the picnic table, it's still here. Exactly as it was nearly seventy-five years ago, beneath the big weeping willow tree."

"You can see it?"

"Even with a bad case of cataracts. But not so much through my eyes as in here," I patted my heart.

"Is Alicia here?"

"Oh, yes." I nodded in the direction of the tree where Wilson sat at the child-sized picnic table pretending to have tea with Alicia Mae and her doll. "You remember our spirit guide from the night of séance?"

"Is he here too?" Zoey face's brightened.

"He is. His real name is Wilson Thorne. He was the previous owner of my house, and he's having tea with Alicia Mae. She's had a surprisingly good effect on him. Between you and me, I thought he might be a lost soul, but I'm beginning to think Alicia's helping him to find it. I believe he considers himself her guardian."

"And you're his?" Zoey arched her brow.

"In a sense, yes. It's a bit complicated, but it's my job to help him. In return, he helps me."

"Does Wilson know why Alicia's here? Has she told him?"

"She has."

I paused.

"Well, what is it? What's she waiting for?"

"Her mother," I said. "She's been waiting for her mother for a very long time."

"But I don't understand." Zoey shook her head. "If Alicia's a ghost, can't she just go find her? Isn't that what ghosts do?"

"Sometimes when people die suddenly, they don't realize they've passed on. They return to those places they knew best, and felt most at home, and wait. In my line of work, we call them shades. You might think of them as being in limbo. Frequently, they don't recognize they're dead. They're just waiting."

"And you think that's what she's doing here? Just waiting for her mother to return."

"There's a belief the mother-spirit greets us at birth, and again at death, and guides us home. For Alicia I believe that time may be drawing close. But because she's attached herself to you, I don't believe she'll leave until she knows you're happy."

"Happy? I'm not even sure I understand what that is anymore."

"I think Alicia does. When you moved in she bonded with you. For her, you were like her make-believe friend. Together, you shared a loss. You had both lost your mothers at a very critical age. I think she believes you're waiting for your mother to return too. Just like she is."

"That's ridiculous. I'm not waiting for my mother to return. I miss her, or the thought of her anyway, but I certainly don't expect her to come back. People just don't do that. That's impossible."

"Not in the sense that you expect her to walk through the door. But in your heart, Zoey," I put my hand on her heart and tapped my fingers, "you miss her, I can feel it in your being. You have an emptiness. You miss her exactly like Alicia misses her mother. That longing, that need to reconnect, is what's keeping Alicia here."

Zoey sat back in the chair and held the pink sweater to the side of her face. "And this all happened because I put in a pool and unleashed her spirit?"

"There are cultures that believe some ground is hallowed. I think when you moved in and built the pool, you unsettled Alicia Mae's spirit. She's been here all along. Heather knew her as her imaginary friend. They shared the same front bedroom. After Heather left, Alicia may have befriended others who lived here, or perhaps she grew dormant, waiting for the right time. I don't know. The universe works in strange ways, and time as we know it is very different on the other side. Yesterday is today, and tomorrow is already gone and past. All I know for certain is that when you moved in and unearthed the pool, Alicia connected with you. She recognized an emptiness in you. The same emptiness she's been living with all this time."

Zoey stared out at the pool. The late afternoon sun sparkled on the water's surface. "What is it Alicia wants me to do?"

"I'm not certain yet. I need to talk to Wilson. I'll know more once we've spoken and he's shared with me what Alicia's told him, but it may require another séance."

The patio door opened, and a young woman poked her head outside. "Zoey? You ready for your massage. I'm set up in the studio upstairs when you want."

Zoey put the baby sweater back in the box and kissed me on the cheek. "Misty, whatever Alicia Mae needs me to do, I'll do. But could you do me a favor?"

"Whatever you need."

"Chad forgot his jacket when he moved out. I can't have it in the house. Not anymore. I put it in the closet in the guest room where Crystal's staying. Could you take it back to him? He's staying with Zac and Kelsey. I was going to ask Crystal, but you're here, and it's on your way. Their address is in the pocket. Could you please?"

Chapter 28

I couldn't turn Zoey's request down. Taking Chad's jacket back to him was exactly the excuse I needed. I had been worried ever since I had last talked with Chad and seen Lacey's ghost in the bedroom, that Lacey had some kind of score to settle with her illicit lover. Because I felt it was partly my fault Lacey had followed Chad home, I was compelled to go and try to collect her spirit and return her to the spirit world.

I waited until I was certain Zoey had gone upstairs with the masseuse to go back into the house, then entered through the French doors off the dining room. With Zoey upstairs, the downstairs was oddly quiet, but not empty. I sensed another presence in the room. I closed my eyes and felt the afternoon light reflected through the great room's floor-to-ceiling windows and took a deep breath. When I opened my eyes, a beam of light danced from the windows directly onto the baby grand piano.

More breadcrumbs.

I crossed the room and stood in front of the piano and brushed the tips of my fingers lightly atop the keys. They were smooth and cool to the touch. I closed my eyes and allowed whatever presence was in the room to embrace me. A soft, slow, almost bittersweet melody filled my head. Without realizing what I was doing, my fingers began to tap out the first notes of "Clair de Lune." I don't play the piano, yet the tune came to me as though I had known it all my life. My fingers knew exactly what keys to press. I stopped and looked up from the keyboard out through the big arched window at the pool. *Who are you?*

With every fiber of my being, I could feel the presence about me. I couldn't see it, but I knew it was there, just as surely as my fingers had known which keys to strike. It beckoned to me, as though it wanted to show me something.

Behind the piano, an antique dressing screen with a triptych scene from a 1930's movie Zoey's grandmother had appeared in, fluttered. And then...

Bang!

Behind the screen, something had fallen to the floor. I moved, quickly as I could, to the narrow space between the screen and the oak-stained shelves that lined the wall. The shelves were thick with books and memorabilia. An old-fashioned movie reel. Black and white photos of Zoey's grandparents. A photo of Zoey's father and mother. A rusted horse spur engraved with the name of the horse Zoey's father had ridden in his last movie. On the floor, a photo of Zoey and Lacey. The glass had shattered, cutting a diagonal line between the two girls.

The frame couldn't have tumbled from the shelf by itself. All of the photos had been neatly lined up against the wall, with better than two feet of space between them and the edge of the shelf. This was no accident. This was a message. The photos on the shelf were Zoey's family. All of whom had died young or accidentally. For the first time, I wondered if perhaps I had been wrong. Was the Chamberlain Family Curse real? Had Lacey been mistaken for Zoey after all?

I backed away from the shelf. Whatever spirit had been in the room had vanished. Its presence no longer directing me. I still had to get Chad's jacket from the guest room closet where Crystal had moved her things, and I knew I best hurry.

The room was equally as plush as the first guest room where Crystal had originally stayed. With a large king-size bed, antique armoire, walk-in closet, and private bath, it looked like a luxury suite at the Ritz Carlton.

The better part of me told me I should ignore my urge to search the room and go directly to the closet and retrieve Chad's jacket. Time was running tight and I sensed Crystal might return at any moment. But as soon as I put one foot inside the room, I knew Crystal had hidden something there, and I needed to find it. I could sense it, like daylight on my eyelids or the smell of rain in the air before a downpour.

I had no idea what I was looking for, but I knew whatever it was, it was there. The bed had been made up, and the room looked neat and tidy. Too tidy. I searched the dresser drawers and the nightstands. Nothing out of the ordinary. I ran my hands along the bedspread, then bent down to feel beneath the mattress. It wasn't until my foot hit something under the bed that I knew I'd found something.

Partially hidden beneath the skirt of the spread was Crystal's day planner, a medium-sized black notebook, she was seldom without. The fact it was on the floor and not with her made me think it had accidentally fallen off the bed in her rush to make it to her doctor's appointment. Several letters and miscellaneous papers that had been stuffed inside the notebook were scattered onto the floor. I picked them up and sorted through them. Some of it fan mail. A few autographed headshots of Zoey. A doctor's prescription for Xanax. Nothing the star's busy personal assistant wouldn't be carrying around for her client. Except for a letter postmarked three months earlier. Addressed to a P.O. Box with a return address from the Department of Corrections.

I placed the notebook, along with the other items I'd picked up from beneath the bed, on the dresser and took the letter from within the envelope. Inside were several Xeroxed pages— official-looking documents—all stamped and notarized, pertaining to Adam Johnson, aka AJ, prison number J876503, followed by an equally judicious looking document form that informed Zoey of AJ's early release.

The letter Crystal claimed to have never received.

I put the letter down on the dresser and went back through the notebook. Like a bloodhound in search of a body, I could smell there was something more. I began by sorting through Crystal's calendar. Several loose pages from the notepad slipped and fell onto the dresser. On them were notes Crystal had taken. Random numbers and some doodlings—not very good cartoon sketches of faces and flowers—things she had probably drawn while waiting for Zoey to finish a scene or an interview. Such is the life of an assistant. Always waiting. I leafed through the pages, then—

"Ahem." From behind me, someone had entered the room. I closed my eyes, held the notebook tight to my chest, and turned expecting to see Crystal.

Wilson. I let out a deep sigh. "Don't ever do that to me again. You know I don't like it when you sneak up on me like that."

"Why, are we playing detective?" Wilson walked over the dresser and picked up several of the pages I'd laid out on the top.

I snapped them back from his hand and placed them on the dresser top. "Look at this." I pointed to a handwritten note. "It's an exact copy of the message included with the flowers Zoey received after Lacey's memorial."

Sorry for your loss. Maybe we can begin again. Love, AJ.

"Is this Crystal's handwriting?" Wilson ran his hands across the note and waited for my verification.

"It appears so, but that's not what's strange. It's this here."

Beneath the note Crystal had written an exact copy of it, written in the same architectural style lettering used in the note sent to Zoey with the flowers. "Look at the lettering, it's exactly like AJ used when he first made contact with Zoey and was later accused of stalking her and sent to jail."

"How do you know?"

"After Detective Romero and I visited AJ I did a little online research. Borrowed your computer and looked up a couple of news stories about Zoey's stalker. The press nicknamed him the Stencil Stalker because of the unusual style of lettering he used. There were photos of some of the notes AJ had written in the paper. It was all block-like lettering."

"Which would have been easy to copy," Wilson said.

"Particularly if you had the original to copy from." I grabbed the notebook and began leafing through it, certain I'd find another clue. Something that would convince me Crystal had copied the real thing. I ran my hand over the inside back cover and found a hidden flap, nearly invisible to the eye. Inside were two small, yellowed note cards. I pulled them out and placed them on the table. "I'd say she did a pretty good job."

Wilson looked over my shoulder. "Are these the originals?"

"I think so."

"But how did she get them?"

"Same place she got the letter. The court would have mailed them to her. After a trial, you can petition the court to turn over any material relevant to the case. Crystal probably told the court she wanted to make sure nothing got into the hands of paparazzi or something like that. However it happened, here they are, and this is what she did with them."

"And Zoey never would have known?"

"Not if the notes, like the letter from the DOC, were sent to Zoey's mailbox. Crystal picks up Zoey's mail. I doubt Zoey even knows where her P.O. Box is. She's too busy."

Wilson studied the notes. "The Ice Queen set AJ up. But why?"

"I don't know. But based upon this letter, I'm convinced Crystal knew all along AJ was out of jail."

"Which is where you're going to be if Crystal finds you in her room." Wilson took the letter from my hand and pulled me toward the door. "Come, we need to get going."

"Why? Is she here?"

"Somebody is. I just heard Zoey's new security gate opening."

I grabbed Crystal's notebook and loose papers off the top of the dresser and stuffed them inside my bag. Then stopped. "Quick. Chad's jacket, it's in the closet. Zoey asked me to return it to him. Get it."

Wilson ducked into the closet and was out with the jacket before I could decide what to do next. I looked around the room. What was I missing?

"Sorry, Old Gal, we need to get going." Wilson grabbed me by the elbow, lifting me onto the tips of my toes, and scooted me down the hall like a suitcase on wheels.

When we got to the living room, Crystal was at the front door. "You're still here?"

"Not for long," I said. "I'm on my way out. Zoey asked me to return Chad's jacket. I nearly forgot it. Talk soon."

Chapter 29

"Step on it, Wilson." I took the note Zoey had written with Zac and Kelsey's address on it from Chad's jacket and read off the address. Within moments, Wilson's Jag was winding the narrow streets through the Hollywood Hills. Houses on either side of the road hugged the hillside. Little more than overbuilt boxes balanced on stilts, with big picture windows and views of the valley floor below. No yards. Just balconies. And that awful sinking feeling I get when LA's next big one hits; they'll all go sliding down the mountainside. Zac and Kelsey's small stilted bungalow wasn't much different.

While Wilson parked the Jag, I approached the house. I hate heights. With great trepidation, I walked across a narrow wooden bridge, with sheer drops on either side, to the front porch and knocked on the door

"Chad? Chad, it's Misty. We need to talk."

I waited for a response. When there was none, I knocked harder. From within the house, I could hear movement. Soft, muffled noises. Someone was moving around inside. Then, from the other side of the door, a thud. Followed by the sound of someone moaning.

"Chad? Chad, is that you?" I stood on the tips of my toes and peered into the peephole. Not that I could see in, but I could see a shadow. "Chad, it's me, Misty Dawn. Open up."

"Go away." From behind the door, Chad groaned. I had a vision of him with his hands and head against the door, not knowing what to do next. "I don't want to talk to you."

"Chad, please. Zoey sent me. Just let me come in. I can help."

Bam! The door vibrated. I jumped back.

"Are you okay?" I asked.

"I hit my head."

There was a long pause.

"Chad?"

Wilson joined me on the porch. Realizing my dilemma, he walked through the door, as shades and ghosts can do, and in seconds reported back to me. "It's Chad alright, and he looks miserable."

"Chad, let me in. We need to talk."

Silence. I looked at Wilson. "What are we going to do?"

Wilson shrugged. From behind the door, I could hear the chain as it unhooked, followed by the sound of the deadlock slide open. The door opened halfway. Chad, with his hair in his eyes and looking like he hadn't slept or shaved, squinted out from behind.

"What do you want?"

"I have your jacket. Zoey wanted me to return it." I held up the jacket so Chad could see it.

"Leave it on the porch." Chad started to close the door.

I put my hand against the door, and with Wilson behind me, we pushed the door open.

"What the—" Like a drunken sailor, Chad fell back against the wall and slid down to the floor with his legs and feet splayed in front of him.

"Now, now, Chad. There's no need for language. I'm here to help."

With Wilson's assistance, we righted Chad to a standing

position and held him until we felt he was steady enough to stand on his own.

"Did you just—" Chad's eyes blurred, and he pointed to the door.

"Push my way in here?" I smiled at Wilson. His ability to walk through walls or muscle objects in my way made us a good team. "I suppose you could say I did. Sometimes I don't know my own strength."

"But how?" Chad looked as confused as he did disheveled. Bare chested, barefoot, and dressed in a ratty pair of sweatpants with nothing but a blanket hung around his shoulders, he smelled as bad as he looked.

"Good grief, Chad. When was the last time you showered? Or ate?" I pulled the blanket away from him and stared at his midriff. The man was skin and bones.

"How's Zoey?" Chad tucked the blanket back around his shoulders and hung his head.

"Better than you are. Are you alone?"

"Yeah. I guess." Chad's eyes searched the room, then the ceiling, no doubt looking for signs of Lacey.

"Where are Zac and Kelsey?" I asked.

"I don't know. What time is it?"

"Almost four," I said. "You have anything to eat in the house?" From what I could see scattered across the floor—glass bottles and half-empty bags of chips—Chad had been surviving on beer and chips.

"There's eggs in the fridge. Bread too, I think."

"Good. Then while you get yourself cleaned up, I'll make you something to eat. We need to talk."

I whispered to Wilson to start the shower.

"What?" Chad asked.

"I said you need a shower."

Wilson moved down the hallway. From where I stood I

could hear the sound of water running.

"Yeah. Guess so." Chad wrapped the blanket around his shoulders. "But, Zoey, could you—"

"Shower!" I pointed again in the direction of the bath.

Chad took a step toward the bathroom, then stopped. "You hear water running?"

I didn't have time to get into the mechanics of things. I snapped my fingers. "Shower, Chad. Now. We'll talk later."

I was counting on the fact Chad was too hungover to question my ability to overpower him and push my way into the house or to magically start the shower when he appeared in the kitchen thirty minutes later. When it comes to men, I'm old school. Food, particularly something hot and savory, works wonders when trying to divert their attention. Chad was no different, if not a little bit easier, due to the fact he hadn't eaten in several days.

I put a plate of freshly scrambled eggs on the table with toast, butter, and black coffee, and told him to sit. When he finished, I explained I needed him to focus.

"Chad, I need you to tell me what's been going on."

"Going on? Zoey's what's going on. Or not going on." Chad sighed. "Dammit I've been a fool."

"Poor boy." Wilson appeared from the bath and leaned against the hallway door to the kitchen. "Women can be such a bother."

I scowled at Wilson, then poured Chad another cup of coffee. "I'd have to agree with you about that."

"Has she asked about me?" Chad stared down at the table.

"I'm afraid that boat's sailed, Chad. That's not why I'm here. I need to talk to you about Lacey."

Chad's eyes shot up at me. "I didn't kill her if that's what you're thinking."

"I didn't ask if you did."

"Yeah, well, the police have. Plenty. I even took a lie detector test. Passed it too." Chad straightened in the chair.

"I'm not the cops, Chad. I'm not here about who killed Lacey, but I am here to ask you about her."

"What do mean?"

"The night of the séance—"

Chad groaned. "You mean her ghost."

"You interrupted the séance before I was able to finish. As a result, I'm afraid Lacey followed you home and—"

"She's real then? I'm not just crazy. You know about her?"

"I've suspected."

"You've got to help me, Misty." Chad stood up and started to pace the room, alternating between scratching his head and wrapping his arms around his body. "You've no idea what I've been going through. I can't sleep. Can't eat. Can't perform. There must be something you can do."

"I could send her back if I did another séance."

Chad stopped pacing and looked over my shoulder. At first I thought the idea had frightened him, that he couldn't possibly. Then I realized, it wasn't his fear of another séance, but Crystal. She was standing in the doorway behind me. Neither Wilson nor I had heard her come in. She glared at me.

"Another séance, Misty? Really?"

"How long have you been here?" I asked.

"Long enough to know you're up to no good." Crystal leaned her back up against the kitchen counter.

My eyes went from her to a knife block just inches behind her. I wasn't sure she knew, but I wasn't about to risk her grabbing the big butcher's knife and coming after me with it. I took the high road and answered mildly.

"On the contrary. I came by just as I told you I would. To

return Chad's jacket. It's on the couch if you want to check."

While Crystal glanced back into the living room for Chad's jacket, Wilson ghosted to her side. Slowly, without her noticing, he slid the knife block from behind her until it was out of reach.

"As far as a séance goes," I said. "I think another might be a good idea. That's up to Chad to decide." I grabbed my bag and pushed past Crystal.

I got as far as the front porch. Crystal pushed me to the railing. Her face inches from my own. "Look, Misty, I don't know what you've done, but for whatever reason, Chad believes you've put some type of curse on him. I'd tell you to leave him alone, but from what I just saw in there, I think Chad's convinced you can help him."

"I'm not a witch, Crystal." I pulled my hand from hers and took a step back toward the railing. "I don't cast spells on people."

"But you do read people." Crystal moved closer to me. "You know he's tormented."

"No more than you," I said. I gripped the railing behind me. The only divide between the porch and a hundred-foot drop to the hillside below.

"You're a cheap carnival trick, Misty. You don't know anything about me."

"Tell that to your doctor. I'll bet he agrees with me. Your OB-GYN that is. You're pregnant, aren't you? Have you told Chad, yet?"

Crystal put her hand on her belly.

"This isn't about Chad, it's about you and me." I could feel the warmth of her breath on me, and the look in her eye...was she really going to push me?

Wilson stepped forward. I shook my head.

"You sure you want to do this, Crystal? I fall, and you'll be left to explain to Detective Romero what happened. And I don't think Romero will believe it was an accident."

Crystal stepped back. My gamble that the Ice Queen had more logic than malice in her veins proved right. "Fine, do it your way. Do a séance. I don't care. But it better work. Chad needs to get back to his music."

"Oh, it'll work. Because this time, Crystal, you're going to be there as well."

"Me?"

"Yes, you. And Zac and Kelsey too."

Crystal bit her tongue. "When?"

"Tomorrow night."

"Fine, but Zoey can't be there. I'll schedule something so she's out of the house. She can't know about Chad and me. You can't tell her that I was here or any of the rest of it. You do, and I'll ruin you. I'll run smear stories on social media that will make you look like a pariah. Your name will be mud in this town. And you know I can do it. You're a has been, Misty Dawn, and by the time I'm done, everybody's going to know it."

"You don't need to threaten me. For what it's worth. I'll give you a little prediction. Free of charge. I'm not going to tell Zoey about you and Chad. When the time comes, you'll do that yourself."

Chapter 30

Wilson and I arrived home from Chad's to find a young woman on the porch, dressed in a long, gray duster, boots, and a cowboy hat. She had settled herself on one of the green striped rockers and with her hat pulled low on her brow and a book in her lap, she appeared to have come prepared to wait. And in disguise.

Breadcrumbs.

"Now that looks interesting." Wilson reached into the console and took out the remote for the garage.

"More than interesting, Wilson. She's exactly what I've been waiting for. It's just taken her longer to get here than I expected." I left Wilson in the garage and greeted my caller on the steps. "Nora?"

"You remember me?" Nora looked surprised.

"I'm good with faces," I said. "We met at Zoey's. You were with Lacey's cousin Joel. I remember thinking how uncomfortable you looked. I gave you my card. I knew you'd come around." I opened the door and pointed Nora in the direction of the living room. Wilson slipped in behind us and sat on the edge of the sofa. Anxious as I was to hear what our mystery caller had to say. "But I sense you're not here for a reading."

"Not quite," she said. "In fact, the reason for the cowboy hat is because I didn't want anybody to recognize me." Nora took her hat off and placed it on her lap. "Joel doesn't know I'm here, and I'd rather he didn't. Ever since I heard the news about Zoey's arrest, I knew I had to talk to someone."

"And you can't talk to the police?" I sensed I knew the answer to that.

"Joel and I have already spoken to the police. Or Joel has anyway. He told Detective Romero he thinks Zoey killed Lacey. He never bought into the idea that Lacey and Zoey were running lines the night Lacey was murdered. He thinks they were arguing, and things got out of hand."

I had heard that much before. When Detective Romero and I parted ways, it was one of the reasons the DA had pushed for Zoey's arrest.

"So that puts you and Joel on opposite sides," I said.

"Joel thought his cousin could do no harm. I'm afraid I see it differently. Lacey lived with us. She was no angel, and all she ever talked about was Chad. She said she hadn't meant to fall in love with him. That she was sorry about Zoey, but that she couldn't help herself."

"And Zoey, far as you know, never had any idea about their affair?"

"I don't believe Zoey would have believed you if you told her. Zoey's as close as it gets to Hollywood royalty. In her world, Chad would never leave her. Not for someone like Lacey. A stand-in? It wouldn't happen." Nora played nervously with the brim of her hat.

"Even so, Lacey was convinced Chad loved her." If Zoey hadn't been Lacey's best friend and deceived her, I might have almost felt sorry for the girl.

"I think Lacey wanted to believe it. Joel and I both tried to tell her Chad would never leave Zoey. Everybody knew Chad was nothing without Zoey's money. Zoey made it all possible. The band. The trips. The promotion. Everything."

This wasn't the first time I had heard about Chad's lack of financial independence. Hearing about it from Nora made me wonder if Zoey's financial aid may have somehow been connected to Lacey's death.

Nora continued, "Lacey said when Zoey was making a movie she forgot about everything else, Chad included. He was lonely. I think Lacey thought if she got pregnant, it'd change things. That Chad would leave Zoey for the baby and a different life."

"You think he promised her that?"

"No." Nora shook her head. "He told her he was working on a plan, that he'd tell Zoey and for her not to say anything. That's why I'm convinced Zoey and Lacey weren't arguing that night. Lacey wasn't confrontational. She never would have told Zoey without Chad there. In my opinion, Chad was waiting for Zoey to leave for Europe. I think he would have paid Lacey off and sent her away."

"If you don't think it was Zoey who killed Lacey, and we know Chad was at the studio that night, then who? Crystal?"

Nora bit her lip.

"Crystal knew Lacey had fallen in love with Chad. And according to Lacey, Crystal did what she could to break them up, including seducing Chad herself. She's a cold and calculating bitch. She loves her role as Zoey's personal assistant, she'd do anything for her. But murder? She wouldn't risk upsetting Zoey and the millions of dollars that are on the line if Zoey fails to complete the current movie she's working on. She's not going to upset the status quo. Not like that."

"Then who else?" I asked.

"I've been asking myself that same question. I keep wondering if maybe Kelsey might have done it."

"Kelsey? Don't tell me Chad had an affair with her too?"

"Hardly. Kelsey and Zac, they're solid. Kelsey's relationship to Chad is purely financial. She's his writing partner. He writes the melody. She does the lyrics. The trouble is, once Chad and Lacey started to fool around, Chad stopped focusing on his music. Kelsey called him on it. Told him he was throwing his career away and needed to get back in the game."

"Do you think maybe Kelsey was angry enough to do something about it?"

"According to Lacey, Chad thought Kelsey and Zac were taking advantage of him. Before they hooked up with Chad they were nobody. Just a drummer and his girlfriend writing cheap melodies."

"That's a good theory," I said. "But not enough to prove murder."

"I didn't think so either, and I've been hesitant to say anything. Particularly since Joel's convinced Zoey murdered his cousin. Except, I remembered Lacey saying how she'd written a poem for Chad, that she wanted him to put it to music. I didn't pay much attention to it until I was cleaning some stuff up in her room and found it. I thought if I showed it to you maybe you might be able to do something with it."

Nora took a notebook from her bag and set it on the table. On the cover, Lacey had scrawled her name in pink magic marker with a heart above it.

"Inside are a bunch of poems Lacey wrote and the lyrics to a song she and Chad were working on. Chad wrote something in the margins." Nora opened the book and flipped to a page. "Here, take a look."

Nora handed me the book and I read the comments out loud so Wilson could hear. "Crazy good lyrics—the one about the jealous lover is a hit! Better than anything the band's done before. I'll lay down tracks on our next session. You rock, babe!"

"Kelsey knew Lacey was sleeping with Chad. What if she found out it was more than that—that Lacey was writing lyrics as well—and it was too much for her? I think she worried she and Zac might be replaced and decided to do something about it."

The notebook gave me pause. Nora was like a missing piece to a puzzle or a breadcrumb the Universe had placed in my path. I never felt Nora fit in with Zoey's friends. From the moment we met I sensed she was an outsider. Yet here she was, right in front of me with the very clue I needed. Lacey's poems with Chad's scrawls promising to record her missives on his next visit to the studio. Had Kelsey felt threatened and murdered Lacey in a jealous rage? Or was it Crystal who feared Lacey had gotten too close to Chad and put an end to their affair because she knew Chad couldn't? I wasn't sure.

Chapter 31

I thanked Nora for coming and closed the door behind her, then told Wilson to bring me my bag. I needed to call Detective Romero right away.

"Not so fast." Wilson took my hand and led me back to the couch. "You should sit down. There's something I have to tell you."

"Whatever it is, it'll have to wait. I need to talk with Detective Romero. He needs to know Crystal had AJ's original notes and release papers from the DOC all along, and she's hidden them from Zoey. And I need to tell him about Kesley. I can't imagine how Romero missed it. This writing partnership between Chad and Kelsey...it goes to motive. And—"

"Stop! Misty. Sit down." Wilson grabbed my bag off the coffee table, held it above his head, then gently shoved me back onto the chair. "Sorry, Old Gal, but you're not calling anyone until you've heard me out."

"Why? What's going on?" I leaned forward, but Wilson put his hand on my shoulder and refused to let me up.

"I wasn't quite sure how to tell you, but while you were talking to Zoey and searching Crystal's room, I made a discovery of my own."

I expected the next words out of his mouth to be that he had stumbled across some long-lost artifact from the

Chamberlain's movie history, but the gray look of concern on Wilson's face told me this was much more serious than a newly found souvenir. I braced myself. Perhaps he had learned the universe was about to call him back, and he was going to bid me farewell. I wasn't sure I was ready for that, but Wilson wouldn't be the first shade I'd be forced to say goodbye to unexpectedly. "Okay," I said. "What exactly did you find?"

"A portal."

"A what?" I fell back into the chair. Of all the things Wilson might have told me, news of a portal was the last thing I expected, and it was a shocker. Portals aren't exactly commonplace, and I hadn't had a lot of experience with them.

"It's some type of passageway."

"I know *what* a portal is, Wilson. My question is, exactly where did you find it? And when?"

"Inside the playhouse. Alicia found it. She said she's known about it for a while, and when she showed it to me, I thought perhaps it was the beginnings of a small sinkhole. You know how sinkholes are, particularly with all the rain and the recent construction Zoey's done on the property. Alicia's afraid her playhouse and her world are about to collapse into the abyss. She's frightened, Misty."

"I imagine she would be. What made you think it's a portal and not a sinkhole?"

"Alicia said she had seen a spirit come through. That whoever she was—"

"She?" I asked.

"Yes, Alicia was quite adamant the ghost was a she, and that *she* had come and gone several times. That's when I knew it wasn't just a sinkhole, but a portal."

"And I assume you explained the difference and assured Alicia she had nothing to worry about?"

"I did, but unfortunately I'm afraid I wasn't much help. You see when I told her how ghosts use portals to come and go between the worlds, she wanted to know why her mother hadn't come through."

"Augh," I sighed. Of course, Alicia would think that. She had been waiting for so long. The surprise of seeing a spirit come through and the disappointment it wasn't her mother, must have been overwhelming. "I assume you told her there could be any number of reasons why she hasn't."

"Yes, but she says the other ghost is Zoey's mother and—"

"Of course!" I slapped my thighs. "Cora Chamberlain. I knew it. She's here. Zoey's willed it, and it's happened. I felt her presence in the great room this afternoon. I could feel her standing behind me at the piano. So strong in fact, that when I brushed my fingers across the keys, they picked out the tune 'Clair de Lune.' The tune she used to play for Zoey."

Wilson sat down on the chair opposite me. "Alicia thinks Cora's been here before. But that something new is happening. Something unfamiliar and it's making Alicia very nervous."

"She shouldn't be. It's all as the universe intends it to be. Cora's here because Zoey's willed it to be. That's the way energy works."

"Yes, but I'm beginning to wonder. If Alicia's right and Cora's been here before, maybe we've got Lacey's death all wrong?"

"What do you mean?"

"What if Zoey's mother killed Lacey? If she knew about the affair, she might have wanted to protect her daughter."

"Nonsense. Ghosts don't kill people. Mortals do. Ghosts may haunt people and cause them to do crazy things out of fear. But they don't kill people."

"You're sure?"

"About Zoey mother's killing Lacey? A hundred percent. If Cora was going to kill anyone, she wouldn't have killed Lacey.

She would have killed Chad."

"Umm..." Wilson got up and paced the room. "I'm sorry to hear that. Personally, I was rather looking forward to settling a few old scores once I officially crossed over."

"Wilson!" Had all my efforts to rehabilitate the man gone for naught?

"Is that wrong?" Wilson winked then handed me my cell phone from within my bag. "Here, call your Detective Romero. I'm sure he'll be delighted to know you've eliminated all possibilities it was a ghost who killed Lacey, and that we're in hot pursuit of Kelsey or is it Crystal? I just don't know."

I snapped the phone from Wilson's hand. I didn't need any smart-aleck remarks concerning our investigation. What I needed was time to think. With everything Wilson had just told me about the portal beneath the playhouse, and from what I had discovered in Crystal's notebook and Lacey's poems, my head felt like a pinball machine. One idea ricocheting off the other, and a scoreboard that kept coming up zero.

I held the phone in my hand. I had been channeling the detective since the moment I found Crystal's notebook beneath the bed in the guest bedroom. But I hadn't called him. I sensed he was about to reach out to me and considered that the better of the two scenarios. Particularly since Romero and I had parted ways after Zoey's arrest.

I waited for the phone to ring. While I did, I considered the purpose of the portal beneath Alicia's playhouse.

Was the portal a sign? Was it really Zoey's mother who had come through? Was Alicia's mother next? If so, would Cora Chamberlain, Margaret Mann, and Alicia Mae all walk back through the portal together and leave Zoey and the Pink Mansion alone? Or would Zoey's mother stay behind? And what about Wilson? What would become of him? Limbo is a temporary state. Was the portal there for him as well? Would

Wilson walk through the portal with them, and once he did, would the portal and the playhouse disappear forever?

I was lost in my thoughts when my phone rang. I looked at the screen and smiled.

"Detective, I had a feeling you were about to call."

"Why, your ears burning?" Romero chuckled.

"Should they be?"

"Maybe. Our case against Zoey's falling apart. Forensics can't pinpoint when the cigarette butt we found out by the pool was tossed on the grass. Could have been that morning, maybe that night. No way to prove it. Which means we can't put Zoey in the backyard the night Lacey drowned. Plus, we got hold of the sides, the pages from the script Zoey was working on. It's just like Zoey said. She and Lacey were rehearsing an argument. And now Lacey's cousin Joel's not so sure Lacey would have confronted Zoey about the affair. Not without Chad by her side, and we know Chad wasn't there."

"I won't tell you I told you so," I said.

"Don't get too excited. The DA's not willing to drop the charges. Not yet. But I do have some good news."

If there was good news, I knew it had to be Denise. She hadn't been around as much as usual, which in my mind could only mean one thing: she had captured the detective's attention and he was keeping her busy.

"You're good, Misty. I won't ask how you knew. But yes, it is Denise. She wants you to know I've set up a ride-along for her with my brother-in-law. He's driving Hugh Jackman and his wife to the airport as we speak. She thought you'd be pleased."

"Pleased," I said. "But not surprised. However, there is another matter concerning Lacey's murder I want to talk with you about. Something's come up. It's important, and I'd like to discuss it with you. In person."

"One condition," Romero said. "This thing you want to talk

to me about, it's something I can use. None of your ghost stuff, right?"

"Yes, Detective. Meet me at my place. Soon as possible. I'll explain everything when you get here."

Chapter 32

The problem with being a psychic is that we don't always have a clear picture. We're human, with likes and dislikes. Those likes, the stronger they are, interfere with our ability to read others and make predictions, which I feared had happened to me.

My ability to stay aloof, which is ultimately important for an intuitive, had been swayed by my concern for Zoey and Alicia. Two very different mysteries, but each uniquely tied to the other. I sensed Lacey's killer was close. It troubled me I couldn't see a face or get a clear sense about who it might be. And while I felt strongly the evidence I had uncovered from inside of Crystal's notebook would help Detective Romero secure a warrant for her arrest, I was equally as troubled by the news Nora had shared with me that morning about Lacey's potential threat to Kelsey's career.

Wilson helped me lay out the evidence from Crystal's notebook on the dining room table. Her unexpected return to the Pink Mansion had prevented me from thoroughly going through everything, and I wanted a little time to myself to see if I might get a psychic read on the papers she had hidden away.

On the surface, the evidence presented a compelling case. The letter from the DOC. Crystal's calendar with the date of AJ's release circled in red and annotated with the initials AJ in small block letters. Two postcard-size notes addressed to Zoey and signed by AJ. And several loose sheets of lined paper where it looked like Crystal had tried to copy the same architectural style lettering AJ had used in his original notes to Zoey.

Everything on the table seemed to point to the fact Crystal knew about AJ's release and had covered it up. She had copied AJ's stilted style of writing and sent a note to Zoey along with flowers after Lacey's death. But why? Had she hired AJ to kill Lacey, or was Crystal simply trying to frame him because she had killed Lacey and feared Romero was getting too close to the truth?

Then there was Lacey's notepad full of poems, and Chad's scribbled writing promising to record them. Did Kelsey know? Had the idea Chad might throw Kelsey and Zac over for Lacey caused her murder?

I still had no answers when Romero knocked on the door.

I told Wilson to make himself scarce. I didn't want any disturbances.

"So, what is it you found, Misty?"

"These," I showed the evidence on the table. "One is a notepad full of poems Lacey wrote. The other is Crystal's notebook."

Romero zeroed in on Crystal's notebook and the letter from the DOC. "And where did you find these?"

"The notebook was under the bed in the guest bedroom. The letter from the DOC was inside."

"Did Crystal give this to you?" Romero wrinkled his brow.

"No. I found it."

"You mean you stole it."

"I'd hardly call it stealing. Zoey asked me to get Chad's jacket out of the closet in the guest room. When I was there, I saw the notebook under the bed. It all seems relevant, don't you think? The letter from the DOC? The notes from AJ, and what looks like Crystal's attempt to copy AJ's handwriting?"

"Except, we can't use it. Not any of it. Not unless Crystal handed it over voluntarily. Plus, if Crystal discovers you've taken this, I don't even want to tell you what troubles you might have created for yourself."

I paced back into the living room and sat down in the wingback chair. "What about Lacey's poems, and the note from Chad? Is there enough of an implication there to make you suspect Kelsey?"

"Of being jealous?"

"Murder, Detective. Kelsey was afraid Lacey wasn't just sleeping with Chad, but that Chad would replace her as his lyricist."

"It'd be hard to prove," Romero said.

"So we're no farther along than we were right after Lacey was murdered?"

"Other than Zoey's been arrested and the evidence supporting those charges is falling apart? No."

"Are you satisfied AJ's no longer a suspect?"

"You said yourself you thought as a suspect AJ looked a little too convenient. With what you just showed me on the dining room table, if anything, I'd say that makes Crystal a lot more interesting. But no judge is going to allow me to use the evidence you found to prove it. As for Lacey's poems and Chad's scribbles about making her a songwriter, it's a bit of a stretch to think Kelsey or even Kelsey and Zac murdered her because of it. Unless you can convince me a ghost did it, I don't see any other likely suspects."

Wilson sat down next to me on the arm of the chair. "All's not lost, Old Gal. The power rests with you. You still have the notebook and tomorrow's séance."

"The séance?" I asked.

At first, I wasn't certain what Wilson meant. Then I realized he was right. Under the proper circumstances, with Wilson's help, I might be able to solicit anything I wanted from those around the table. Whether I did an actual séance or not, nobody attending tomorrow night's meeting would know. Only Wilson and myself.

"Are you talking to yourself again, Misty?" Romero looked at me oddly.

"Actually, I was thinking out loud. What if I could secure a confession from the killer? If whoever murdered Lacey told me, and you heard it, would it be enough for you to make an arrest?"

"And how do you propose to do that?"

"A séance," I said. "It's what got us into this in the first place. And I think it's what's going to get us out."

"You're serious?"

"Very. In fact, I've already arranged for it. Chad will be here tomorrow night. He believes Lacey's ghost has been haunting him and he wants me to do a séance to get rid of her."

Romero sat down on the couch and put his hand to his head. "I don't believe what I'm about to ask, and the department may never understand, but explain to me, exactly how it is you think this séance idea of yours will secure a confession?"

"I'll save the details for the séance until later. But for now, I've asked Zac, Kelsey, and Crystal to be here tomorrow night. One of them could have killed Lacey. When they're sitting around the table tomorrow night, I believe we can get whoever killed her to confess."

"We?" Romero raised his brows.

"In your line of work, I believe you call it a sting." I explained to Romero I was sure, from all the cop and robber shows I'd watched, that he would want me to wear a wire so he can have everything on tape. I'd want him at the Pink Mansion early enough so we can set up the dining room for the séance, and nobody would know he was there.

"There's an antique dressing screen next to the piano.

Zoey's grandmother used to use it. It's big enough for you to hide behind, and from there you should be able to hear everything I say. More importantly, everything anyone says to me."

"And Zoey?" Romero asked. "If you're going to do this, I'd like to have her there as well."

"Zoey can't be at the séance. I doubt she and Chad could be in the same room. Not after everything that's happened. But don't worry, I'll clue Zoey in to my change of plans and have her here well ahead of time. She can hide upstairs in the gym. She's as anxious as you are to know who murdered Lacey, and we should wire the gym so she could hear as well."

"And if you don't get a confession?" Romero asked.

"If I don't get a confession from one of those around the table, I promise you, if Zoey killed Lacey, I'll find out. I'll get her to confess to me. You have my word."

"This is highly irregular, Misty."

"Like I told you before, Detective, I'm highly irregular. But very effective."

Chapter 33

The following morning I called Chad to remind him of the séance. In his present state, I wasn't convinced he hadn't remembered anything about our meeting yesterday. Chad grunted agreeably, and before he hung up, I reminded him Zac and Kelsey needed to come along as well. I then called Crystal. Despite the fact Crystal didn't believe in ghosts, she did believe I had some magical hold on Chad, and for that, I reminded her how important tonight's séance was. She agreed and told me she had set Zoey up for a facial in Beverly Hills at six p.m. Both Crystal and Chad would be at the mansion by seven p.m. After I hung up with Crystal, I called Zoey. I instructed her to cancel her appointment with her facialist and meet me at the Pink Mansion precisely at six p.m. I told her I'd explain why later, but for now, not to tell anyone. Particularly Crystal.

While I was doing all this, Wilson was having a meltdown. He came down with a bad case of stage fright. Like a director on opening night, he had the jitters and had begun to obsess over what it was I expected him to do and when. I told him not to worry. All he had to do was to babysit Alicia Mae and make absolutely certain no ghosts came through the portal until I cued him I was ready.

Wilson and I arrived at the Pink Mansion slightly ahead of time. While I waited at the front gate for Detective Romero,

Wilson slipped the bars and went around to the backyard to find Alicia Mae. Detective Romero arrived a few minutes later. With him was another, much younger detective of junior rank. Romero introduced him simply as Detective Richards and explained he was here to back him up, should the need arise.

I didn't feel that would be a problem—at least I hoped not.

At precisely six p.m. Zoey pulled up in front of the big security gate. With a quick wave to us, she punched in the lock code then pulled her Audi convertible into the garage and closed the door. With the garage door closed by the time Crystal returned to the mansion with our guests, no one would suspect Zoey was home.

The detectives and I walked up the hill and met Zoey in the front courtyard.

"Why's he here?" Zoey looked nervously at the detective then back at me.

"I'll explain later," I said. "Right now, we need to get inside before anyone sees us. Trust me, when you understand what I have in mind, you'll be happy he's here."

With her hands shaking, Zoey unlocked the front door and ushered us inside.

Once behind closed doors, Romero took Richards on a tour of the house, including the upstairs studio where they set up a listening post so that Richards and Zoey could monitor everything going on downstairs. While the detectives went about setting up what they needed, I explained to Zoey I had taken the liberty of asking Chad, Crystal, Zac, and Kelsey here under the pretext of doing another séance.

"Another séance? I don't understand. Why would Crystal agree to such a thing?" Zoey looked confused.

"Because she didn't want you to know." I put my arm around her and walked her into the great room. "This isn't about making contact with Alicia Mae. What's about to happen here tonight, it's not a real séance. It's about securing a confession from whoever killed Lacey."

Zoey jerked away from me. "You really think it's one of my friends?"

"I know it's not you, and if I'm going to prove it, I need a confession. So, young lady, much as I know you want to be here, I need you to go upstairs and make yourself scarce."

"And Detective Romero's okay with this?"

"He's agreed it's unconventional. But if the real killer confesses, he's down with it."

Romero returned from the upstairs studio. "We're ready. Zoey, if you go upstairs I'll put a wire on Misty, and you'll to be able to hear everything that happens down here."

I put a hand on Zoey's shoulder. "It's going to be fine. I promise. Whatever happens, trust me, you're going to be okay."

Zoey exhaled. "And where are you going to be Detective?"

Romero pointed to the folding screen behind the piano. "Over there. Soon as we get a confession, I'll make my move."

"And if you don't?" Zoey asked.

"Then next time you and I meet, it's going to be in court."

By six forty-five p.m. the house was quiet. Everyone was in place. Detective Romero had equipped me with the wire, an itchy thing that caused my heart to race. Zoey was upstairs in the studio with Detective Richards and could hear my every breath through her headphones. Romero was crouched behind the changing screen next to the piano, which, given the low light in the great room, proved to be a remarkably effective hiding place. With nothing left to do but wait, I went outside to the courtyard and sat by the koi pond.

Crystal and Chad arrived a few minutes later and appeared surprised to see me on the front porch. I told them I had remembered the passcode to the security gate and had let myself in.

"I hope that's okay?" I said.

Crystal huffed, looked at me like I was a necessary distraction, and fumbled through her purse for her key to unlock the front door. "Fine for now, I guess. But remember, after tonight, Misty. No more. You and Zoey, you're done."

I didn't answer. Zac and Kelsey arrived before we were barely through the door, and I instructed everyone to take a seat in the dining room.

Crystal sat next to Chad and placed her hand on top of his. "What's next, Misty? I assume you're going to light a candle or something?"

I didn't appreciate the snarky attitude and pulled a matchbook from within my bag. "It's not necessary, but if you like, be my guest."

Crystal snapped the matches from my hand, lit the two long tapered candles on the table, and sat back down. "Nothing like a little atmosphere. Now what else do you need? I'd like to get this over with as soon as possible."

"I'm sure you would, but I've one small problem," I said.

"Why am I not surprised?" Crystal looked up at the ceiling.

I bowed my head and patted the sides of my long skirt. Finding my cell phone, I pulled it from my pocket. "I'm sorry. I really thought I'd be able to do this tonight, but I'm missing a fifth person."

"A fifth person?" Crystal squinted. "What do you need a fifth person for?"

"I can't do a séance without six or any number of participants divisible by three. Together you, Chad, Kelsey, and Zac are four, and I'm five. I need six. I asked my friend Denise if she'd sit in. She was at my last séance. Chad remembers, don't you, Chad?"

Chad nodded. "Yeah, I guess."

"She promised she'd be here, but she's running late. LA traffic. She called right before you arrived, but what can we do?" I held the phone up and shrugged. "I don't suppose you'd all mind if we just talked a spell? I'm sure she'll be along shortly."

In truth, I hadn't asked Denise at all, but the lack of the sixth person for my séance made for a good excuse.

Crystal sat back and folded her arms. "Whatever. As long as this doesn't take too long. I promised Chad he wouldn't run into Zoey here. It really wouldn't be a good idea if he did."

"I get it," I said. "Chad's hurt and Zoey would go crazy if she thought you'd let us in the house without her permission."

A thin smile crossed Crystal's face. "Yeah, something like that."

"Well, then. Since we're here to help Chad convince Lacey's ghost to leave him alone, perhaps Chad, you might help by sharing with me how you met Lacey and what's been going on. It may help me to understand how deep the connection is."

Chad looked around the table. "You mean with her ghost or how we met?"

"Let's start with before Lacey died. How is it the two of you got involved?"

"I don't know. Lacey was hanging around a lot. Even at the other house, 'fore we moved in here. She was always there. She'd come over and sit out by the pool. She and Zoey spent a lot of time together. Sometimes I got the feeling Lacey thought she lived there. Then after Zoey and I moved in here, Zoey was gone all the time, working on the movie and stuff. And Lacey, she'd come by and lay out by the pool. 'Fore I knew it, things just happened. I told her it wasn't supposed to, but—"

"It did," I said. "And then Lacey got pregnant."

"That was an accident. It shouldn't have happened. I told her it was a mistake and she could do whatever she wanted, but then she said she wanted to tell Zoey and get married. I mean it was crazy. Married? I wasn't going to marry Lacey."

"And you weren't tempted to stop her?"

"I didn't want her to tell Zoey, but I didn't kill her if that's what you mean. I told her I'd pay for the baby and she could go away for a while. I was willing to do whatever it took. But kill her? No way!"

"Stop it. Stop it right now." Crystal slapped her hand on the table. "Misty, what are you doing?"

"I'm just trying to understand the relationship. The more I understand, the easier this will be." I smiled sweetly at Crystal and turned back to Chad. "You weren't here the night Lacey drowned. You were at the studio, right?"

"You know full well who was here," Crystal said. "It was just Zoey and Lacey."

"And you," I said.

"Yeah, I was here. So what? But only until Zoey and Lacey finished dinner. I went home right after so they could run lines."

"So you say." I put my cell phone back in my pocket.

"What do you mean, so I say?" Crystal stood and put her hands on her stomach. She looked pale, as though she were about to be sick.

"I mean, you say a lot of things." I looked around the table. Zac and Kelsey's eyes were following mine. "Didn't you also tell Detective Romero you didn't know Zoey's stalker had gotten an early release from jail?"

"I don't know what you're talking about." Crystal gripped the back of the chair, her knuckles white.

"No?" I took the letter from the LA Department of Corrections from within the pocket of my skirt and put it on the table.

Crystal's eyes widened. "Where did you get that?"

"I found it in your notebook under the bed in the guest

room. Did you think you had lost it?"

Crystal grabbed the letter off the table and crumpled the paper in her hand.

"Go ahead. Tear it up if you like. It's a copy. Detective Romero has the original."

Crystal threw the letter back on the table. "It doesn't mean anything. I got busy. Zoey knows how crazy things get when she's filming. I forgot to tell her, that's all."

"Maybe so, but I also found this." From my other pocket, I took the pages Crystal had used to copy the note attached to the flowers from AJ, and placed them in front of her. "You wanted Detective Romero to think AJ had sent the flowers. That AJ had killed Lacey, mistaking her for Zoey. So you copied AJ's cryptic lettering, wrote the note yourself, and then put it with the flowers on the front porch. Thing is, you might have pulled it off if I hadn't found these."

Crystal shoved the pages back across the table. "I had to do something. Romero was asking too many questions."

"You thought he was coming after you?" I asked.

"Me?" Crystal shook her head. "I didn't kill Lacey, but I thought maybe Chad had. I had to protect him."

Chad looked like he had been hit in the stomach. "You thought I killed Lacey? How could you think that? I was at the recording studio all night. I didn't clock out until after two a.m. The coroner said Lacey died before midnight."

Crystal put her hand on Chad's arm. "I didn't know that then. I tried to get you to talk about it, but you wouldn't say anything."

"What did you want me to say? You and I weren't exactly buddies. We didn't spend a lot of time talking."

"Chad stop!" Crystal screamed at him. "I'm pregnant."

"You're what?" Chad jerked away.

"You heard me." Crystal glared at Chad. "I'm pregnant. I

didn't mean to get pregnant, but I am. So listen to me. Stop talking, let's just get out of here. This is all stupid anyway. Just some trick Misty's worked up."

Chad slapped the table. "Look, Misty, I didn't intend for any of this to happen. I don't know how Crystal got pregnant, but—"

"Probably the usual way, Chad." I patted him on the shoulder. "That's how those things happen."

"Yeah, right. I'm a jerk, okay? But I didn't kill anyone. When the cops started talking about AJ, I figured it was him. That he was stalking Zoey again, saw Lacey in the spa that night, and mistook her for Zoey."

I turned back to Crystal. "To save Chad, you resurrected AJ, knowing the cops would think AJ was good for the murder."

"I didn't know what the cops would think. I just wanted to get Detective Romero off our backs. He was asking too many questions. Zoey had a movie to finish, and you're right, I still had the letter from the DOC. I had forgotten all about it until I was moving in with Zoey, and when I found it again, I thought, why not? It's my job to protect Zoey. It's what I do. Everything I did was so that Zoey's world wouldn't fall apart."

"Zoey's world or yours?" I asked.

"Is there a difference?" Crystal sat back in the chair and stared at me coldly. She hadn't cracked, not like I had expected her to.

I turned to Kelsey. "Crystal wasn't the only one who understood how important Chad was to Zoey, was she, Kelsey? You write with Chad, you knew how important Zoey was to Chad's music. He called her his muse."

"So?"

"You also knew Lacey was coming between Chad and Zoey. You knew about their affair. It wasn't the first time. You had probably seen it before. Band on the road. Lots of late-night gigs and young groupies around. Chad wasn't the most loyal of boyfriends, but this time it was different. Zoey was gone more than usual, and you could hear it in his music. Something had changed. You knew it was Lacey. She had a pull on him, and when you found out about her poems, you were afraid Chad was going to replace you."

"Replace me?" Kelsey laughed. "Lacey could barely write her name. Her stuff was crap. Chad wasn't serious about anything she wrote."

"Except the night of Lacey's murder, you began to wonder if maybe Chad didn't think so. You and Zac were at the studio with Chad. Chad was having trouble with the lyrics you'd written. He wasn't excited about them. It wasn't working for him, and he wanted to try some of Lacey's stuff. You couldn't handle that. You told Chad you weren't feeling well and you wanted to cancel the session. Only Chad didn't want to leave. He wanted to stay and put some of Lacey's poems to music, and it upset you."

"I don't know what you're talking about. We left 'cause I wasn't feeling well. I had a headache."

"A headache? You told Detective Romero you had a stomachache."

"What difference does it make? I wasn't feeling well."

"You left the studio but didn't go home. You told Zac you wanted to talk to Lacey, see if you could talk some sense into her. You knew Lacey was at the mansion running lines, so—"

"Stop!" Kelsey pinched her eyes pinched shut.

Zac grabbed Kelsey's arm. "Kelsey, don't."

"I'm sorry, Zac. I can't go on like this." Kelsey pulled her arm away from Zac and looked at me. "Zac and I knew if Chad didn't stop his affair with Lacey that it was only a matter of time before Zoey found out. Lacey was tearing him apart. Chad couldn't write. The music sounded flat. Nothing was getting done. Everything we'd worked on was going down the drain. We knew we had to do something."

"What happened?" I asked.

Zac looked at Kelsey. "Let me explain." Kelsey nodded. "Kels and I never planned to kill Lacey. The idea never even crossed our minds. We just wanted to talk to her. Tell her how important Zoey was to Chad's work. We figured if we talked, she'd get it and back away. We knew Lacey and Zoey would be running lines and we planned to wait in the backyard until they were done and we could talk to Lacey alone."

"How did you get in the yard?" I leaned a little closer to Zac. I wanted to make sure Romero had this word for word.

"Chad and I like to hike the trails, and I always had a key to the back gate 'cause Chad never remembered his. Kels and I parked on the street 'bout a block away, hiked up through the park, and came in through the back."

Kelsey continued. "When we reached the yard, I went to sit on the chaise and nearly sat on one of Zoey's dolls. Somebody had left her there, and it made this kind of whiny cry-baby like sound. Like a cat's meow."

"I told Kels to be quiet," Zac said. "I could hear Zoey and Lacey talking. They were in the kitchen, right above us. Lacey said she thought she heard a cat outside. Zoey said something about feral cats in the area and that maybe it was a kitten. I figured this was our chance, so I took the cry box out of the doll and lured Lacey into the backyard."

"When Lacey came outside I called her over to the spa where I was sitting." Kelsey looked nervous, but Zac squeezed her hand, and she continued. "I told her we needed to talk. I thought for sure woman-to-woman, she'd get it. She would realize Chad was a mistake. But she wasn't having any of it. She told me I was riding Chad's coattails. That Zac and I were nothing but backup singers and she could write better. I don't know what came over me. She turned and I grabbed the doll and hit her over the head. I didn't mean to. Honest. It all happened so fast. Next thing I knew, Lacey fell into the spa. The drain caught her long hair and pulled her under. Zac and I tried to pull her free, but her hair was stuck. We couldn't save her."

"And then you dropped the doll and ran," I said.

Zac answered. "We didn't know what else to do. We went out through the gate to the park and went home."

"Later I told Zac I had to go back to the house to find the doll."

"And when you did, that's when you met Detective Romero and discovered someone had already found the doll and put it in Crystal's room." I nodded to Crystal.

"I probably should have said something." Kelsey bit her lip. "But I couldn't. I was too afraid. I'm sorry."

"So am I," I said. "Detective Romero, do you have what you need?"

Romero came out from behind the screen. "I do."

Before it had even registered with Zac and Kelsey what was happening, Romero asked them both to stand and put their hands behind their backs. He announced they were under arrest for the murder of Lacey Adams.

While Romero read them their Miranda Rights, Zoey rushed into the room with Detective Richards behind her.

Crystal stood. "Zoey! You're here?"

"Surprised?" Zoey was flushed. "What were you thinking? You and Chad?"

"Zoey, please. You don't understand, I was only trying to help."

"By sleeping with my fiancé?" Zoey asked.

"He's a jerk, Zoey."

"Get out! I don't ever want to see you again. You're fired!" Then turning to Chad, Zoey pointed to the door. "You too. Go!"

Chad refused to move. "Zoey, please."

"Out!" Zoey screamed.

Crystal got as far as the door. "Chad, we need to talk."

"Not now, Crystal." Chad refused to move.

"You idiot!" Crystal yelled at Chad.

Romero opened the door. "Looks like your work's done here, Crystal." Crystal stomped through the entry. Then with a nod to me, Romero added, "Nice work, Misty. We'll be in touch."

"Good night, Detective."

I watched as Romero and Detective Richards left with Zac and Kelsey in handcuffs, then turned my attention back to Chad. He had refused to move and was trying one last time to convince Zoey how sorry he was.

"Please, Zoe. I never meant for any of this to happen."

Zoey backed away, both hands up. "Don't even try to explain. What are you, the most fertile man on the planet? You knock up Lacey and Crystal and think I'd forgive you? Get out of here. I don't ever want to see you again."

Chad looked at me. "Misty, please."

"I'm sorry, Chad, I can't help you."

Chad walked slowly toward the door, then stopped. "What about the ghost, Misty? What about Lacey? What am I supposed to do about her? You promised you'd help."

I couldn't believe after Kelsey and Zac's confession and arrest, and Crystal's surprise announcement she was pregnant, that Chad was still thinking about Lacey. I didn't have a lot of sympathy for Chad, but even a ghost deserved a better host.

"There is no magic spell to release Lacey from haunting you, Chad. I confess I lied to get you here, you don't need me to perform a séance to remove her from your life."

"What do you mean? I don't understand. I thought you could help?"

I put my hands on Chad's shoulders. I had no sense of any spirits about him, just a dark aura of worry, and maybe a little shame. "Lacey's not here with you now. She wouldn't be. She knows better than to return to the scene of the crime. Not that of her death, mind you, but where you and she began your affair, right here under Zoey's roof."

Chad shut his eyes.

"If you see her again, it won't be here. And if you don't see her again, it won't be because she doesn't exist, but because you have decided not to allow her into your life. Just as you should not have allowed her into your bed in the first place. That's when she began to haunt you, Chad. In life. You allowed your erotic fantasies about her to open the door. Until you decide to close it, she'll continue to haunt you."

"But isn't there something you can do? Something you can give me to make her go away?"

"I can't give you anything you can't give yourself. Ghosts can't exist on our plane. They are only here because we allow them to be. Your guilt and fantasy about your past exploits have invited her into your life. If you really don't want Lacey to pursue you, tell her to leave. Shelve those fantasies you have about her, along with any souvenirs you've kept, and toss them away."

"Souvenirs?"

"The red negligee? Trash it. And you might want to burn a little sage."

"That's it? I go home, burn a little sage and tell her to go, and she'll be gone?"

"It's not much more complicated than that. Shutter those thoughts. Stop with those erotic fantasies you carry around about her, and she'll be gone. Live in the here and now. Not in some fantasy world. Now, if you'll excuse me, I've still got some work to do here with Zoey. You need to go."

Chad turned to Zoey one last time. "Zoey I'm—"

"Save it, Chad. We're done. Leave!"

Chapter 34

Chad slammed the front door behind him. The sound of it echoed throughout the great room.

"This is it then. My best friend is dead. My assistant's gone, and my fiancé and I are done. Everybody who was anybody in my life is gone." Zoey sounded as though she were about to cry.

"Not everybody," I said.

"I'm sorry, Misty, I didn't mean to sound rude. You're here, and I appreciate it. I really do."

"You're not rude. But you're wrong. The house isn't empty, not at all."

"Is Alicia Mae still here?"

"For a little while. Come. Sit with me. I want to show you something." I took Zoey by the hand and led her to the couch in front of the big picture window where our view of the backyard was illuminated by the dappled moonlight as it shimmered through the big weeping willow onto the pool. "The other day when we sat on the patio, I told you about Alicia's playhouse, how it's still there."

"Except I couldn't see it." Zoey shook her head.

"But you asked me if it would ever be possible."

"Is it?"

"Now more than ever. But first, I need you to listen to me very carefully. Do you remember the box of things I brought by that Zac and Kelsey had accidentally taken from your house when Chad moved out?"

"I do."

"And the photos we found in the box? Particularly the one of you and your mother at the piano, and another of Alicia Mae with her mother?"

"I love that picture of my mother and me."

"Love plays a powerful role in the mystic world. It's the tie that binds, through good times and bad times. Across generations, and far beyond the here and now. It's what ties you and Alicia Mae together. The desire to reconnect with a bond you lost far too early in your life."

"What are you saying?"

"You've both had the same wish. You both want to be reunited with the mother-spirit, a kind of guiding light or guardian angel if you will." I put my hand on Zoey's face and brushed the hair from her blue eyes. "You missed that as a child. And consciously or subconsciously you wanted that love in your life again. When we put that much energy into something, we create opportunities far beyond our mortal world."

"You really think so?"

"There's a portal beneath the playhouse. It allows the transfer of spirits from this world to the next. Wilson believes Alicia's been waiting to—"

"What? Leave? Why? This is her home. Why would she want to go?"

"You need to understand, Zoey, the Pink Mansion was her physical home. Alicia's home is bigger than this. She's waiting for her mother's spirit to come and lead her there."

"If that's true, then why hasn't she come before? She could have come anytime. Alicia's been here for seventy-five years. Why now?"

"Because Alicia's mother wasn't dead. Margaret Mann only

recently passed. After she and her husband sold the Pink Mansion, they moved away. Years later, Margaret moved back, and lived in a retirement home not far from here. It's the same retirement home where Heather's mother is living. It was Heather who brought Margaret Mann's passing to my attention. She was ninety-seven."

"Alicia's going to leave me now too? I'll be all alone?"

"I don't think so. I believe your mother's been here. Not permanently like Alicia. But temporarily. The piano music you thought you heard? It's your mother, Zoey. She's visited here several times since you moved in, and she's been watching over you."

"Then it wasn't my imagination?"

"No, not at all," I said.

"Will she come back?"

"With the universe there are no guarantees. We can't hang onto a spirit because we're afraid of being alone or of letting go. It isn't healthy for either the spirit or our own growth. But I believe your mother wants to be here. She's been trying to come through."

"I hope so."

"Alicia Mae needs to leave first. In order for your mother to join you here, Alicia's mother must come through the portal first and take her daughter home. There's a balance of power in the universe. I don't claim to understand it, it's as though there's only room for so much energy from the other side to be here at any one time. So until Alicia leaves, your mother either can't or won't come through the portal for anything more than just a short visit. The time is upon us now, Alicia is about to go home."

"Can I see her before she goes? Just once?"

I looked out at the patio and beyond to the playhouse where Wilson sat at the picnic table by himself. He was dressed exactly as I had seen him that first day on the staircase, in pleated pants, a collared shirt with suspenders, and a bowtie. But this was not the same man. He was much kinder now. Not nearly so arrogant or self-serving. The man seated at the table wasn't solely focused on himself or his possessions as he had been. This was a different Wilson Thorne, and he was thinking about Alicia and what he needed to do for her.

"Take my hand," I said. "If you really want, I can lift the veil between our two worlds for a short spell. Do you want me to try?"

Zoey nodded.

"Look out at the yard and make a picture of it in your mind. When you think you've got it, close your eyes, then try to recreate that same picture in your head. Everything. The colors, the light on the water. The drape of the weeping willow. Right down to the shadows beneath the tree. Can you do that?"

Zoey took my hand and stared out at the yard, then closed her eyes. I waited until I could feel the image embrace her. Like a 3-D picture, I could visualize her sitting next to me looking at the same scene I saw in front of me.

"Do you have the picture in your mind?"

Zoey squeezed my hand, her eyes pinched shut.

"Good. This is your mind's eye. It sees beyond our own dimension to the spirit world around us." Zoey's eyelids fluttered. "Don't worry. You can trust it. There's nothing here to harm you. You're in complete control. Just stay with it." I waited until I saw the corners of Zoey's mouth turn up in a slow smile. I knew we were looking at the same scene. "Now look beyond the pool, beneath the big weeping willow. There's a small playhouse. It's white with pink shutters and a candy cane frame around the doorway. Do you see it?"

Zoey nodded. "Yes. It's exactly as I imagined it'd be."

"Good. You can open your eyes now. You're beyond the veil, between our world and the spirit world and everything you see is exactly as it's supposed to be."

"There's a man sitting at a picnic table. He's in front of the playhouse. Is that Wilson? Your spirit guide? I was hoping I'd see him too."

"Yes," I said. "That's Wilson."

"What's he doing?"

"He's waiting for Alicia Mae and her mother."

"But where are they? They haven't left yet, have they?"

"No, not yet. But soon." I wondered if Wilson was as prepared for this moment as I hoped I was. My throat tightened. Saying goodbye is never easy. Sometimes the suddenness of it is all too unexpected, even when we know it's coming.

We sat in silence and waited. Then, like a little fairy from within the playhouse, Alicia Mae appeared. She was dressed exactly as she had been the night of the séance, with her long hair curled in ringlets to her waist and her doll Mariposa in her arms.

"Ahh!" Zoey inhaled suddenly, a short quick breath. "There she is! Look at her. She's real!"

Alicia ran to Wilson and climbed up onto his lap. Wilson put his arms around her and lowered his head to hers, their brows touching. He whispered something to her. Alicia smiled and put her small fingers to his lips. Wilson kissed them, then took her fingers in his hands and held them close to his heart. The tears in my eyes started to blur my vision, but not before I saw her put her doll down, put her arms around his neck, and kiss him lightly on the side of the face. I brushed the side of my own face with my fingers. It was as though I could feel the kiss too.

"What are they talking about? She looks so happy."

"Wilson's explaining she's going home." My throat tightened. I blotted a tear from my eye with the side of my finger.

Zoey reached toward the window. "Look, he's pointing at us. Wilson knows we're here."

Alicia climbed down from Wilson's lap, took a few steps in our direction, then stopped and looked back at Wilson. He gestured with the back of his hand, a small wave. *Go on, it's okay.*

"Go," I said. "Put your hand on the window. Alicia wants to say goodbye."

"Can I touch her?"

"If you put your hand on the glass, you'll be able to feel her."

Zoey went to the window, crouched down so that she and Alicia would be eye-to-eye, and placed the tips of her fingers on the glass. Alicia ran toward the window, then stopped three feet away and crooked her head while she played with one of her long curls.

Zoey slowly placed the palm of her hand flatly against the window and waited. "It's okay," she said. "Don't be shy. Put your hand on the glass. I just want to say hello."

Slowly, Alicia put her small fingers on the glass and giggled. Then quickly, she pushed the palm of her hand against the window until it was covered by Zoey's larger hand.

Suddenly, there was an aura-spill. A blending of energies. Colored lights like fireflies danced around their hands, then settled into a golden hew that filled the caverns of the great room from the floor to the ceiling. It was time.

"You need to tell her to go, Zoey."

"But how?" I could see Zoey didn't want to say goodbye but knew she had to.

"Just like you would a small child whose bedtime has come. Tell her it's time for her to go. That she'll always be welcome, but her mother has come to take her home, and you wish her well."

"That easy?" Zoey laughed lightly.

I nodded. "Ghosts are amazingly responsive when you take charge."

Zoey pressed her hand harder against the glass, then put her forehead to the window. Alicia did the same. The two a mirrored image of each other. Zoey paused. This wasn't a rehearsed role. This was real. And it was hard. The words didn't come easily.

"Thank you, Alicia. Thank you for being here. I'll never forget you. You can come back, often as you like." I caught a catch in Zoey's voice. "But your mother's here now, and you've been waiting for her for a long time. Just like I have mine. So you can go with her now. I don't need you anymore. She's come to take you home. Go."

Zoey let go of the glass and stood up, then put her fingers to her lips and blew Alicia a kiss.

Alicia stepped back from the window. Her thick lashes wet with tears. She giggled, then waved and ran back to Wilson's waiting hand. From within the playhouse, Alicia's mother appeared. Like a ghostly spirit, she swept from the entrance and materialized in front of Wilson and Alicia. Then Margaret Mann picked up her daughter and placed her on her hip. With one arm around her mother's neck, Alicia smiled and waved goodbye. Margaret gave a slight nod, then turned and the three of them, Margaret, Alicia, and Wilson, disappeared back into the playhouse. Like a sprig of dandelion seeds, the wind had blown them from my view and they disappeared in the spirit world beyond.

"Are they gone?" Zoey asked.

I gazed into the yard. The playhouse. The picnic table. Everything was gone. The yard was once again as it was before I had lifted the veil. Back to its modern form.

"I think so," I said.

"Wilson too?" Zoey turned to me, a look of concern on her face.

"I don't know." I sat back on the couch and closed my eyes. I tried to replay my last vision of the three of them in front of the playhouse. Had Wilson waved to me before they left? Was he trying to signal me? Was this goodbye for me too? My eyes burned. I was going to miss the man. This selfish limboed shade of mine. I could only hope he had gone on to a better place. That I'd somehow helped him to find his higher self.

Zoey put her hand on mine. "Are you okay?"

"I'm fine," I said.

"Do you think it worked? Do you think my mother came through?"

I exhaled and squeezed back a tear. I didn't know. I felt spent and suddenly very tired.

"You may not know for a while," I said. "But I think so. Do you mind if I sit a minute? These things sometimes take their toll."

"Are you going to be okay?" Zoey sat down next to me.

I squeezed her hand and released it. "Just sit with me a moment. Close your eyes and open yourself up to the energy around us."

I felt a warmth sweep the room and opened my eyes. The candles flickered on the dining room table. And then...music. From the piano came the soft sounds of "Clair de Lune."

"She's here, Misty. You hear that?" Zoey stood and spread her arms as though she could embrace the room. "That's 'Clair de Lune,' my mother's favorite."

"She is," I said. "You may not see her right away, but I suspect over time you will. You don't need to worry about the Chamberlain Curse anymore. She'll take care of you. You're not alone."

I took a deep breath. My work was done here. I needed to

get home to my cat and Denise and whatever else waited for me there. I determined I should probably call an Uber. I certainly couldn't drive Wilson's car. I was about to tell Zoey I didn't think I was up to driving when I heard a voice.

"'Bout time you and I headed home, don't you think, Old Gal?"

Wilson! I turned around to see him standing in the entry.

"It appears I've more work to do. So unless you've any objections, I believe we ought to get ourselves home. Tomorrow's another day, and perhaps the universe will know what to do with me next time. As for now, I believe our adventures are just beginning."

NANCY COLE SILVERMAN

Nancy Cole Silverman credits her twenty-five years in news and talk radio for helping her to develop an ear for storytelling. But it wasn't until after she retired that she was able to write fiction full-time. Much of what Silverman writes about is pulled from events that were reported on from inside some of Los Angeles' busiest newsrooms where she spent the bulk of her career. She lives in Los Angeles with her husband, Bruce, and her standard poodle, Ali.

Mysteries by Nancy Cole Silverman

The Misty Dawn Mystery Series

THE HOUSE ON HALLOWED GROUND (#1)

The Carol Childs Mystery Series

SHADOW OF DOUBT (#1)
BEYOND A DOUBT (#2)
WITHOUT A DOUBT (#3)
ROOM FOR DOUBT (#4)
REASON TO DOUBT (#5)

Henery Press Mystery Books

And finally, before you go...
Here are a few other mysteries
you might enjoy:

STAGING IS MURDER

Grace Topping

A Laura Bishop Mystery (#1)

Laura Bishop just nabbed her first decorating commission—staging a 19th-century mansion that hasn't been updated for decades. But when a body falls from a laundry chute and lands at Laura's feet, replacing flowered wallpaper becomes the least of her duties.

To clear her assistant of the murder and save her fledgling business, Laura's determined to find the killer. Turns out it's not as easy as renovating a manor home, especially with two handsome men complicating her mission: the police detective on the case and the real estate agent trying to save the manse from foreclosure.

Worse still, the meddling of a horoscope-guided friend, a determined grandmother, and the local funeral director could get them all killed before Laura props the first pillow.

Available at booksellers nationwide and online

Visit www.henerypress.com for details

MURDER IN G MAJOR

Alexia Gordon

A Gethsemane Brown Mystery (#1)

With few other options, African-American classical musician Gethsemane Brown accepts a less-than-ideal position turning a group of rowdy schoolboys into an award-winning orchestra. Stranded without luggage or money in the Irish countryside, she figures any job is better than none. The perk? Housesitting a lovely cliffside cottage. The catch? The ghost of the cottage's murdered owner haunts the place. Falsely accused of killing his wife (and himself), he begs Gethsemane to clear his name so he can rest in peace.

Gethsemane's reluctant investigation provokes a dormant killer and she soon finds herself in grave danger. As Gethsemane races to prevent a deadly encore, will she uncover the truth or star in her own farewell performance?

Available at booksellers nationwide and online

Visit www.henerypress.com for details

FATAL BRUSHSTROKE

Sybil Johnson

An Aurora Anderson Mystery (#1)

A dead body in her garden and a homicide detective on her doorstep...Computer programmer and tole-painting enthusiast Aurora (Rory) Anderson doesn't envision finding either when she steps outside to investigate the frenzied yipping coming from her own back yard. After all, she lives in a quiet California beach community where violent crime is rare and murder even rarer.

Suspicion falls on Rory when the body buried in her flowerbed turns out to be someone she knows—her tole-painting teacher, Hester Bouquet. Just two weeks before, Rory attended one of Hester's weekend seminars, an unpleasant experience she vowed never to repeat. As evidence piles up against Rory, she embarks on a quest to identify the killer and clear her name. Can Rory unearth the truth before she encounters her own brush with death?

Available at booksellers nationwide and online

Visit www.henerypress.com for details

MURDER AT THE PALACE

Margaret Dumas

A Movie Palace Mystery (#1)

Welcome to the Palace movie theater! Now Showing: Philandering husbands, ghostly sidekicks, and a murder or two.

When Nora Paige's movie-star husband leaves her for his latest co-star, she flees Hollywood to take refuge in San Francisco at the Palace, a historic movie theater that shows the classic films she loves. There she finds a band of misfit film buffs who care about movies (almost) as much as she does.

She also finds some shady financial dealings and the body of a murdered stranger. Oh, and then there's Trixie, the lively ghost of a 1930's usherette who appears only to Nora and has a lot to catch up on. With the help of her new ghostly friend, can Nora catch the killer before there's another murder at the Palace?

Available at booksellers nationwide and online

Visit www.henerypress.com for details